Where the Dead Men Lie

Also by Hugh Capel and published by Ginninderra Press

Kiandra Gold

Hugh Capel

Where the Dead Men Lie

The Story of Barcroft Boake,
Bush Poet of the Monaro

Acknowledgements

Some of the material in this book is provided with the kind permission of the National Library and the Mitchell Library, State Library of New South Wales. The texts of Barcroft's poems can be found in copies of *The Bulletin* (1891 and 1892), held by both libraries. The Mitchell Library's reference for the letters by Barcroft Boake to his father is A849, volume 4 of the *Bulletin* manuscripts, copied as CY reel 1540. The handwritten text of 'To a Hatpeg' is also in the Mitchell Library, in the A.G. Stephens papers at ML MSS 4937/8.

The 1897 and 1913 editions of A.G. Stephens' edited collection of Barcroft's poems, *Where the Dead Men Lie and Other Poems*, (Angus & Robertson) were invaluable sources for information and it is only through Stephen's work that Barcroft's story can be told today. The 1897 edition is held by both libraries.

Where the Dead Men Lie: The Story of Barcroft Boake, Bush Poet of the Monaro
ISBN 978 1 74027 135 6
Copyright © text Hugh Capel 2002
Cover design: Helen Walker

First published 2002
Reprinted 2016

GINNINDERRA PRESS
PO Box 3461 Port Adelaide 5015
www.ginninderrapress.com.au

Dedicated to Honor Capel

Contents

Preface

This is the story of Barcroft Boake, bush poet from Australia's colonial past. As with his poetry, it is a story based on the truth. A story of his love for the bush, of his love for a girl, of his love for the people of the bush. A story about life and death. A story of what might have been. Like a leaf swept along by life's stream, the deep currents of the time took him where he could not choose.

In this story, apart from some minor editing, Barcroft's poems and his letters are reprinted as he wrote them.

1

Sydney Harbourside Residence, 1892

'Ladies and gentlemen. Silence, please. Mr Stephens will now read *Where the Dead Men Lie.*'

Mr Stephens waited for the chattering to subside. He adjusted his glasses and began to read.

'Out on the wastes of the Never Never,
That's where the dead men lie,
There where the heat-waves dance forever,
That's where the dead men lie;
That's where the Earth's lov'd sons are keeping
endless tryst – not the west wind sweeping
feverish pinions, can wake their sleeping –   *pinions: wings*
Out where the dead men lie!

'Where brown Summer and Death have mated,
That's where the dead men lie,
Loving with fiery lust unsated,
That's where the dead men lie;
Out where the grinning skulls bleach whitely,
Under the saltbush sparkling brightly,
Out where the wild dogs chorus nightly,
That's where the dead men lie.

'Deep in the yellow, flowing river,
That's where the dead men lie,
Under the banks where the shadows quiver,
That's where the dead men lie;
Where the platypus twists and doubles,
leaving a trail of tiny bubbles;
Rid at last of their earthly troubles,
That's where the dead men lie.

'East and backward pale faces turning,
That's how the dead men lie;
Gaunt arms stretched with a voiceless yearning,
That's how the dead men lie;
Oft in the fragrant hush of nooning,
Hearing again their mother's crooning,
Wrapt for aye in a dreadful swooning,
That's how the dead men lie.

'Nought but the hand of Night can free them;
That's when the dead men fly;
Only the frightened cattle see them –
See the dead men go by;
Cloven hoofs beating out one measure,
Bidding the stockman know no leisure,
That's when the dead men take their pleasure,
That's when the dead men fly.

'Ask, too, the never-sleeping drover,
He sees the dead pass by,
Hearing them call to their friends – the plover,
Hearing the dead men cry.
Seeing their faces stealing, stealing,
Hearing their laughter pealing, pealing,
Watching their grey forms wheeling, wheeling
Round where the cattle lie.

'Strangled by thirst and fierce privation –
That's how the dead men die.'

After a moment's silence, a slightly uncomfortable silence, the small audience responded with polite clapping. Mr Stephens bowed slightly, then resumed his chair in the front row.

The gentleman who had introduced him stood up and addressed the audience. 'Thank you, Mr Stephens. That was a moving rendition. I hardly need tell the people present today, this work comes from the fertile field of bush balladry. The poem has all the hallmarks of our bush hinterland, almost in too striking a fashion. I am told the verses are the work of a young bush poet, a Mr Boake. Can you tell us something of him, Mr Stephens? Will he be the next Adam Lindsay Gordon?'

Mr Stephens stood up. 'That I could not say. We have seen but little of his poetry yet. Indeed, he has been in print for less than a year. I myself only recently became aware of his work. The poem I just read is not entirely representative. I chose it for the strength of its imagery, and for the way it evokes the spirit of our vast inland. Other rhymes of his have been published in *The Bulletin*, as well as *The Sydney Mail*. I am not a regular subscriber to *The Bulletin*, I hasten to add. As to his fame, well, time and history will be the judge.' Mr Stephens sat down.

'Thank you, Mr Stephens. Ladies and gentlemen, that concludes our presentation for this afternoon. I thank you most sincerely for your attendance. On behalf of all here today, I extend our warm thanks to Mr Stephens and to the Reverend Mr Watkins for their thoughtful renditions from two very disparate poetic realms. Tea will now be served on the patio, through the French doors. The next meeting of the North Sydney Literary Association will be held in a month's time, at this location, commencing at two p.m. sharp. Thank you once more for your attendance. We look forward to your company again. Please enjoy your refreshments.'

It was a bright, clear, summer's day. Perfume wafting by from the garden flowers mixed in the air with the smell of fresh scones. The leafy wisteria drooped from its trellis. Fragments of conversations could be heard above the quiet rustle of dresses and the occasional squeaking of cane chairs as they moved across the flagstones. The chink of cups and saucers and the occasional tinkle of silverware drifted across the neatly clipped lawns. Beyond the patio, the lawns rolled gently down to the water's edge. Beyond them, on the harbour, an occasional white sail dotted the sparkling blue sea. It was a picture-postcard scene.

The serving maids busied themselves replenishing teapots and bringing out fresh supplies of hot scones and jam. Their white starched pinafores matched the neatly folded napkins on the tables.

'Aunt Cecily, what *is* the Never Never?' asked a young girl seated at one of the tables.

'That's what they call the vast interior of Australia,' her aunt replied. 'They say it's where the pioneers venture, never to return. So they call it the Never Never land.'

'It sounds very harsh,' asked the girl. 'Is it really like that? Do lots of men die out there? Have you ever been there?'

'I can only tell you what I've heard, dearie. I've never been there myself. From all accounts, there are many privations. Fortunately, you needn't bother yourself about such things.'

'It does sound exciting,' said the girl. 'Even if quite dangerous. I think I must go there one day. This bush poetry is so romantic,' she said with a sigh.

At another table, two ladies in billowing dresses were discussing the merits of the chinaware as they sipped their tea.

'Most exquisite, most exquisite,' exclaimed one, holding up her cup to inspect the miniature painting on its side. 'The subject and the aspect suggest a French derivation, don't you think?'

'You may be right,' replied her companion. 'I saw a similar scene recently. It was on the china at Government House. Mrs Hetherington told me it had been imported directly from France.'

'Is that so? I had a not dissimilar piece myself, but one of the serving maids broke it. I was most upset. It really is so hard to get reliable help these days.'

'Excuse me, miss,' her companion said to the maid passing by. 'Could you please bring me a clean napkin. This one has a dirty stain on it.'

Mr Stephens and the Reverend Mr Watkins were walking side by side on the lawn.

'Mr Stephens,' said Watkins, turning towards him. 'I must tell you, I am not entirely comfortable with the inclusion of Mr Boake's work in our recitals. *The Bulletin* is hardly the type of source we should be drawing from, given the content and the attitude of that scurrilous magazine.'

'My dear reverend,' replied Mr Stephens. 'You can be assured I would never include any polemical material in our presentations. I am most scrupulous in that regard.'

'I'm slightly puzzled, though,' said Mr Watkins. 'Can you enlighten me? I previously heard tell of 'Where the Dead Men Lie' as a diatribe against our society and its best citizens. Yet the words you recited are quite uncontentious in that regard. Even so, it is somewhat too strident for my liking.'

'Reverend, I should share a secret with you. I did some judicious editing before my presentation. There are a further two verses in the original written by Boake. They do not sit well with the rest of the work, in my view. They contain some base radical sentiments that could only serve to engender discord in a listener. Without them, the poem is much improved and has merit enough to warrant general publication.'

They came to the edge of the neatly clipped hedge and turned around.

'My gosh, what a nuisance,' said Mr Watkins. He had brushed against a post, leaving a brown mark on his cuff. 'Dear me, you do need to be careful, don't you? Even in a well kept garden.'

A young couple seated in the shade of the wisteria just outside the French doors were also discussing Mr Boake's poetry.

'It's too much about death. I didn't like it,' said the young lady, carefully adjusting her bonnet.

Her companion, an earnest-looking man and a student of theology, mused, 'I wonder, where does a poet get such inspiration. To speak with such force about hardship and death? Particularly in one so young. I'm told Mr Boake is not yet thirty years of age.'

2

Surveyors Camp, Riverina District, 1891

It was hot. It was dry. It was thirsty. And it was dusty. The three horsemen were covered from head to toe in a fine brown film. Their horses stirred up dusty plumes each time their hoofs hit the track. Turning the last corner, they came in sight of their camp beside the dried-up billabong.

As they dismounted, clouds of dust drifted lazily to the ground in the still warm air. To finish off, they banged their hats against the stock rails, brushed their pants and stamped their feet. Then they unsaddled their horses, hobbled them and let them loose to look for scarce feed. When that was done, they walked across to their tent, moving stiffly after a long day in the saddle.

The sun was low on the horizon, though sunset was yet to come. Around the billabong, the river red gums stood gnarled and waiting. The dry grass flats were a faded straw yellow. The near hills were a dusty brown. In the distance, the mountains on the horizon were pale blue-grey.

There was no spare water for washing at the camp. Only enough to boil the billy. It was a couple of days since the riders had taken a trip to the river to get fresh water. It was over a week since they'd been able to clean up properly and even longer since they'd put on clean clothes. It was something they got used to.

'Mr Raymond, you'd better draw up those maps now the wind has dropped,' said Mr Lipscomb. 'It'll still be light for long enough.' Lipscomb was the surveyor in charge. His remark was addressed to one of his assistants. He didn't expect a reply.

'Mr Boake, you start the fire and prepare the meal,' he added. Lipscomb was always formal when he gave orders. His assistants took it in turn to do the chores.

Soon, wood fire smoke drifted upwards, losing itself in the overhanging branches of the river red gums. Not long afterwards, the smell of cooking damper wafted towards the tent.

The New South Wales Government Survey Board had recently asked Lipscomb his opinion of Barcroft Boake. It was their task, the board wrote, to seek regular reports on those who may have aspirations to practice as a licensed surveyor. Lipscomb replied,

Mr Boake is a good horseman, and a first class bushman. In my opinion he is thoroughly qualified to be a surveyor. In the field he is sufficiently capable and he is a particularly good draughtsman. His work in the field books outlining the topography of the country is the best I have ever seen. He is very temperate, except in the use of tobacco – his pipe is hardly ever out of his mouth. He is fond of reading whenever he gets the chance, though a surveyor's life gives little opportunity for study. His health seems good but his habits are solitary, his disposition melancholy – even morose. He has few friends, and he dwells overly on his past experiences on the Monaro and as a drover. In short, he has the talent but would benefit from a brighter and more positive disposition towards the profession.

There was a touch of boyishness in Boake's nature and appearance. In figure he was slim and loosely knit; tall rather than short. It was generally agreed that he looked infinitely better on a horse than off. His eyes were dark, his hair dark brown, almost black, and his face was made remarkable by a deep scar on the right brow, the result of a fall in childhood.

After dinner, Barcroft sat hunched in front of the fire, encased in a thick cloud of pipe smoke. He held his pipe by the bowl, cupping it in front of his face, his elbows resting on his knees. He was far away in thought as he stared into the fire.

There was no moon tonight. The only light came from the flickering fire and an oil lamp slung from a pole outside one of the tents. On the other side of the campfire, Raymond sat on an upturned stump, idly poking the embers with a stick. He was a complete contrast to Barcroft, in appearance as well as character. He was a short, rather stocky young man, with a reddish sunburnt face and the makings of a ginger beard. His hat was set back jauntily on his head, his face fringed with short curly red hair.

'Hey, grumpy,' he said to Barcroft. 'How about coming down the pub tomorrow?'

There was no answer.

'What d'you reckon? There's likely be a dance on. Sure to be a few sheilas too. What d'you say?'

Barcroft kept staring into the fire. His mind was far away.

Raymond tried again, this time more loudly. 'Boakie! Hey, Boakie. What about it?'

Barcroft looked up, puzzled. 'What did you say?'

'How about we go down the pub tomorrow afternoon – after we do the books? We could clean up in the river on the way.'

Barcroft paused before answering. 'No, you go. I'll stay here and mind the camp.'

'Come on. You hardly ever come,' said Raymond. 'You need a bit of company now and then. A few ales would do you good. There'll be some girls there too. Good-lookers for sure.'

'No, I'll be right. I'll stay here.'

'What'll you do, then?'

'I'll do some reading.'

'You're always reading,' said Raymond. 'You'll go blind from it – what with that poor lamp light and all. Jenny has a friend. I'm sure she'd like to meet you. What d'you say?'

'No, thanks, all the same. I'd prefer to stay here this time.'

'What is it? Are you saving yourself for your special Monaro girl?'

'No,' said Barcroft defensively.

'Bet you are,' said Raymond. 'Come on. No use pining away. There's more than one fish in the sea. You should come and try some other girls. Otherwise, how will you know if you've got the right one? Anyway, that one of yours is a long way away. She's probably got another fella by now. She'd never know anyway. Same as my Susie. What they don't know can't harm 'em, eh? Come on.'

'No, really. I've got a book I want to finish.'

'All right. Have it your way then.' Raymond gave up. He thought Barcroft must be one of the most reserved, even grumpy individuals he'd ever met. Not that he was selfish, but he was entirely self-absorbed, and brooding continually. He gave definition to the saying 'wrapped up in your own thoughts'. Despite that, Raymond thought he was a likeable enough chap – when he came out of his cocoon. That was mainly in the day. At night he would sit and smoke. Sometimes he'd sit there just smoking. Other nights he'd read while he smoked, or he'd write while he smoked. Whatever he was doing in the evening, his pipe was always in his mouth.

During the day, when Barcroft was on his horse, he came to life. It was as though he was meant for the purpose, thought Raymond. He seemed to become one with his mount, moving in harmony with the animal. His conversation also came to light then. While riding, you could talk with him. He would tell stories from his droving days. In the evenings, without a spur to action, he retreated into his shell, surrounded by his thick cloud of pipe smoke.

Early next morning, the light chill of dawn caressed the ground, leaving a faint dampness on the dusty ground. Wisps of mist hid low in the river gullies. All about was stillness and silence, except for the occasional distant bird call. Without the direct light of the sun, the surrounding hills were a pale pastel grey.

Barcroft and Raymond stamped their feet as they came out of their tent, both to squeeze into their boots and to get the circulation moving.

The sun edged over the horizon as they saddled up. Momentarily, as the sun bathed the hills and flats in gold, a stark beauty struck the land. Barcroft took in the view as he looked around and breathed in the fresh morning air. The smell of early morning was also the smell of horses. The sights and smells of the bush always made him feel alive.

By mid-morning he and Raymond were riding along a sparsely treed ridge, on their way to Brookong Station.

Raymond turned to Barcroft. 'Why d'you say you hate surveying?' he asked. 'What's wrong with this?'

'There's nothing wrong with this,' replied Barcroft.

'What is wrong, then? Why are you always complaining about surveying?'

'It's fine so long as we're on the move,' said Barcroft. 'It's the waiting round I don't like – and the measuring and the calculating.'

'I don't mind the waiting,' said Raymond. 'At least you can have a blow. What about the draughting? You're pretty good at that.'

'It's tedious – and it's boring. I'd prefer to be out doing something.'

'What d'you mean?

'I'd prefer to be out droving,' said Barcroft. 'I could be riding with the wind in my face. Wheeling and cutting out cattle. Trying to guess their next move. Racing to cut them off. There's never a dull moment when you're with the herd.'

'If droving's so good, how come you're not doing it? Why stay round here?'

'I don't have a choice,' said Barcroft.

'How come?' said Raymond.

'I promised my father.'

'What did you promise?'

'It's a long story,' said Barcroft. 'I had a bad experience droving. It was before I started here with Mr Lipscomb. I lost all my savings. I promised my father I'd finish my qualification as a surveyor. That's why I took this assignment.'

They rode about a mile further along the ridge before coming to the track that would take them to Brookong Station.

'So you'll be setting up by yourself, then?' asked Raymond.

'I don't know,' said Barcroft. 'I'd still have to get accepted for a licence. Then you need capital to start up. I'm not sure I want to. Maybe I'll go droving again. Maybe I'll go back to the Monaro.' Barcroft laughed nervously. He really didn't know what he would do. He knew what he would like to do, and that was to write. But he wasn't about to share his private thoughts with Raymond.

On their way to Brookong, they had to pass by Jim Dolan's selection. It was scrubby country, in amongst the ridges before you got to the broad river flats. Mostly rocky and a fair bit hilly. There wasn't much feed in the gullies, mostly wombat holes. It was tough country in which to make a living.

Jim was fixing the yard fence when they rounded the track bend. He looked up as they approached, and tipped his hat to greet them. 'Hey there, young fellas. Where are you lads going?'

'Just off to Bookong. To get the weekly supplies,' said Raymond.

'Why don't you come in and have a cuppa?' said Jim. 'Sally'll have the kettle on. She's over at the homestead. You've got time, have you? It's mid-morning so tea's in order.'

'Yes, we've got time.' said Barcroft. 'If you don't mind, we'll take up your offer.' They were both pretty thirsty, having ridden for a couple of hours already.

'Here – give your horses a feed while you wait.' Jim heaved a bale over the fence to the horses. He made it look easy, although city-bred men would have had trouble even lifting it. 'Best you have a drink of water first. You look pretty dry.' He held out a water bottle.

'Sure you've got enough to spare?' said Raymond. 'Water's pretty scarce these days.'

'Not a worry. If you look after your mates, the Lord will look after you,' said Jim. That was his basic theory of bush hospitality.

They took turns to drink from the bottle but were careful not to take too much.

As they walked across the yard to the homestead, Jim asked them if they'd seen a mob of cattle on their way. 'There's a dozen missing,' he said. 'Reckon they'll be heading back up Tumbarumba way. Can't afford to loose 'em.'

'We seen none, did we?' said Raymond.

Barcroft shook his head in agreement.

'Better not be those Gardiner bastards again,' said Jim. He gave his words emphasis by spitting into the dirt.

The homestead was a slab hut. It had a wood-shingle roof and veranda. Its front windows were framed with hessian bags for curtains. A wisp of smoke drifted skywards from the iron-clad chimney.

The veranda floorboards squeaked as Raymond and Barcroft stepped onto them. Barcroft noticed they were freshly cut, with the bark still showing at the sides.

Sally was waiting for them on the veranda. Her dress stretched out in front over a soon-to-be member of the family. She was smiling broadly at them, with the contented look that pregnant women sometimes have.

'You know my Sal, don't you?' said Jim.

'Yes, we do,' said Barcroft. 'Good to see you.'

'How about a cuppa?' Jim said.

'It's on its way,' said Sally. 'Make yourselves comfy,' She gestured towards a rough-hewn bench on the veranda. 'I've just put the kettle on. I saw you coming.'

The men sat on the bench and looked out over the yard. They discussed the weather. Soon, Sally brought out mugs of tea. When they'd finished drinking, Jim asked if he could join them for part of the way to Brookong. He said maybe he'd come across the missing cattle.

On their way to Brookong, they had to cross Harrigan's Creek. It was dry, except for a few pools of stagnant muddy water.

'We need rain bad,' said Jim. 'If it don't come soon, I'll start losing stock. The ones I've got are in poor enough condition. No use trying to sell 'em. There's no one'd buy 'em.'

They urged the horses up the far bank.

'See those sticks,' Jim said, pointing to a collection of debris lodged at head height in the fork of a branch. 'That's how high the creek was in '88. Lost nearly half my herd then. They were cut off this side of the creek and swept away.'

Raymond and Barcroft looked, then nodded.

They followed the track out into the open where the country flattened out.

Jim kept musing. 'It's tough out here. I've had to borrow too much. The Australasian Pastoral Company owns more of my run than I do. Can't afford another flood like '88.'

They kept on riding to the west – away from the hills.

'What d'you fellas know about these hard financial times they reckon we're having now?' asked Jim.

'Only what the papers say,' replied Barcroft. 'They say capital's lost its confidence in Australia.'

'All I know is I can't get a fair price for my stock. We're not working any less. The beasts are just as good, but those bastards at Australasian won't pay their true value. I'll tell you, though – the bastards haven't reduced the interest they're charging me.'

They crossed another dry creek bed. They could tell its course from the line of river red gums that snaked across the plain. On the far side there was a grassy mound beside the track, not far from the creek bank. The initials J.C. were carved into the trunk of a nearby tree. Jim pulled back on his reins. Raymond and Barcroft joined him as he stopped and looked down at the mound.

'We never did find out his name,' said Jim. 'There he lies, at peace, poor sod.'

'What happened?' asked Raymond.

'Thirst. He died of thirst. That was five year ago. Lost his horse. It was summer then and the creek was dry. His horse turned up at Brookong. They didn't find him for near a week. He'd been well gone by then. All we know 'bout him are the initials carved in that tree.'

They rode on in silence.

It was two weeks more before it finally rained. Not heavily. Barely enough to wet the ground. Just enough to make the mud stick to Barcroft's boots. The creeks stayed dry.

Raymond wondered why Barcroft was often scribbling on bits of paper. Even when they were in the field taking bearings, he'd see Barcroft jotting down notes on a scrap of paper. It seemed as though whenever Barcroft had a spare moment he'd be writing something. As soon as Lipscomb came into sight, he'd quickly shove the notes into his pocket.

Eventually, Raymond asked him what he was doing. Barcroft hadn't told anyone about his writing before. He felt ambivalent towards it. He wasn't sure how good it was. He hadn't told Raymond, in case he'd make fun of him. When Raymond finally asked him, he decided there was no choice but to tell him all about it.

'I'm trying to write about the bush,' said Barcroft. 'It works best for me as verses. Not soppy stuff. Bush ballads, like Adam Lindsay Gordon.'

'Really?' Raymond was impressed. He knew some of Gordon's poems. From then on he was willing to make some allowance for Barcroft's moodiness.

Barcroft carefully copied his verses from the scraps of paper into his manuscript book in the evenings. Then he'd rewrite them to polish them. As he wasn't good at punctuation, he asked Raymond if he'd mind checking the punctuation in the final versions. Raymond agreed, so he was the first to see Barcroft's work.

'I'm not good at writing. I won't suggest any changes,' said Raymond.

'You can if you want to,' said Barcroft.

'No, it's your work. It wouldn't be right.'

Sometimes, Raymond did make a comment. When Barcroft wrote 'Jack's Last Muster', Raymond recognised the influence of Gordon's 'How We Beat the Favourite.'

'You're really taken with Gordon, aren't you?' said Raymond. 'You've even copied his metre from 'How We Beat the Favourite', haven't you?'

'I really admire what he's done,' said Barcroft.

'I didn't mean it badly.'

'That's all right. I make no apology. In my opinion there's no man in the last century who's achieved such lasting fame. His poems don't just appeal to one class of cultured minds, like Tennyson or Browning and that lot. There's not a bushman or drover who doesn't know a verse or two of 'How We Beat the Favourite' or 'The Sick Stock Rider.' I call that fame,' Barcroft said with feeling. 'Don't you think so?'

'I guess so,' said Raymond.

'Gordon's the favourite of the bush. He's the only poet of the back-blocker. You'd have to agree, wouldn't you?' said Barcroft.

'So you want to be a new Gordon?'

'I'm not sure about that,' said Barcroft.

'You know, if you do want to be a second Gordon, you'll have to complete the business properly and finish up by committing suicide – that's what he did.'

Barcroft laughed quietly in reply. Raymond said no more. It was late, so they turned in for the night.

3

Boake Residence, Sydney, 1885

'Bartie! Did you pass? Did you pass?' Evie, Barcroft's youngest sister, tugged at Barcroft's coat sleeve as he stood in the hallway. 'Are you going to be a surveyor now?' she asked.

'Wait on, wait on,' said Barcroft, trying to get out of his coat. 'Let me get out of this first.' He wriggled out of his coat and hung it on the peg in the hall.

Evie persisted. 'Tell me first. Tell me first,' she pressed.

'All right. I think so,' he said, giving in – as he usually did.

Evie ran into the kitchen ahead of him. His father looked up from his newspaper with an inquiring look. His other sisters, Addie, Violet and Clare and his Gran all looked up as he stood in the doorway. Suddenly Evie became shy.

'Tell us, then,' said his father.

'It was hard. But I think I passed. I answered all the questions.'

'When will you know?' asked his father.

'Next week sometime,' Barcroft replied. 'But Mr Sheldon looked at what I'd done when I'd finished. He told me to come to the Government Survey Office next Tuesday. He must've thought my work was all right.'

'That's good to hear. You can help me in the studio on Monday, then,' said his father.

'All right.' Barcroft was happy to agree. It would be a break from the office work he'd been doing.

'Now sit down and have some dinner,' said Gran, taking charge.

His father went back to his reading and his sisters found something interesting to talk to each other about.

Barcroft was eighteen, the oldest and only son in the Boake family. His father owned a photographic studio in George Street, where he also painted miniature portraits. After his mother died in childbirth five years earlier, his Gran had taken over the household, her own husband having passed on some years before.

The photographic business was unreliable, so his father insisted young Barcroft take a placement in the office of a Sydney land surveyor. During this time, Barcroft learned sufficient draughtsmanship to sit for the examination for admission to the New South Wales Government Survey Office.

Barcroft had briefly attended Sydney Grammar School before being taught for five years by a private tutor, Mr Edward Blackmore, of Hunter Street. His school reports said he was 'a quiet, reserved boy, by no means mopish; fond of reading; noticeably honourable, generous, and constant with his affections'. There was no mention of the depressive moods that sometimes overwhelmed him. To the onlooker, he was not so different from other boys his age.

After a few weeks, Barcroft settled into a routine at the Government Survey Office. Each morning he'd catch the early morning ferry from Milson's Point to the city. After a day in the office, he'd return on the afternoon ferry. Barcroft soon decided it was boring. The work of a temporary draughtsman was more tedious than onerous. Most of the other draughtsmen were family men. They put their heads down and kept their own counsel. The supervisor, Mr Braithewaite, was a stickler for detail. He had a chip on his shoulder from being passed over for promotion. Neatness and order was his catch cry.

Barcroft found himself chided by Braithwaite for talking too much to the office assistants. He thought this was unfair, as Braithewaite himself spent much of his day complaining to all and sundry about the various injustices in his life. Fortunately, there was another trainee surveyor in the office, William. He'd also been a victim of the Braithwaite's displeasure. Together, he and Barcroft plotted a trick on Braithwaite.

Braithwaite's office was beside the main draughting room. It also doubled as the map storage room, so there was a fair traffic of office staff through it. One of the functions of the assistants was to keep the inkwells full. Braithwaite's desk had three wells clearly labelled Black, Red and Blue. Barcroft remembered a trick from school. Early one morning, before the supervisor arrived for work, he and William crept into Braithwaite's office and swapped the contents of the three inkwells round, so that each had a different colour in it. Then they waited.

It was mid-morning before the inevitable occurred. Quite a commotion followed. The first to be accused was the office assistant. He vehemently denied it and said he had witnesses that he'd never been in the office that morning. Secretly, he wished he'd thought of it himself. The head surveyor, who happened to be passing by, saw the comic side. He added to Braithwaite's woes by chiding him for his inattention to detail, though clearly with tongue in cheek. Braithwaite did not take this kindly. William and Barcroft made sure they kept their heads down drawing and were lucky enough to escape suspicion. They had a good laugh about it at lunchtime.

Except for Gran, the Boake family were not early morning people. When Barcroft woke up, Gran was always busy in the kitchen. The noise of her banging pots and pans usually woke him. If it didn't, his father would do the job. At breakfast, Barcroft usually kept quiet, so as to avoid a quarrel with his grumpy sisters. Girls, in his experience, were best to be avoided in the morning.

After breakfast, Gran fussed a bit. 'Have you got your warm vest?' she'd ask. 'Now don't forget your lunch.' She cut lunches for all the children and she made sure they took them in their bags. She always included some home-made biscuits and a piece of fruit.

As Gran loved reading, she made sure the household always had a fresh supply of books, which ranged from Jane Austen and Dickens to Sir Walter Scott. Barcroft was most impressed with *Robinson Crusoe* when he first read it.

On Sunday, if everyone was home, they'd have a roast dinner. This was a family affair. Barcroft and the girls would help prepare the vegetables, which their father had grown in the backyard. Depending on the season and the weather, there were potatoes, carrots, parsnips and pumpkins, and peas, beans or spinach for greens. The children would have competitions to see who could shell the most peas. Barcroft got to cut up the vegetables when they'd been washed. Gran said he could be trusted with a sharp knife. After dinner, the girls helped with the cleaning up, often reluctantly.

Occasionally at the weekend, they had visitors over for afternoon tea. One was Mr Nugent, a client of Mr Boake's from his photography business.

'Good day. Good day,' said Nugent cheerfully as he took off his hat and shook Mr Boake's hand. He was a portly man with a full set of whiskers, well dressed but in an opulent manner.

Barcroft and his sisters waited in the drawing room.

'Do we have to be here?' complained Evie. 'How long will it take? When can I go and play?'

'Quiet, dearie,' said Gran. 'You need to be polite for visitors. You'll like the fresh tarts I've made.'

Evie squirmed on her chair. She felt uncomfortable in her good dress.

'Look at your sisters,' said Gran. 'See. They're behaving like proper little ladies.'

Evie looked at her sisters sitting beside each other on the settee. They didn't look very happy to her.

'Well, now. How are we all today?' said Nugent as he was ushered into the drawing room.

The girls replied politely.

'And how about you, my fine young man?' Nugent asked Barcroft.

'I'm well, thank you,' replied Barcroft, also politely.

'We must see some more of each other, eh?' said Nugent. 'Though your father tells me you're now at the Government Survey Office. Do they keep you out of mischief, eh?'

'I'm kept busy enough,' replied Barcroft.

'You must tell me some more about it later. Ah, Mrs Clarke. It's good to see you. You are looking well.'

'Thank you, Mr Nugent,' replied Gran. 'Please do take a seat, and I'll bring in the teapot.'

Nugent eased himself into one of the good chairs. It creaked under the load as it took his full weight.

Gran brought the tarts in first. 'Please help yourself, before these children eat them all,' she said, with a wink in the direction of the girls.

Nugent took two. The girls were then allowed to help themselves, but only to one at a time. Nugent and Mr Boake then talked business and local politics. Barcroft listened politely, but did not join in. He was no longer a boy, but he didn't feel part of their world. After the tea and the tarts were all finished, the older men adjourned to the porch to smoke their pipes. Barcroft took the opportunity to escape to the veranda on the other side of the house. He was soon joined by Addie, his oldest sister.

'Bartie, why don't you like Mr Nugent?' she asked.

'Why do you say that?'

'I can tell. You had that look.'

'What look?'

'Just that look of yours,' said Addie.

'Was it that obvious? I was polite, wasn't I?'

'Of course you were. I don't think he noticed. He doesn't seem to notice much, except himself.'

'You don't like him either?'

'Not really. He's too...oh, I don't know what. I just don't like him. But you were in Noumea with him for two years. How was it you stayed so long with him there?'

'I didn't have any choice. I was only nine when I left. Father thought it would be good for me. Mother wanted me to learn French. But it was horrid!' Barcroft spoke the last words vehemently.

'What happened?' asked Addie. 'You never talk about it. I always wanted you to tell me about Noumea. All you ever did was put me off. Then Mother died. Was that it? Is that why you never want to talk about it?'

'Not really. I don't know. I remember visiting Mr Nugent then.'

'I was very young,' said Addie 'I don't remember it well – 'cept that we were all sent to stay with Gran. When we came back home, Mother was gone.' She shrugged. 'It was a difficult time. I missed Mother terribly. Father didn't talk for ages. He's still not quite the same.'

'Maybe it was worse being away,' said Barcroft. 'I remember being told the news by Mr Nugent. He put his arm around me.' Barcroft winced. 'I hated the way he touched me.'

'He was only trying to help, wasn't he?'

'It wasn't that.'

'What was it, Bartie?' she asked quietly, knowing he was upset.

'Bad things happened to me. I can't tell you about it. I just can't. Sometimes I wake up and want to kill myself.'

'Please, don't ever do that,' she said, sounding very concerned.

'I don't really mean it – I think. But sometimes I feel so useless, so depressed. There just doesn't seem any point in living. Everything seems so pointless, so meaningless.'

'Is that when you've got the grumps? Is that when you shut yourself in your room?' she asked.

'Yes.'

She moved closer to him and put her hand on his arm. 'I don't know what to say, Bartie. We all love you. We don't want you to do anything silly. You know that.'

'I know, but somehow that doesn't help. Nothing helps. It's as though the light's been put out. Nothing seems good any more. Everything seems so pointless.'

'What can we do?' she asked.

'Nothing, really. It usually goes away. Listen, don't tell anyone else what I've told you about Noumea and Mr Nugent. Promise.'

'I promise.'

'Maybe I shouldn't say this, Addie, but you're my favourite sister.' He looked at her.

'I sort of know,' she said, returning his gaze. 'You're special to me too, Bartie.'

They didn't need to say any more. They just sat there. Barcroft was very fond of Addie – almost too fond, he sometimes thought. He hoped one day he could find a girl of his own – like her. At least with her kindness. That was the type of girl he'd like to marry. Addie was attractive, too, especially now she'd developed a woman's shape. But you couldn't marry your sister, he said to himself.

By July 1886, Barcroft had spent twelve months as a temporary draughtsman in the Government Survey Office. His efforts were rewarded by the offer of a field assistant appointment. He could hardly wait to tell everyone at home the news.

'Gran, Gran. Where is everyone?' he asked as soon as he came in the door. I've got some exciting news.'

His sisters were in the kitchen.

'You're getting married,' said Clare.

They all laughed.

'No, silly. I've been offered a field assistant position.'

'What's that?' said Evie.

'Where?' said Addie.

'It's on the Monaro – up in the Snowy Mountains,' said Barcroft. 'Near Adaminaby. I'll be getting my own horse too!'

'Really?' Clare was most impressed. She was keen on horses.

'How long will it be for?' asked Gran. 'Your father will be pleased. He's always been worried about you being temporary.'

'I had to promise Mr Commins I'd go for two years. But he said I could come home sometimes – for a holiday.'

'When do you go?' said Addie. 'We'll miss you.'

'We leave in two weeks' time,' said Barcroft. Then he added, 'I'm going to miss all of you too.' He suddenly realised he'd be leaving home for good. The thought unsettled him for a moment.

'I'm not going to miss you,' said Evie, pouting.

'Why not?' asked Barcroft.

''Cos I won't have frogs in my lunch,' said Evie.

The other girls laughed. On Tuesday, Barcroft had hidden a frog in Evie's lunch box. She had got a fright when she opened it at school.

'It was a joke, Evie. He was a nice frog, anyway, wasn't he?' said Barcroft.

'You shouldn't have done it,' said Gran.

'How would you like a frog in your lunch?' said Evie.

'All right, all right, I'm sorry.' He gave her a hug. 'Is that okay now?'

She buried her head on his chest. 'Mmm. Maybe.'

'What clothes will you need?' asked Gran. 'You'll need plenty of socks and some warm undergarments. It's sure to be cold up there. The Snowy Mountains, you said?'

'Not now, Gran. Let's think about that later. What's for dinner? How about a cup of tea first?'

Barcroft's father was very pleased to hear the news when he arrived home. 'Now you're going places, son. Here's the start of a real career. Make sure you do your best.'

'Of course I will.'

4

The Monaro, 1886

The train rattled and snaked its way up through the hills. The further they went from Sydney, the browner the country became – and the colder it got. At Goulburn, an icy wind swept across the station platform.

'It's always freezing here,' said Mr Bourke. 'Damned miserable place.'

Barcroft wrapped himself in his coat as he huddled over his pipe with his back to the wind. The wind tried to suck the smoke out of his mouth before he could inhale it. He was glad now that Gran had insisted he take plenty of warm clothes.

The next major station was Queanbeyan. Here, they changed over to horse and carriage. Then on they lurched, through Michalago, Bredbo and Bunyan, from hotel to hotel. Bourke remarked to Barcroft that travellers and their drivers seemed an awfully thirsty lot. So were the locals, too, Barcroft noticed.

'How they get so thirsty in this damned cold is a puzzle,' commented Bourke wryly. He was an abstemious man himself.

As they rocked along, Barcroft took in the images of the countryside as it passed by the carriage window. It made a vivid impact on him, the way things do when you set forth on an adventure.

The bush was unlike any he'd previously seen. From Michalago and Bredbo onwards, the Monaro grasslands opened out beside and ahead of them. Stark, frostbitten grasslands, edged with sparsely treed brown hills. Blue-grey rugged mountains fringed the skyline beyond. Above them, thin wisps of cloud stretched across the pastel sky.

They finally reached Cooma. It was a bustling town of well over a thousand people – the centre of the Monaro district. A busy scene met them. The town was spread over a few hills, with the churches keeping watch from the heights. Government confidence in the town could be seen from the construction of substantial public works buildings. Blacksmiths were banging, masons and carpenters hammering and the mill rumbled away by the creek. Horses and pedestrians ambled down the streets.

Mr Commins had arranged for Barcroft to be met in Cooma by one of the Rocklands Station hands, Tim Boyd. Tim would show him the way to Rocklands Station, wrote Commins, and bring him to join Commins at his survey headquarters. Rocklands was twenty miles or so along the road to Adaminaby, up in the hills, Commins explained in his letter.

Tim was waiting to meet the coach when it arrived late in the afternoon at the Royal Hotel. He was younger than Barcroft expected. He had blond hair, blue eyes and a boyish look. He couldn't be any older than himself, Barcroft thought, maybe even younger.

'I'll give you a hand with that,' said Tim, picking up one of Barcroft's bags. 'We're sharing a room. It's upstairs, round the back of the hotel.'

'Thanks,' said Barcroft. He took his other bag as it was handed down from the coach.

'We'll collect your horse tomorrow,' said Tim. 'Now let's get this up to the room. They're just about to serve dinner.'

As they clumped down the stairs, he said over his shoulder, 'The food's good here. Better than you'll get at Rocklands. There's heaps of vegies.'

Barcroft agreed with Tim about the food. It was good. After dinner, Tim suggested they join the crowd at the bar. They walked down the corridor and into a room full of heat, noise and smoke. A large fire was roaring away on the far side. Faces were flushed. The talk was loud and boisterous. They squeezed their way to the bar. When they'd been served, they took their drinks to a table in the corner. Before Barcroft could light his pipe, an unstable old bushman joined them, spilling his drink as he sat down.

'Ain't I seen yer before?' he said, peering at Tim. His face was weathered red from the sun and the wind. Spikes of iron-grey hair stuck out untidily from beneath his battered hat. His bushy grey beard was stained yellow with nicotine from the pipe clenched between his teeth. Despite his unsteadiness, Barcroft noticed that his watery blue eyes were piercing and direct.

'Where yer going, now?' he asked. He fumbled as he tried to light his pipe.

'Right now? We ain't going anywhere, right now.' said Tim. 'Just having a drink, same as you.'

'That's not what I mean,' said the old man, then he paused. 'I mean, what's y'business? Y'know.'

Tim thought about stringing him along, but changed his mind. 'I'm just in town to collect Mr Boake here. He's a surveyor. I'll be taking him up to Rocklands Station,' said Tim.

'G'day, then,' said the old man. He insisted on shaking their hands, spilling more of his drink in the process. 'I'm Barnie – Old Barnacle. Used to be at sea – get it?' He started to chuckle but ended up coughing.

'Rocklands? Rocklands?' He repeated the words slowly, followed by a hiccup. 'That's on the road to Seymour, ain't it? The Seymour–Kiandra road?'

'It's twenty mile along the Kiandra road, before Adaminaby,' said Tim.

'Yer mean Seymour,' said Barnie.

'No, it's called Adaminaby now. They changed it,' said Tim.

'Baloney! They can't do that! It's Seymour. None of this Adaminaby rubbish. Sounds like a black's name. Can't have that,' he said indignantly.

'Well, it's called Adaminaby now,' said Tim. He explained to Barcroft the town's name had just been changed so as to avoid confusion with Seymour in Victoria.

'I don't care. Yer can't change a town's name,' the old man said, raising his voice. 'No good'll come of it. God'll punish them. He'll smite 'em down. He'll drown 'em in a great flood! Mark my words!' He shook his finger at them, then slumped back in his chair.

Barcroft was taken aback by his tirade. He wondered what could be the cause of it.

One of the drinkers at a nearby table had overheard the old man shouting. 'Don't take any notice of him, he's crazy in the head,' he whispered to Barcroft.

'Ain't been up Kiandra way for years,' said Barnie, mumbling into his beard. 'Not since the easy gold ran out.' He peered at Barcroft from over his drink. 'I were there in the big rush, y'know. In the sixties.'

'Really?' said Barcroft.

'Yeah. Them were the days.' He looked pensive.

Tim got up from the table to get another round of drinks.

'Now what's yer business again?' said the old man, leaning towards Barcroft.

'I'll be doing surveying for Mr Commins,' said Barcroft. 'He's based at Rocklands.'

'I know,' said Barnie with a wink. 'Yer off to Kiandra. Yer gonna survey claims, ain't yer?'

'No, not to my knowledge,' said Barcroft. 'We'll be doing farm selections.'

'Yer can't fool me.' The old man leaned forward. He whispered hoarsely, 'Yer don't have to tell me. I know there's gold in it. They'll kill for it. But I'll keep mum.' He paused, then added conspiratorially, 'Yer can trust an old digger.'

They sat for the next few minutes without talking. The old bushman finished off his drink. Barcroft lit his pipe.

Then the old man whispered at Barcroft again. 'Yer got to watch out for them Chinese in Kiandra.' He leaned forward and held onto Barcroft's arm tightly.

Barcroft could feel the old man's fingers biting into him. He had surprising strength.

'Them Chinese at Kiandra, they'll take yer in the night!'

Barcroft could see a look of fear in his eyes.

'Watch out. Yer've been warned,' he said. 'Take it from me. I know. You young fellas need to be told. Yer mayn't think so. But I've told yer now.' He let go of Barcroft's arm and sat back – as if his conscience had been satisfied.

Tim returned with the drinks. Peter, a stockman friend, was with him.

'Hey, Old Barnie's not bothering you?' said Peter.

'No. It's fine,' said Barcroft.

'Don't worry 'bout him. He goes on a bit – lives in the past. He's harmless, but. Never been the same since his accident. Can't ride now. It banged his head.'

After a couple more drinks, Tim and Barcroft turned in for the night.

The next morning, they were up early for a solid breakfast, finished off with a mug of hot tea. Their horses had already been saddled for them when they reached the stables. They thanked the stable groom. Barcroft spent a few minutes getting to know his new companion, a brown mare called Sweetbriar. They hit it off immediately. She was a good-looking horse. Not a racehorse, but a sturdy mountain horse, like her wild cousins in the hills.

Cooma was fog-bound as they rode briskly up the hill towards Mount Gladstone. The frost crunched under their horses' hoofs and their breath made clouds of steam in the crisp morning air. Twisted scrubby white gum trees lined the track. By the top of the rise, they had warmed up and were out of the fog. From here, in the far distance they could see white snow-capped mountains on the horizon. Immediately ahead stretched the pale yellow Monaro grasslands, now lightly dusted with a white frost.

'That's the main range, over past Jindaboine,' said Tim, pointing to the far mountains. 'We go the other way. Over there towards Kiandra.' He gestured to the west.

'Will there be snow at Rocklands?' asked Barcroft.

'Could be.'

'I've never seen snow before. What's it like?'

'Just like frost, only thicker. You'll soon see,' said Tim.

The Travellers Rest nestled in a hollow ahead of them. It had been well patronised during the Kiandra rush but it didn't get much custom now. They rode past without stopping, except to nod at the landlord standing on the front veranda. At the four-mile junction, they turned west.

Across the undulating grasslands they rode, and up amongst the low hills. From the heights at Rhine Falls, they stopped and looked back. The Monaro plains stretched for miles behind them. Traces of smoke from the fires of Cooma hung lazily in the air in the far distance. It was a superb view. Barcroft took a deep breath of the cold mountain air.

'We'll be at the top of the Great Dividing Range soon,' said Tim. 'It's not so high here, but you might see some snow.'

As they rode further, isolated snowdrifts appeared beside the track. Mostly they were in the shade of fallen tree logs. Barcroft dismounted to feel the snow. It was just like ice – sort of crumbly and wet.

The track wound its way through stands of white-trunked trees and over the top of the hill. Again they could see the snow-capped mountains in the distance, only closer now. A few miles further and the trees started to thin out, retreating to the knolls. They rode gently downhill through grassy frost hollows crowded with tussocks. Granite boulders were casually strewn around, like the work of an untidy giant.

Rocklands Station nestled amongst the boulders, surrounded by grazing sheep. Its timber and iron buildings were scattered across a north-facing slope, on a slight rise beside Frying Pan Creek. Barcroft noticed there was even a tennis court.

Commins was pleased to see them. Barcroft hadn't met him before, but he liked him straightaway. He reminded him of his uncle. He laughed in the same way. Barcroft immediately had a good feeling about the place.

The survey party were housed in the shearers' quarters for the winter. Meals were served at the main house. In the spring, when shearing began, they would need to set up tents for themselves. In the meantime, they had the shearers' rooms all to themselves. These were timber-lined, with a north facing veranda. Commins had turned one of the rooms with a window and a fireplace into a draughting room. Barcroft had a bedroom for himself. Quite luxurious, he thought.

Barcroft settled easily into life at Rocklands, except for the cold. A week after he arrived, it stormed. Late in the afternoon, the clouds darkened and became menacing. Then a fierce wind blew. Finally, the snow came. White sheets of driven snow whipped horizontally across the yard. It was so densely white that at times Barcroft couldn't see the main house from his room. At first, the snow melted as it touched the ground, but soon it built up in drifts against the posts and the sides of the sheds. When the wind dropped, the white flakes drifted down in little flurries, ever so quietly. Total quietness followed, as the day ended. All night, Barcroft could hear a soft pattering on the iron roof.

In the morning, everything was blanketed white. It was as though the land had been touched by a white wand and made beautiful. Even the farm sheds looked picturesque under their snow-covered roofs – with delicate icicles decorating their eaves.

The beauty didn't last. By afternoon, the tramping of men and animals had turned the yard into a muddy quagmire. The snow-covered hills, which had started the day so gracefully, returned to their usual faded brown. Barcroft noticed how quickly the appearance of the landscape changed. If you were philosophically inclined, he mused, you could see it as a reflection on life. Beauty can be so fragile and so fleeting – so easily lost. It would make a good subject for a poem, he thought.

After the snow came the cold. The following nights were freezing cold. Bone-freezing cold. So cold Barcroft couldn't keep warm, no matter how many blankets he used. It was so cold he couldn't sleep properly. His nose kept freezing. He had to keep it out of the covers to breathe. He'd always felt embarrassed about his nose – now it didn't even work properly. Not only that – outside in the cold air it dripped continuously.

When the novelty of his new surroundings wore off, he missed his family, especially Addie and Gran. He wrote his family a letter. When they wrote back, their news seemed to come from so far away.

Winter passed. When spring came, his days were mostly spent in the field. He liked it because they were always moving on. Surveying took them riding all over the surrounding countryside. The weather varied, but the open Monaro country gave panoramic views to the distant mountain ranges on all sides. Here you were on the roof of Australia. At times, the clouds drifting overhead were so low he felt he could almost reach up and touch them. It was good to be alive.

Barcroft had never found waking in the morning easy. But now he had Sweetbriar to welcome him. She eagerly waited for her feed of early morning oats. She was always keen to see him and give him a nuzzle.

At Rocklands, Barcroft had little opportunity to brood over things. There was always someone to yarn to or something to do. There were horses to feed, sheep that needed yarding, or tennis to play. The farm was a thriving little community. Commins had been joined by his wife, who was a keen tennis player. Miss Mulligan the housemaid also played, and so did Tim. Apart from tennis players, there were Jack and Charlie the stockmen, Ted the rouseabout, Miss Brooks the other housemaid and Peng the Chinese cook, not to mention the station manager, Mr Williams – and, at shearing time, the shearers.

'Come on, you lot,' shouted Williams. 'Come and give us a hand.' He waved his hand at Barcroft, Tim and young Ted. He was wheeling a barrow loaded with tree seedlings. 'Let's see if we can give the yard some shelter,' he said. 'Here, take these spades.'

They took a spade each and followed Williams. He led them around the far side of the stockyard railings. 'Best we plant them here, on the southern side,' he said.

They were each allocated a planting site. He'd already marked each site with a stake. They started digging. It was hard work and they struck rock at some of the sites.

'Do we really have to do this?' said Ted. He was never a willing worker. 'Why bother? The sheep'll only eat 'em anyway.'

'Yeah. It'll be years before they give any shelter here – if they survive at all,' said Jim.

'That's the trouble with you youngsters,' said Williams. 'You never think of the future. Always looking for the easy way out.' He had a captive audience, so he kept going. 'When you're older, you'll realise. You've got to invest in the future right now. If you don't, the future won't happen. There isn't an easy way out. The future is only what we make of it now.'

'I won't be here,' said Ted. 'Not if I can help it.'

'Don't bet on that,' Williams said. 'Fate plays strange tricks. Even so, someone will be here. They'll appreciate the work we're doing. There'll be big beautiful trees here one day.'

'I hope we all live to see it!' said Tim.

In all, they planted twenty trees, poplars, elms and pines.

The weekends were the highlights for Barcroft. He and Tim would ride down to Adaminaby. Mostly, they'd end at a pub. The publican at the Commercial Hotel got to know them well. He offered them cheer and company. It was in his interest, of course.

Adaminaby lay in an open valley, not far from the Eucumbene River. It was the last town before the road to Kiandra wound its way up into the hills. Like the Traveller's Rest, it had seen the glory days of the Kiandra rush but was quieter now, almost sleepy.

The New Chum claim at Kiandra was still operating. Sometimes, miners from the claim would pass through. In front of a blazing fire and warmed by a potent brew, the old timers would tell tales from the heyday of the rush. They told how men had frozen to death in their tents. How the gold coach had to run the gauntlet of the bushranger gangs. How men had fought to defend their claims, or just for the hell of it. They told of times when gold nuggets had been lying around for the picking. Late in the evening, by the flickering light of the fire, it didn't seen to matter if the stories were true or not.

Apart from the attractions of the pubs, another other reason to visit Adaminaby was to attend church on Sunday. The women at Rocklands were most keen on this. Barcroft suspected their interest was prompted more by the opportunity to dress up and meet friends than by the call of God. He was happy enough to accompany them, though. Unlike some men, he didn't feel uneasy in the company of women, once he got to know them. It reminded him of his sisters.

Sitting in church, Barcroft would reflect on the wider purpose of life. He believed in a god of sorts. But if there was a god, he must work at some high level. There was little evidence of his workings in everyday life. It was easier to see the influence of the Devil in the general affairs of man. The suggestion that the meek and downtrodden, the selfless and the deserving would inherit the earth didn't ring true to him. In his view, this precept was only used by the powerful and the greedy as a ruse to dupe the common people while they exploited them.

Barcroft took more than a passing interest in the young women he met. In this he was no different from other men his age. He viewed women with a keen eye and was a critical judge of looks. Madge Mulligan was good company, he thought, but she had the face of a pudding. Sometimes, he wondered if he'd ever meet his ideal girl. She would be attractive, of course – but intelligent too. She'd have a mind of her own but would be kindly and care about people, a bit like Addie. His shyness worried him. What if he met his ideal girl but couldn't tell her how he felt?

There was no time for reflection the first time Barcroft saw the McKeahnie girls. He felt an immediate sensation – like an electric shock. His heart raced. The McKeahnies didn't always attend church. This Sunday, Alex McKeahnie and his wife were accompanied by all their children, including the oldest girls, Jenny, Jean and May. The McKeahnie children radiated the glowing good health of the bush. Hats and ribbons akimbo and skirts rustling, they laughed and chatted amongst themselves as they arrived, stepping lightly across the damp church lawn.

It was Jean and May who caught Barcroft's eye. Briefly, the rain had stopped. A ray of sunlight danced on the church wall as they walked past. That moment was marked indelibly into his memory. He noticed their fresh faces, their sparkling eyes and their captivating smiles. He didn't know what to do. He must have looked awkward.

'Are you all right?' asked Mrs Commins, who had invited him join her on the ride to church.

'Yes, I'm fine, thanks,' he replied.

The McKeahnies sat in the opposite pew. Barcroft spent much of the sermon looking sideways at the McKeahnie girls, as surreptitiously as he could. He noticed their long brown hair, falling in tresses down their backs, and their hazel eyes. They didn't seem to notice him. He didn't hear a word the minister said. After the service, everyone gathered outside to exchange news and pleasantries. Mrs Commins knew the McKeahnies, so she walked over to join them.

'Good day, Mrs Commins,' Mrs McKeahnie said. 'Mr Commins not with you today?'

'Not this time,' said Mrs Commins. 'But let me introduce you to Mr Boake. He's been kind enough to accompany me today.'

She introduced Barcroft to Mr and Mrs McKeahnie, and to their daughters, Jenny, Jean and May. The younger children had already disappeared with friends.

Jean looked Barcroft directly in the eye. 'A pleasure to meet you, Mr Boake,' she said. Her glance lingered.

May curtsied in front of him. 'Nice to see you,' she said, with the sweetest of smiles.

Barcroft noticed the intriguing way she curled the corner of her mouth, and the look in her eyes.

Jean was the older of the two sisters. Barcroft guessed she was around his age, or perhaps a bit older. May was a year or so younger. He thought both girls were very attractive, though in different ways. Jean's face had strength and character, with a straight nose and high cheekbones. She was plainer than May and had long straight hair. May's hair was wavy, almost curly. She had a turned-up nose and girlish lips. Lots of teeth showed whenever she laughed or smiled. Both had very pretty eyes. He specially noticed their long dark eyelashes.

Barcroft felt he was going red. He stammered a reply. He didn't know who or what to look at.

'So you're Mr Commins' young assistant?' asked Mr McKeahnie.

'Yes, sir,' said Barcroft, trying to regain his composure.

'We've heard about you. How long will you be up this way?' asked Mrs McKeahnie.

'Till the winter of '88, I think,' he replied.

'You must come and visit us then. You like riding, do you?' said Mrs McKeahnie.

'Yes, I think so,' he said.

'He's being shy,' said Mrs Commins. 'He's a rather good horseman.'

'Young Charlie could do with some riding company,' said Mr McKeahnie. 'Why don't you come over and visit us next Saturday? That's if Commins can spare you.'

'I'm sure he'll be able to,' said Mrs Commins. She had a twinkle in her eye. She could see what was happening.

'If that's all right, I will,' said Barcroft. He felt excited but tried not to show it.

'We're easy to find,' said McKeahnie. 'Just take the road round Locker's Hill and follow it to the Murrumbidgee. We're at Rosedale. It's just the other side of the ford. You can't miss us. There's willows at the ford. You can see them from across the river flats.'

'Yes. It'll be nice to see you,' said Mrs McKeahnie. She spoke in a genuinely friendly tone. 'You can tell us all about yourself then.'

Barcroft had the feeling his life had just been changed. He rode back to Rocklands in a daze.

That evening, he wrote to his father.

Rocklands, Adaminaby

29 May 1887

Dear Father

It gets very monotonous here after being accustomed to shifting every week or so, there is always the change and speculation as to what sort of camp the next will be and besides there is always something going on, but at the farm there is no excitement except to go to Adaminaby on Saturday afternoon.

We are in the middle of winter now. It is excessively cold, a heavy frost every morning, it is cold now the whole day, of course you don't notice it if you are hard at work in the sun but as soon as you go in the shade it is as chilly as possible even at midday. The mountains all round have been covered with snow since the beginning of the month. There was snow on them at the beginning of January and again in May so it is only off them for about four months, hardly that.

I had a pleasant ride today in and out of Adaminaby in the pouring rain – to church. This was a woman's freak. Mrs Commins would go, and asked me; and as I can't refuse a lady as a rule I made a martyr of myself.

I am sure I don't know how I managed to make this letter so long for I have no news. I will give you an extract from my diary for the last fortnight. 'Got up just as the breakfast was going in. Rushed in as grace was finished; ate two chops; bullied Miss Mulligan about the tea being too weak. After breakfast smoke in the kitchen. Did plans till eleven; another smoke; dinner at one – ate a plate of mutton. Another smoke, more plans, more tobacco till 4 o'clock, knock off play tennis till tea time, feed my horse, then eat more chops, another smoke. Mrs Commins and I play young Boyd and Miss Mulligan; and strange to say, always beat them. Mrs Commins retires about nine; I put in the time yarning in the kitchen with Jack and the cook (Chinese) till ten – then bed.'

Of course, on Saturday whole holiday; go to Adaminaby hear the latest yarn from Walter, the publican (mostly discreditable); then home. On Sunday read the papers all day; tennis in the afternoon.

This is the programme, except we have cutlets for breakfast occasionally instead of chops. I think I have had beef once only since the spring. How is Granny give her my love.

Your affectionate son, Bartie.

He didn't mention the McKeahnies. He thought he'd wait and see how things developed.

5

Rosedale, 1887

Mr McKeahnie's directions were clear. Barcroft followed the road round Locker's Hill and down to the Murrumbidgee. Here, the river flowed out of the mountains and into a wide fertile flood plain, bounded by grassy hills. As he rode across the river flats towards Rosedale, he saw three riders ahead in the distance. At closer range, he recognised the McKeahnie girls, Jean and May. His heart beat faster. There was a young man with them. Jean and May introduced him as their brother.

'Everyone calls him Charlie Mac,' said Jean. 'You may as well too.'

'Hello,' said Barcroft.

Charlie nodded, but said nothing.

Barcroft sized him up. He guessed he was a couple of years younger than himself. He had the same bright eyes and clear good looks of his sisters. His gaze was direct and he sat proudly in his saddle, as if to say this was his territory.

'Nice of you to come over,' Jean said to Barcroft. Her words broke the tension, immediately making him feel more at ease.

'My pleasure.'

'We were wondering if we might meet you,' said May, smiling sweetly. 'Our place is over there, just the other side of the river. It's only a mile or so from here.'

They wheeled their horses round and headed in the direction of the homestead.

Barcroft noticed Charlie was riding a big grey mare. She was a strong-looking horse, with clear signs of good breeding. Jean and May were on sturdy mountain-bred colts.

'That's a fair-looking horse you're on there,' Charlie Mac said to Barcroft.

'She's willing enough,' said Barcroft. 'She's no racehorse. But she handles the rough ground well.'

After riding a little further, Charlie turned to Barcroft. 'How 'bout we race home?' he said.

His sisters must have guessed. As soon as they heard the word 'race', they were off like a flash. Barcroft and Charlie galloped after them. Across the grassy flats they raced. Charlie caught the girls by the corner of the boundary fence. Barcroft was just behind. Then down towards the ford they went. Barcroft saw his chance. He pointed Sweetbriar into the thick tussocks to cut the corner. It was a risk, but she took it in her stride. By the start of the ford, he and Sweetbriar were ahead of the rest. Across they all splashed. Barcroft urged Sweetbriar up the far bank, only a couple of lengths ahead. Now they were at the home paddock, with Charlie and his sisters in hot pursuit. The home paddock rails barred their way. Barcroft gave Sweetbriar her head. Straight over she went, clearing them in style. The others followed.

'Hey, you can ride,' said Charlie as they wheeled in front of the homestead, catching their breath. 'I would've cut the corner too if I'd known.'

Barcroft smiled.

'Well done, Mr Boake,' said May, with a touch of admiration in her voice.

Barcroft didn't need to say anything. He felt good.

'Lets give these horses a rub down,' said Jean. 'Then we can go in for a cup of tea. If that's all right with you, Mr Boake?'

'Certainly,' said Barcroft.

As they walked the horses over to the stables, May asked, 'Do we have to call you Mr Boake? It sounds very formal. What do your friends call you? Have you got a nickname?'

'Sometimes people call me Boakie. My sisters call me Bartie.'

'I'm really Mary – but you can call me May,' she said, with a smile and a toss of her head. 'I think I'll call you Bartie.'

Rosedale was a substantial station. It had a commanding view across the Murrumbidgee flats and was tucked into the lee of a hill for protection from the western winds. Inside, Barcroft could see the McKeahnies had all the comforts of modern living. The kitchen had a large centrally located table. There was a separate dining room and through it Barcroft could see that the drawing room was tastefully decorated, with a carpet and a comfortable settee. There was even a piano in the corner.

The cook was making hot cakes as they walked into the kitchen. She immediately bustled them out.

'Hey, hey,' she said. 'There's much too many of you to be in here! You sit yourselves down on the veranda and I'll bring you some tea. Off you go.'

She was clearly the boss in the kitchen, so they did her bidding.

Mrs McKeahnie joined them on the veranda. When the food appeared, so too did the two youngest girls, Dolly and Lem.

Barcroft was the centre of attention. They all wanted to know about his family. He told them about his sisters, and his father's photography business. Jean asked questions about the technical details of photography. She also wanted to know about surveying. Mrs McKeahnie was interested in the latest news from Rocklands.

Barcroft felt at home with the McKeahnies, even though he'd only just met them. The atmosphere at Rosedale reminded him of his own family, except there were more of them here. Jean had a sharp mind, he could tell. She wasn't satisfied with half an answer. He found that attractive. He really liked her. But he also found May very attractive. She was gentler, but carefree and full of life. He felt a strong physical attraction towards her.

Mrs McKeahnie said he must visit them again.

'Next time you come, how 'bout we look for wild horses up the range?' said Charlie Mac. 'It's rough up there but that little filly of yours'd go well.'

'Charlie's always looking for an excuse to go after wild horses,' said Jean. 'You'll need to take care.'

'Where's the range?' asked Barcroft.

'It's up the river, in the hills between here and Kiandra. Our uncle's got an outstation there,' said May. 'We sometimes go up in summer. It gets too much snow in winter. There's lots of wild horses up there, though.'

'Sounds interesting,' said Barcroft. '

'It's done, then. We'll go next week if it doesn't snow,' said Charlie Mac.

Barcroft rode home that afternoon all buoyed up. He hardly noticed the developing chill in the air. It was some time since he had been down in the dumps, he reflected. The fresh mountain air must be doing him good.

It snowed next week. It snowed so heavily that everyone was trapped at Rocklands for two full days. When conditions improved, it was a job and a half travelling in to Adaminaby. Riding after wild horses was put off until the spring. Mrs McKeahnie would not allow it till then.

Barcroft wrote to his father, still without mentioning the McKeahnies.

Rocklands, Adaminaby

31 July 1887

My Dear Father

I could not answer your letter last post as I was away last Sunday. I have not much news to tell you - everything is very dull always through the winter. The principal topic of course is the weather which has been simply fearful for the last two months.

We have had snow every week without fail, if we do happen to get a fine day it blows a hurricane. It is bad enough here but in Kiandra they are finally snowed in for the winter. The traffic in and out has ceased for some time with the exception of the mail and last Sunday it could not get in on account of the snow, so now he has to take it as near as he can on horseback and a man comes out from the town on snow shoes and takes it in.

I don't think I ever told you about these before, fancy having to use these in sunny Australia, but in Kiandra and the mountains they are the only means of travelling. They have been able to use them in Adaminaby for pleasure, not necessity, it is great sport.

They are about seven feet long, just a Mountain-Ash paling 4 inches wide steamed and turned up at the point with a leather strap in the middle for the feet. They travel at a tremendous pace on falling ground: of course on the level they can only go slowly.

I saw in the Kiandra letter today that there is 3 feet of snow on the level and further up at Nine Mile workings 6 feet; in the drifts this means 20 feet or over.

We get a magnificent view of the mountains from the top of the paddock extending in one unbroken line of white along the horrizon.

Give my love to Granny and Addie and the children and write soon.

Your affectionate son, Bartie.

Over the next few months, Barcroft became a regular weekend visitor to Rosedale. He began to feel he was part of the family. On Sundays, he'd sit on the floor of the drawing room with the younger children and read them stories. Even though they were old enough to read for themselves, they liked him to read out loud to them. Sometimes he'd read from *Alice in Wonderland*, or a Grimms' story. At other times he'd make up stories. They were usually variations on the Grimms' tales but with the cruel bits left out.

One evening when they were all sitting round the dinner table, Mr McKeahnie said to Barcroft, 'I hear you're a bit of a storyteller. It's about time I told you a story. You can tell this one to the city folk when you get back home.'

'Not the one about the miners?' said Mrs McKeahnie, apprehensively.

'No, not that one. This one's a true story. It's about what happened right here. Here in this district a few years back.'

'It's the one about Jack Corrigan,' guessed May.

'Yes. It's the story of Jack,' said McKeahnie.

'It goes on for a while,' said May.

'Let your father tell it,' said Mrs McKeahnie.

McKeahnie began. 'Well, there was this fella called Jack Corrigan. He used to live down the river here – down past Flat Rock. He'd taken up some land there but it wasn't enough to make a living.'

May leant over and whispered in Barcroft's ear. 'It's got a sad ending,' she said.

He liked it when she came so close. He could smell her hair. He wished he could touch her.

'Jack was a bit of a character,' went on McKeahnie. 'He was popular with the locals. A top horseman he was, too. They reckon there was no horse known who could unseat him – and that's saying something. The mountain horses round here can buck like crikey.' McKeahnie paused before going on. 'Generous to a fault was Jack. And d'you know why?'

'No,' said Barcroft.

'Well, Jack wasn't too fussy about property. He was generous to everyone – but it wasn't his property he'd be giving away. The squatters round here reckoned he was a complete rascal. You see, it was their beef his wife used to salt for his table.'

'What did happen to his wife?' asked May.

'She left the district. Let your father continue, or we'll never get to the end,' said Mrs McKeahnie. 'Go on, Alex.'

'Jack thought his neighbours wouldn't notice the occasional beast gone missing,' said McKeahnie. 'Well, he was wrong. They did. And, to cut a long story short, they set the troopers after him.' He paused again.

The younger girls started fidgeting. Mrs McKeahnie frowned at them.

'It happened like this,' McKeahnie resumed. 'Jack was having a drink at the Squatters Arms. He liked a tipple or two. He must've got word that trooper Fraser was coming for him. The way I heard it, one minute he was having a drink, the next he was on his horse racing down the street. Trooper Fraser was after him as fast as he could. Over at the showground they saw Jack and his filly go clear over the big swing gate. It must've been a sight.'

'That's not there any more, is it?' said Charlie.

'No, it isn't,' said McKeahnie. 'Well, Jack was clearly heading for his place down the river. The Lockers tell me they saw Jack and the trooper go past their gate at a furious pace. The river down here was up in flood but Jack and the trooper still swam it at the ford. Then off they went down past O'Rourke's, down past Flat Rock, till they were almost at Jack's place. Jack was probably aiming to change his horse there. The trooper was catching him and his horse was failing.' He paused for a drink.

'At Jack's place there was a punt to get across the river. And there was a wire rope to pull it across. Well, Jack leapt off his horse and rushed down through the scrub to the punt. But when he got there the punt was gone. It'd been washed away in the flood. The trooper was right behind, almost in range for a shot. I don't know whether he fired or not. It doesn't matter. Jack jumped into the river and started to pull himself across by the rope. He didn't get far when a big branch came down the river and swept him away.' McKeahnie paused for emphasis. 'They never saw him again.'

'What happened to his place?' asked Charlie.

'He never owned it. The government took it back. It was Crown land.' McKeahnie turned to Barcroft. 'See, it hasn't always been quiet here. We've had our share of excitement.'

'We can do without that kind of excitement,' said Mrs McKeahnie.

'That's a story you can take back to Sydney when you go,' said McKeahnie.

'I don't know if I'll be going back to Sydney,' said Barcroft. 'But, you know, that story could make an interesting poem.'

'A poem?' said Charlie, screwing up his face.

'Well, a bush ballad anyway – like Gordon's poems,' said Barcroft.

'Are you going to write bush ballads?' asked Jean.

'I don't know,' said Barcroft. 'I'd like to be able to.'

'Writing poetry is all right,' said McKeahnie. 'But it doesn't pay the bills. I wouldn't want a daughter of mine marrying someone who's just a poet.'

He had a twinkle in his eye, but Barcroft thought he sounded half-serious.

'I think your daughters will want to make up their own minds about who they marry,' said Mrs McKeahnie.

'I'll certainly be making my own decision on that matter,' said Jean, quietly but firmly.

'That's enough,' said Mrs McKeahnie. She could see trouble brewing. 'Let's talk about something else.'

It was bright moonlight as Barcroft rode home to Rocklands. The river at the ford was only a foot or so deep and flowing gently. There was no need to swim it tonight – though you could see on the banks how high it sometimes rose. Barcroft found it hard to imagine the power over life and death it could wield.

The night was clear and calm. He could feel the cold air settling in the hollows as he rode along. The overnight frost was on its way.

When he arrived at Rocklands, Tim was eating in the kitchen. Tim suggested they ride to Kiandra next Saturday. 'There's still plenty of snow up there,' he said. 'The boys at the Commercial tell me they have snowshoe races. Why don't we go take a look?'

Barcroft agreed.

Early next Saturday, Barcroft and Tim set off early. They were well prepared. They packed provisions in their saddle bags and wore plenty of layers of warm clothing. There was no snow on the ground at Adaminaby, only frost, but not far up the Kiandra road snowdrifts began to appear beside them. By Sawyer's Hill, the snow was deep across the track and the horses were slowed to a steady plod.

They finally sighted Kiandra across the far side of the Eucumbene valley. It was a snow-white vista. Where they stood, the sun was shining. Over past Kiandra, the horizon was darkened by billowing dark grey snow clouds, hovering ominously over the mountain ridgetops.

'What a view!' said Tim, with uncharacteristic emotion. He wasn't often moved by the sights of nature.

Barcroft had been taking in the scenery as they travelled. Nothing he'd seen before compared with the beauty of this mountain landscape. There was a special beauty in the twisted grey and white snow gum trunks, with their feet buried in the snow and their tops capped with it. Leaves poked out from underneath their white snowcaps like an untidy fringe. Delicate icicles hung from their branches, sparkling in the pale sunlight. All around, the sharp contours of the land had been softened by a gentle white blanket of snow.

'It sure takes some beating,' said Barcroft. This is truly beautiful, he thought to himself.

Down they rode to the freezing waters of the Eucumbene River, then up to Kiandra township. The township buildings were strung out along either side of the road, hiding under their snow-laden roofs. Plumes of wood smoke rose from the chimneys. Further up the hillside, at New Chum Hill, the derrick in the New Chum claim was like a giant gallows, looming darkly over the white landscape below.

The action was at Township Hill, on the slope above the town. A small crowd of spectators were dotted across the hillside. Tim and Barcroft tied up their horses at the hotel and joined them. Not without some difficulty. It wasn't easy walking across the drifts. Every few steps the soft snow would sink under their feet with a jolt.

The spectators were spread out in two rows lining the slope, all the way down to and across the road. Most were rugged up in thick woollen clothes, many with thigh-high boots. Some were balancing on long narrow snowshoes made out of planks of wood with the ends turned up, like the prows of Viking ships. Others had stuck them upright into the snow beside them. Barcroft noticed the snowshoes had bindings in the middle for attaching to your boots. As the skiers moved across the snow, they used a long sapling, cut from a straight mountain tree, to steady themselves.

'What's going on?' Tim asked one of the onlookers.

'It's the Australasian championships,' the man replied.

'What's that?' asked Barcroft.

'The Australasian Snowshoe Championships,' said the man. 'They start at the top of the hill and race each other down there to the finish.' He pointed to the crowd over the road at the bottom of the slope. 'Watch out! Here they come!'

Two skiers came swishing down the hill towards them, legs apart, crouched over their long timber skis. At the road crossing, one of them lost his balance as he took the bump. He ended up cartwheeling into a snowdrift on the far side.

There were shouts and cries from the crowd.

'Someone's done their money,' said the man beside them.

'They bet on the races?' asked Tim.

'They sure do. And the winner gets a prize, too. That's the overall winner, of course. These are the heats. The losers get eliminated and the winner is the best in the final.'

Tim and Barcroft watched two more races before it was time for the final. Their companion introduced himself as Harry, a miner from the New Chum claim.

'If I had money, I'd put it on Carl the Dane,' said Harry. 'They live and breathe the snow where he comes from.'

'Who's he up against?' asked Tim.

'A local lad, Davy Eccleston,' said Harry.

'I know him,' said Tim. 'He comes from down our way.'

The final was an anticlimax. Carl sped down the slope with grace and speed. Davy was never in the race.

'I told you,' said Harry. 'That Dane knows all the secrets. I heard him tell how he waxes his snowshoes with a special mixture.'

'Really?' said Tim.

'But he's good, anyway. He's got terrific balance. You saw him,' said Harry.

'Yes, he's got class. Pity about Davy,' said Tim. 'But it can't be easy.'

'It sure isn't,' said Harry. 'You should give it a try.'

'Maybe we should,' said Tim.

'Time for some hot food now, don't you reckon?' said Harrry. 'Why don't you come and join us at the pub? They serve good tucker.'

Barcroft had been watching the men on their snowshoes. There weren't many with Carl's control. Spills were frequent. When they came down the hill and wanted to brake, they put their saplings between their legs and rode them like witches brooms. You wouldn't want to hit a rock with your stick, thought Barcroft. You could do yourself some serious damage.

'Come on, Boakie, let's get some tucker,' said Tim.

Inside the hotel, the fire was roaring. A crowd of hardy-looking men and a few women were sitting around solid wooden tables. It was hot and smoky. Harry and his friends took over a table. They were well known to the publican. Barcroft sat at the end. Tim got talking to Harry. Barcroft was happy enough to warm his hands around a steaming hot mug of soup and listen.

In no time, hot toddies were shouted all round and the conversation got boisterous. Nothing like as boisterous as it used to be, if the stories Barcroft overheard were even half true. In the old days, it seemed that fighting and stealing were the rule, when the lure of gold and the temptation of easy riches took hold of men and women alike.

The miners at the table took turns to tell tales.

'Let me tell you a story from the old times that'll bring tears to your eyes,' said the old miner sitting opposite Harry.

'It's the story of Kitty McCrae,' he said. 'Her dad had the contract for the Greytown mail. In those days, that's how the government gold was sent down the mountain from here. That's after it got collected by the gold commissioner.'

He took a long swig from his drink. 'Kitty was a fine young lass – with a full head of curly red hair. I knew her well meself.'

He paused, and a faraway look momentarily passed his eyes. Then he continued, 'Well, one day Kitty's dad got sick and couldn't make the mail run. She was a great little horsewoman was Kitty. She'd been riding since she was a tot.'

'Here, give the man another drink. It's thirsty work telling tales,' said Harry.

'Well, Kitty leaps on this big strong mail horse. No one listened to the mine manager – a bloke called Brown. He'd heard the Mulligan gang were up this way. It was all the talk round Golden Gully. I was there. I heard 'em sayin' it.'

By now, all the men at the table were listening.

'Kitty's dad must've known it was risky. On his way up, he'd left the coach at the change post and rode the lead horses. But he was worried. If he didn't deliver the mail, he'd lose the contract. It was getting dark and he thought Kitty would be all right if she rode Postboy.'

'Who was Postboy?' interrupted someone.

'He was the best mail horse, a strong mountain-bred nag. Anyway, off goes Kitty on Postboy. Things were okay till she got over the far side of O'Connor's Hill. The forest opens out there.'

'You mean past the rock flats?' asked Harry.

'It was past there. The Mulligan boys were waiting for her. We seen their tracks after. They must've called on her to halt but she must've ignored them and charged on. She was like that, never had a fear, did Kitty. Anyway they fired and winged her. She made it all the way down across Warrigal Flat before she fell off, stone dead.'

'The bastards!' said Harry.

'Yeah, the bastards!' shouted the others.

'Here's the amazing part,' said the old miner. 'The horse kept on going. No matter it had no rider. It turned up at the mail post, all covered in blood and dust – still carrying the Greytown mail.' He sat back and took a swig from his drink.

'What happened to the gang?' asked Tim.

'They got theirs. The troopers caught up with 'em soon after. They all got hanged.'

'Serves 'em right!'

The old miner wiped a tear from his eye. 'She was my favourite girl, young Kitty. She was so brave, she was. Here, bring me another toddy.'

The table went quiet. They brought him another drink.

'Just as well the troopers got 'em first!' he said through his clenched teeth.

Barcroft believed he meant it.

Tim and Barcroft didn't talk much as they travelled back down the mountain. They rode silently along the track where Kitty had ridden those years before. Barcroft felt a sadness come over him as he looked at the beauty of the bush. He thought of Kitty's young life cut short.

Suddenly the bush seemed icy cold and lifeless. It was as though there was death in the air.

The next weekend at Rosedale Jean was most interested to hear about the snowshoe racing. 'How did they make the snowshoes?' she asked.

'They say Alpine ash works best, or something like it,' said Barcroft. 'It's got to be dead straight.'

'But you said the ends were turned up.'

'Yes. They wet them and heat them or something. It's so the bend will stay in place.'

'Wouldn't it split them?' asked Jean.

'I don't know. They say it's like boatbuilding. It's how they bend the timbers for ships,' said Barcroft.

'Maybe we could make some. Then we could all go up to Kiandra and try them,' said Jean.

'What's this about going to Kiandra?' said Mr McKeahnie as he walked into the room.

'I was just saying how we could make snow shoes and try them out at Kiandra,' said Jean.

'No one from my family is going to Kiandra.'

'Why not?' asked Jean.

'It's no place for a young lady.'

'Why not?'

'Because I say so.'

'But why shouldn't we go? You have to give me a reason.'

'It's the miners,' said McKeahnie. 'They've got no respect. They're rude and unruly – worse than shearers even. I've heard too many bad things. It's too dangerous.'

'That was a long time ago,' said Jean. 'It's different now. Barcroft's just been. He says they have a Kiandra Ski Club. Gentlemen from Sydney go up there.'

'I don't care,' said McKeahnie.

'I do. I should be able to go if I want to,' said Jean adamantly.

McKeahnie looked exasperated. He found it hard dealing with his headstrong daughter. 'The snow's melting now anyway,' he said. 'Soon it'll be spring and the river'll be too dangerous.'

'Well, in that case I'll go next year,' said Jean firmly.

McKeahnie frowned, but decided to say no more.

Barcroft admired the way Jean stood her ground with her father. Not many women would dare to, even in these liberated times, he thought. She wasn't one to back away. He knew that from his own experiences with her. She was personally brave too. He'd seen that when they were out riding. She never baulked at a jump, no matter how fearsome it looked. When she took a fall, she never cried. He helped her up once and could see she was in pain. He wanted to hold her tight and comfort her. But she just bit her lip and said she'd be all right. Then she got back on the horse and kept going.

He often thought about her when they were apart. He'd close his eyes and picture her face, with her sprinkling of freckles across the bridge of her nose, and her direct, inquiring eyes. It was as though she was right next to him at times. He felt tight in the chest just thinking of her – as he sometimes did when he was with her.

He also thought about May. It was her smile that stayed with him. It was hard to know who he liked the most. He wondered if it was possible he was in love with both of them. Jean was the best company. He knew he could never take liberties with her, but she was a true friend. She was someone you could talk to about anything. She was full of curiosity about the world and willing to try anything. May was more exciting. His heart raced when she was close. At times he felt an animal attraction for her that scared him.

He wished he had the courage to tell them how he felt. But he was too shy. They probably wouldn't understand anyway. How could he tell them he loved them both, but in different ways? And what if they didn't feel the same way?

Lying in bed at night he'd think of them. It would tie him up inside. It wasn't a bad feeling, just a strong, tense, unfinished feeling. He didn't know what to do with it.

6

Adaminaby, 1887

Early summer in Adaminaby was golden. The road from Rocklands wandered past the stooked haystacks on its way to becoming Denison Street. Golden fields of stubble stretched all the way down to the river. The surrounding hills were a faded yellow, dotted with dusty-coloured sheep. Cattle idly chewed their cud and stared as Tim and Barcroft rode past. The town itself was an untidy collection of buildings. Here and there amongst the houses dark green pine trees poked up above the roofs. They looked strangely out of place against the light tones of the native bushland on the distant hills.

Tim was off to play cricket for the local team. Barcroft preferred tennis, but he had come along for the ride. After the match, the teams would go to the Commercial Hotel – for celebrations in the case of a victory and for recriminations if they lost. Neither was taken too seriously.

Barcroft sat on the boundary and watched as the teams played. By mid-afternoon they'd had enough cricket and adjourned to the pub. Barcroft joined them. He sat at a side table and listened.

'Mind if I join you?' asked Mr O'Dowd, sitting down next to him before he could reply.

Barcroft would have preferred to be alone, but was too polite to decline. O'Dowd was a local store owner – a small businessman with the interests of a small businessman. Most notably he was chairman of the Adaminaby Progress Association. 'Great day, isn't it?' he said.

Barcroft nodded.

'Did you play?'

'No, I just watched,' said Barcroft.

'It's good to see visitors in town. It gives a lift to the place, don't you think?'

Barcroft nodded again, and sucked on his pipe.

'We've got a great future here. This town has real potential, don't you think? I've always said so. We can make things happen for Adaminaby. You're at Rocklands with Mr Commins, aren't you? Doing surveying?'

'Yes.'

'That's essential. That's the groundwork. The land needs to be surveyed. Then the settlers will come. There'll be more and more people choosing this district. We've got so much to offer here. So much potential.'

O'Dowd undid his waistcoat buttons and made himself comfortable. You could see he'd been in good pasture these past few years, thought Barcroft, looking at his expansive waistline. He certainly hadn't been short of a feed.

'I can see a time when Adaminaby will be famous,' said O'Dowd. 'It'll be known as the capital of the Snowy Mountains. There's so much going for it. So much more than Queanbeyan, or Cooma – or even Goulburn. We've got the Eucumbene River, with its beautiful sandy beaches, haven't we?'

'I suppose,' said Barcroft, sounding somewhat unconvinced.

'Look at those fertile fields out there,' continued O'Dowd. 'Where else do they have a mountain fed river like ours, replenished every year with snow melt? Where else do they have mountains like we do? Gold was only the beginning. Now there's copper. There must be untold mineral riches in those hills out there, just waiting to be found. Then what about the snow in winter? What an attraction!' He was becoming increasingly enthusiastic. 'Already gentlemen parties from Sydney are coming through. If this keeps on, we'll soon need to build another hotel. Imagine that!'

Barcroft looked around to see if anyone else was likely to join them. He was finding O'Dowd's enthusiasm rather overpowering.

'Then what about our horses? We've got the best mountain horses in the country. Not only that. We've got the best mountain horsemen. There's no match for our riders. We could teach the world how to ride wild horses. I've always said our horsemen are second to none. We need to set up a riding academy. That would be a certain success, don't you think?'

Barcroft nodded as Mr O'Dowd paused to take drink from his mug of beer. He wiped the froth from his whiskers with the back of his sleeve.

'All we need now is the railway,' he said. 'It's coming to Queanbeyan and Cooma soon. We need it here. That's really important. The railway's really important. We've got to get that message to the government. Once we get the railway we'll never look back.'

Mr O'Dowd leaned forward. 'There's so many short-sighted people here. They just can't see beyond their noses. They need to look up, to see the vision. All they do is think of themselves. They've got to think big, think wide. Where do you come from?'

'Sydney,' said Barcroft.

'When you get back to Sydney, you tell them the railway must come here.'

'All right. But I doubt anyone is likely to pay much attention to me.'

'That doesn't matter. If everyone's saying it, the government will pay attention. I'm putting together a petition. It's at my store. You should come over and sign it when you can.'

At this point Barcroft was rescued by the Tim and the cricketers.

'Hey, Boakie! Come and join us. Here, have you met Jack and Charlie? They top scored for our team. Damm good with the bat they are. And just as well. They saved us today.'

'You were pretty handy with the ball yourself,' said Jack.

'Barcroft does surveying. He's based with us at Rocklands,' said Tim.

'Hi. I'm Jack Cosgrove,' said Jack.

'G'day. Charlie Sweetland – from Cathcart,' said Charlie. 'I just came up for the game.'

Barcroft shook their hands. They both had big strong farmers' hands.

'The boys here tell me there's a dance on tonight,' said Tim.

'How 'bout we stay for it? We shouldn't be too late. They tell me the McKeahnies will be coming. Will you stay?'

'All right,' said Barcroft. The mention of the McKeahnies made him feel oddly nervous. He hadn't heard about the dance before. He wondered why. It wasn't long before he found out.

By now it was late afternoon and the heat of the day had passed, leaving the air temperature comfortably warm. The low western sun cast long shadows down the street.

While Barcroft was standing outside the hotel, the whole McKeahnie family, including Mr McKeahnie, Mrs McKeahnie and the young children, turned up in a convoy of sulkies and horses. They were all dressed up for the outing, decked out in hats and ribbons.

As the McKeahnie girls dismounted from their sulky, they saw Barcroft on the other side of the road. Jean smiled and waved to him.

May came bouncing over. 'I was hoping we'd see you,' she said. 'We've just been invited to the Rossiters' for dinner. Then we'll be going to the dance. Will you be there?'

'Yes. Tim and I will be there,' Barcroft said.

'Terrific! Will you have a dance with me?' she said.

'Yes. But I don't dance very well,' said Barcroft.

'That's all right. I'll show you. See you there.' May ran back to her family.

The dance was held in the School of Arts building, one of the largest buildings in Adaminaby. A crowd had gathered outside the hall by the time Tim and Barcroft arrived. Inside, the dancing was already underway. Music was provided by a piano, helped along by a fiddle and an accordion. The dancers were enjoying themselves, with lots of clapping and foot stamping. The timber floor was bouncing up and down as the dancers reeled and waltzed across it.

True to his word, Barcroft was not good at dancing. He stood at the side and watched. May and Jean were both capable dancers. He noticed they were enjoying themselves with a succession of partners. He couldn't help feeling a bit jealous. May took him for a dance, as she'd said she would. He didn't do it very well, but she didn't seem to mind. Jean danced with Jack Cosgrove and May danced with Charlie Sweetland. They all seemed to get on very well with each other. Barcroft felt isolated and out of place, even lonely.

May and Jean each made a point of coming over to say goodnight to him before they left. He still felt uneasy.

Tim was in high spirits as they rode back to Rocklands. Barcroft didn't feel so good. He was glad to get home and curl up in bed.

Next Sunday, Barcroft set off early for Rosedale. It was a grey day, more like autumn than summer. Low-lying clouds scurried across the sky, and light misty rain drifted across the hills. As he rode along, he could feel the rain sprinkling on his face. It glistened wetly on the gum tree leaves, before falling in little droplets onto the dry ground.

Instead of going through Adaminaby, he made straight for Rosedale. This took him across the grasslands of Dry Plain. It was a strange area, almost flat in places. As he passed the few scrawny gum trees on the higher ground, he noticed their leaves hung oddly downwards in strands, like weeping willows. Long Lake was almost dried up. It too was strange. There were no tributaries to explain its existence. Beyond Long Lake, Caddigat Creek began to cut a deep valley for itself. He'd always wondered where this led, so now he followed it downstream. He stayed on the high ground to make for easy going.

As he followed the creek, it cut deeper and deeper into the shale-like bedrock, until it plunged over a rocky ledge and fell as a waterfall into a deep gorge edged by rocky bluffs. A mob of grey kangaroos hopped lazily along the far side of the gorge, dodging in and out amongst the trees. Barcroft stopped to take in the impressive view, then turned Sweetbriar towards Rosedale. He could see Caddigat homestead over to north. He'd taken quite a detour, so he set off at a gallop. It didn't take him long before he was over the ridge and riding down the open slopes of Bolaro Hill, opposite Rosedale.

Charlie Mac met him at the home rails. 'How y'doing?' he said. 'Isn't it time we went looking for those wild brumbies? Remember? We were going to look for them in spring. How 'bout we go next weekend?

'Now it's dried out they'll be round the flats and gullies looking for green grass,' said Charlie. 'What about it? Can you do it next week?'

'Yes, I think so,' said Barcroft as he sent Sweetbriar off for a feed.

'That's done, then. We'll need to stay up there overnight. We can stay at my uncle's place – at his outstation up there. It's a bit rough. Just a slab hut. But it'll do.'

'That'd suit me.'

'I'll fix it with Father,' said Charlie. 'You bring some bedding. I'll look after the provisions. We'll need to start first light on Saturday. Is that okay?'

'Yes, I should be able to.'

'You'll need to get over here as soon as you can. How about I ask if you can sleep here the night before?'

'Okay,' said Barcroft. He left Charlie at the stables and walked across to the homestead.

Jean was reading on the veranda. She looked up as he approached. 'You didn't look too happy last night,' she said.

'What do you mean?' said Barcroft, a little defensively.

'Here, take a seat,' she said. 'Come on, sit down.' It was almost a command.

He sat down beside her.

'Everyone else was enjoying themselves last night. It was pretty obvious you weren't. What was eating you?' she asked.

'I'm not good at dancing.'

'It wasn't that. You looked unhappy.'

'All right. I wasn't that happy. Anyway, you were having such a good time with Jack.'

'You wouldn't be jealous, would you?' she said teasingly. 'It's not as if we're engaged, is it?'

Barcroft didn't know what to say. Jean's directness put him off his guard.

'Only joking, silly. Jack and I are just good friends. We've known each other since we were children. He's good fun but it's not serious.' She paused and looked at him. 'I'd like you to be my friend too. I think we could be the best of friends.'

'Are you sure?' said Barcroft.

'Of course we can. But don't be sulky. I won't put up with that. Anyway, I think you like May more than me. You looked more worried when she was dancing with Charlie Sweetland.'

Barcroft didn't know what to say.

Luckily, Mrs McKeahnie joined them just then. 'Enjoy the dance?' she asked.

'Yes, thanks,' he lied.

Jean looked at him knowingly and smiled. 'Barcroft was just telling me how much he enjoyed it,' she said.

He lay awake that night trying to work out what Jean had meant. Had she been trying to tell him something? He couldn't be sure. Maybe she was just teasing him. She was always very friendly to him – but maybe it was only as a friend. He couldn't work it out. He really wished he could. Even so, it wouldn't solve his problem. He was still unsure who he loved the most, Jean or May. He felt it would be unfair if he didn't make a choice. It wouldn't really be proper to be courting both. He wondered if it would be easier if they made their feelings more obvious to him.

Neither Jean nor May helped him solve his dilemma. Both continued to be friendly to him whenever he saw them. May was even flirtatious at times. At other times she seemed a little cool. He found her moods unpredictable, which only added to his feeling of uncertainty.

The night before he and Charlie set off to look for wild horses, Barcroft slept at the Rosedale shearers' quarters. Jean and May both came over to say goodnight to him. He would have liked to talk to them privately but Charlie was there so he couldn't. It was a missed opportunity, he thought. On the other hand, he usually got tongue-tied when he had a chance to talk to them alone.

He lay awake thinking of them. They were so close. He imagined them sleeping in their beds just across the yard from him. He wondered if they were thinking about him. He didn't sleep well.

The next morning, Charlie woke him before dawn. An hour later, they were saddled up and on the road, just as the sun rose over the eastern hills. The horses and their riders cast long shadows ahead on the dusty track. Charlie was on his favourite grey mare, Empress, the pick of the Rosedale stable. Barcroft was riding Sweetbriar.

They skirted the Goorudee Morass, with its tangle of tussocks and reeds, then headed towards Bugtown.

At McLaughlin's Flat, Charlie said it was best to cut around the ridge and head up Bulgar Creek. 'We'll pick up the track there. That'll take us to Nungar Plain,' he said. 'It's pretty steep up the ridge, but we need a track. The bush is too damned thick on the side of the range.'

He was right. The track was half-overgrown and not easy to follow. They lost it a couple of times.

'It doesn't matter,' said Charlie. 'So long as we stay on top of the spur and keep climbing, we'll find it again.'

In time they did. As they wound their way up the spur, the grasses and swamps of the valleys gave way to tall mountain gums. The air temperature cooled. At the top of the ridge, a high plateau opened up in front of them. Across it they rode, through a carpet of alpine flowers and snow grasses, with snow gums standing guard on the ridges.

After a mile or so, Charlie stopped and beckoned to Barcroft. He held his finger to his lips to caution silence. 'We need to be very quiet now,' he whispered. 'We don't want to give ourselves away. Brumbies have amazing hearing. We'll use signs from here on. The noise of our horses won't matter. They'll think it's one of their own.'

They rode on till they came to Nungar Creek. Here, Charlie motioned to Barcroft to stop. It had taken most of the morning to get this far. He pointed to the provisions in the saddle bags, then to his mouth, indicating it was time to eat. They tied their horses to the nearby bushes after letting them drink from the creek. Hobbles would've made too much noise. There was plenty of fresh grass for the horses to reach. Then they took the bedding rolls off the horses and sat on them while they ate lunch.

When they'd finished eating, they stacked their bedding and

saddlebags beside a large rock before setting off again to look for brumbies. They were disappointed. They found plenty of fresh horse tracks. A whole network of them. And plenty of fresh dung. There were mounds of it where the horses had marked their territory.

They followed the tracks with the freshest dung. Every so often, startled pairs of rosellas flew squawking into the surrounding bush. Enough to warn any wary horses, thought Barcroft.

As the sun sank low in the sky, they called it quits for the day.

'I dunno where they are,' said Charlie. 'They can't be far. By the look of it, there's a big mob of them somewhere round here.' He spat on the ground in disgust. 'The one I'm after is the Lord of the Hills,' he said. 'That's what Uncle calls him. He's a beautiful stallion. They yarded him once. But the cunning devil got away. Now he's super-shy.'

They headed for the hut. It was very basic. It had an unlined iron-sheetd roof and slab walls, an iron-sheeted chimney and a rough stone hearth. There was no timber floor and no windows. The only opening in the walls was a rough-hewn door. Luxury inside was limited to a couple of canvas stretchers.

'We'll try again at first light,' said Charlie. 'Now let's get the fire going.'

It was cosy once the fire was alight. After a filling meal of damper and Mrs McKeahnie's cakes, they turned in early.

Charlie really meant first light. They set off for the headwaters of Nungar Creek in semi-darkness. An eerie landscape surrounded them as they rode through the swirling morning mist.

This time they were in luck. As they approached Nungar Creek, the mist lifted. In front of them were a startled a mob of wild horses.

'There he is!' shouted Charlie, standing in his stirrups. 'It's the Lord of the Hills!'

The brumbies made off with a snort. Empress needed little prompting. She sprang forward at the touch of Charlie's hand on the rein. Over the creek she leaped. Barcroft and Sweetbriar were close behind.

Across the flat the wild horses raced, with a furious drumming of hooves, their wild manes and tails streaming behind as they headed straight for the green timber belt.

Empress and Sweetbriar were close behind when the brumbies reached the cover of the trees. Along the side of the ridge they raced after the wild horses – through the low branches and the undergrowth all the way to the high side of the spur. Here, the ground fell away sharply. A slip on the loose rocks spelt disaster.

Empress was gaining ground as the mob strung out along the side of the hill. They raced until they came to the steep slope that dropped to the river. Here, the stallion left his mob, wheeling away and charging straight down the hill to the Gulf Plain. Across the plain the stallion galloped. Here Barcroft and Sweetbriar fell behind. Charlie and Empress were closing on the stallion when he wheeled again and made for the Gulf itself, where the Murrumbidgee runs swiftly though the gap in the hills.

Crossing the river downstream from the Gulf, the stallion headed up the far side of the range. Over fallen logs and under low branches he raced – with Charlie and Empress close behind. With every stride Empress was drawing closer. Barcroft and Sweetbriar were well behind now. Every now and then Barcroft caught a glimpse of Charlie and Empress ahead through the trees.

Charlie was riding Empress hard and closing fast. In terror, and with total disregard for his safety, the stallion charged down the river gorge towards Yiack. A deep and narrow track wound amongst the boulders on the floor of the valley, half hidden amongst the shadows.

In fear and exhaustion, the stallion was pushing himself to the limit. His coat was covered with lather as he charged along the path. He could hear Empress only a couple of strides behind. At a sharp bend in the track, a granite boulder hid behind the thick bushes. Misjudging his pace, the stallion ran straight into it, with a sickening thud. It killed him outright.

Charlie saw the danger just in time. With a twitch of the rein, Empress leapt to the side and over the stallion, just grazing her side on the rock. Charlie jumped off and inspected Empress's wound. Quickly, he loosened her girth strap. When he'd wiped the blood from her side with a tussock, he turned back to look at the stallion.

That's how Barcroft found him, standing beside the boulder, looking down at the dead horse, who only minutes before had been the pride of the bush.

Charlie shook his head slowly. The dead horse was still so beautiful, still so sleek and lithe, yet his strong limbs would now be forever motionless. He was at a loss for words.

Barcroft and Charlie stood still while the reality of the death sank in. The loss of such a magnificent animal in its prime was so much more severe, thought Barcroft. No more would he run freely through the hills. No more would he romp with his harem of mares. No more would he kick up his heels in the crisp mountain air. Life could teach such brutal lessons.

On their way home, Barcroft and Charlie rode in silence. They each felt the sadness of the death of the stallion, and the burden of their own contribution.

'You know, it could just as well have been me or you,' said Charlie.

'Or both of us,' said Barcroft. It was a sobering thought.

7

Wedding Reception, Sydney 1888

'Where's that damned photographer!'

Sir Eric Wainwright was on the rampage. At these times, his staff knew to make themselves scarce.

'Smithers! Smithers!' shouted Sir Eric. 'Where'd that blasted butler get to? Never around when you need them. Smithers!'

He stormed across the hall, bumping a table as he went. Silverware clattered to the floor. The serving maids scurried over to pick it up.

'Don't put that back,' barked the head maid. 'Go and clean it first.'

The reception hall was decked out lavishly in the finest luxury money could buy. 'Spare nothing' was Sir Eric's instruction. His wife, Lady Celia, made sure his direction was implemented. She arranged a special order of fine Wedgwood china for the dinner service, and commissioned a complete set of ornamental silver cutlery to be engraved for the occasion. Even the curtains were imported from France. As for the food, the Governor's own cook was the head chef. He had instructions to serve a banquet the like of which the colony had never seen. 'Make it as good as they serve at Buckingham Palace,' Sir Eric said.

The special occasion was the marriage of Sir Eric and Lady Celia's only son and heir, Nigel, to Miss Philomena Laurence. It was the society wedding of the year. As the managing director of the Australasian Pastoral Company, Sir Eric was the richest man in Sydney. His son was a great disappointment to him, having shown little interest in his father's business. That was of no importance when it came to wedding preparations. Lady Celia was in charge. She carefully vetted the guest list to ensure the appropriate quality and balance of invitees. This was a unique opportunity for Sir Eric and Lady Celia to host a function on a grand scale for their friends and associates.

Sir Eric finally found the photographer. It was Mr Boake, Barcroft's father.

'Boake! Where have you been? I told you to be here at nine sharp! Do you want this commission or not?'

Boake tried to reply but Sir Eric cut him off. 'There are plenty of others in your business I could have hired. You should count yourself lucky I've given you this opportunity. The least you could do is be punctual.'

'I did come at nine,' said Boake quietly. 'I've been waiting since. I couldn't find anyone who could tell me where to go.'

'All right, then,' said Sir Eric grumpily. 'Now listen. What I want you to do is to get a good picture of the guests at the main table. Make sure of that.'

'It won't be easy. I'll need a flash. And the guests will need to stay still.'

'What nonsense!' stormed Sir Eric. 'You can't ask them to do that. They're here to enjoy themselves. Not to act like stuffed dummies!'

'The picture will be blurred if they don't stay still,' said Mr Boake firmly.

'I don't want to hear what can't be done. You just make sure you do it,' said Sir Eric and he started to walk away.

'Excuse me,' said Boake, trying to catch his attention. 'But do you have a place where I can take the bridal photographs?'

'What?'

'I'll need a room. Somewhere I can set up my equipment to take the photographs of the bride and groom.'

'Talk to Smithers. Don't bother me with a detail like that,' Sir Eric said curtly as he strode off.

Smithers was receiving directions from Lady Celia. Boake was told to wait in the anteroom. He did so – for nearly an hour. In due course, he was given a chance to explain his requirements to Smithers. He was then provided with access to a drawing room where he could arrange the props for the photographs.

Lady Celia came in while he was setting up his equipment. 'You're the photographer, are you?' she asked haughtily, looking down her nose at him.

'Yes ma'am.'

'What's that cloth thing doing there?' she demanded, pointing at the wall hanging Boake was arranging.

'That's a backdrop, ma'am,' he said. 'The subjects stand over there. Then I take their picture in this direction.'

'That won't do. It's dowdy. Smithers!'

'Yes, your ladyship.' Smithers jumped to.

'Make sure you find some suitable drapery for this wall.'

'Yes ma'am.'

Lady Celia turned to Boake. 'I want the bride to be sitting and Nigel to be standing. She's nearly as tall as he is. It wouldn't do for her to be standing. It would look awful.'

She turned again to Smithers. 'Get me a chair. Make sure it's not one of those plain ones. Hurry up, we're just about to leave for the church.'

Amongst the wedding guests waiting at the church was May McKeahnie. She'd been invited by an old school friend, Emily. Emily was one of the bridesmaids in waiting. May was surprised to receive the invitation, as she hadn't heard from Emily for some time. They hadn't been close friends at school.

May made the long journey to Sydney with one of her aunts, who had to travel there for family business. Emily met them at the station the day before the wedding. Her family lived in a large house on the waterfront at Hunter's Hill. It was set amongst leafy gardens and surrounded by harbourside views. May hadn't been there before as she only knew Emily from boarding school. She was amazed at how green the gardens were, and how the sea was so blue. Everything was so brightly coloured compared with the pale tones of the Monaro.

She was also amazed at the crowds of people in Sydney. There were so many buildings, and so many people. May specially noticed the bright clothes and the different styles. It was so overwhelming it made her head spin.

'I'm so lucky to be one of the bridesmaids in waiting,' said Emily. 'I still can't get over it. This has to be *the* place to be seen this year.'

'Thank you for inviting me,' said May.

They were sitting in Emily's bedroom.

'I thought of you when I was told I could bring a friend – so long as she was pretty.'

'Did they really say that?' exclaimed May. 'I'm not that attractive, am I?'

'I'm only joking,' said Emily. 'They said so long as my friend's not ugly. Anyway, I thought of you because of when we were in that play together. Remember? They called us the princess twins. They said we looked alike.'

'Yes, I remember,' said May. 'I forgot my lines.'

'And my make-up ran,' said Emily, giggling. 'Tell me, what have you been up to? Have you met your prince charming yet?'

'I'm not sure,' said May.

'There'll be some very eligible bachelors at the wedding tomorrow. I think that's why we were invited really. I'm sure Richard Woolford had something to do with it. He's so handsome. And he's very rich, which doesn't hurt! You make sure you stay away from him.'

'I don't know him,' said May.

'Keep it that way – only joking – sort of,' said Emily.

May thought she did mean it.

'Anyway, tell me about your prince charming. What's he like?'

'There's a young surveyor in our district,' said May. 'He's got a silly name – Barcroft. But he's really nice. I like him a lot. I'm still not absolutely sure, though.'

'He sounds interesting. Is he rich?'

'No, I don't think so.'

'Pity. My mother says money makes an attractive man more handsome. Is he good-looking?'

'Sort of. I think so, anyway. He makes me feel funny when we're near.'

'So what's happened?' said Emily expectantly.

'Nothing really. He's a bit shy. I don't know how much I should encourage him. I don't want him to think I'm too forward. He might think I'm cheap.'

'It's hard, isn't it? Men are s'posed to take the initiative. But they're so bad at it. It'd be so much easier if it were our job, don't you think?'

'I don't know. He mightn't like me, then I'd make myself look silly. He might like my sister more.'

'Really? How awful.' Emily made a face.

'Maybe not. It's hard to know. I'm sure he likes me a bit, though.'

'Good luck, then. You can invite me to the wedding,' said Emily.

'Don't say that.'

'It must be time for us to sleep now. There's lots to do in the morning.'

'Yes, I'm rather tired,' said May. 'I'd best be off to bed. Goodnight. I'll see you in the morning.'

'Yes, see you in the morning.'

At the wedding reception next day, the bride and groom were nervous for the photographs. They kept fidgeting. It took three attempts before Boake was happy with the result. The wedding guests weren't much better. He wouldn't know for certain whether the pictures had been successful until he developed the plates at his studio. He hoped there were no failures. As for the photograph of the main table, he was much less confident the outcome would be satisfactory.

'I don't know what all the fuss is about,' Lady Celia said loudly to her companions. 'It's not as if we're having our portraits painted. I'd understand that. I can see the need for skill in portraiture. Where's the skill in this photography business? All that's required is for someone to point a black box at you. I hope your commission isn't excessive, Mr Boake.' She didn't expect a reply.

When the photographic sessions were completed, Boake reported to Smithers to ask about his payment.

'Sir Eric never told me about that. You'll need to talk to him yourself,' said Smithers, as Sir Eric came into the room.

Fortunately, Sir Eric was in a jolly mood. The ceremony had gone well. The banquet had lived up to expectations and all the guests were enjoying themselves.

'Payment? You want to discuss payment? I thought you were doing it for free,' said Sir Eric jokingly.

Boake was less amused. Like his son, he took life fairly seriously.

'Tell me,' said Sir Eric, 'Smithers says you'd like to update the facilities at your studio.'

'Yes, but I can't afford to. My equipment needs upgrading. And I could do with more space. I was just dreaming.'

'I can help you,' said Sir Eric.

'How?'

'What you need is capital,' replied Sir Eric. 'And I've got capital. I'm always looking for a good place for it. What say I give you all the capital you need?'

'Just like that? I can't afford to pay much interest,' said Boake apprehensively.

'I'll tell you what I'll do,' said Sir Eric. 'I'll lend you the capital, but you needn't pay me any interest until I get the capital back.'

'When would that be?'

'So long as you're doing well, it can stay for the next five years.'

'Can I think about it?'

'Certainly,' said Sir Eric. 'If you want to take up the offer, come and see me at the club. I'll get Smithers to settle your account for today.'

The following Tuesday at the club, Sir Eric leant back in his armchair and sipped his glass of claret. A fellow director of the Australasian Pastoral Company was sitting next to him. He was a florid portly gentleman, with a bushy white beard and a prominent gold fob watch.

The waiter brought Sir Eric a telegram. It was news of the shearers' strike.

'Outrageous! How dare they!' He shouted so loudly all the other patrons in the club looked up. Sir Eric turned to his fellow director. 'Listen to this! The shearers at Brookong have refused to work until we increase their pay rate – and they demand better conditions. What a hide!'

His colleague read the telegram. 'Where's Brookong?' he asked.

'No idea,' said Sir Eric. 'And I don't give a damn! How can we make a decent profit with this kind of blackmail. It's those radical elements stirring up trouble. We should never have allowed the union onto our stations.'

The waiter returned. 'Excuse me, there's a Mr Boake to see you.'

'Tell him to come back tomorrow,' said Sir Eric. 'Can't you see I'm busy now? What does he want? Oh, it's that photographer fellow. Tell him I'll give him the money tomorrow.'

8

Adaminaby, 1888

It was Saturday afternoon and it was raining. Tim and Barcroft were sitting in the Commercial Hotel. Most of the cricket team were also there.

'Tell us one of your stories, Don,' someone asked.

Don Lette was the captain. He was a true bushman and never short of a tale to tell.

'Yes, come on, Don,' said a drinker at the next table.

'All right,' said Don. 'Have you heard the one about Joe Riley?'

'No. Tell us.'

'It goes like this. There was this Englishman, Joe Riley was his name. Well, Joe was in this pub in Sydney. The rum was flowing and there were wagers in the air. But there was something odd about Joe. D'you know what?'

'No. What?'

'Joe wasn't drinking. He was in a pub and he wasn't drinking! Imagine that! Now, let me tell you, never trust a bloke in a pub who isn't drinking.'

'No! Never!' was the noisy response from the drinkers at the next table as they banged the table with their glasses.

'Bring us another!' shouted someone.

Barcroft tried to make himself inconspicuous. He wasn't drinking. He lowered his head and sucked on his pipe.

'Quiet,' said Don. 'Now listen carefully. Joe put his purse in the middle of the table. Just like this.' He put his glass down in the middle of the table. ''Here's a wager,' said Joe. 'Foot racing is what I do. I'll bet my earnings here that I can run three hundred yards against your fastest horse and win. I'll even let you choose the course.''

Don took a drink from his glass, tilted back his hat and went on.

'You can imagine the interest that caused. Some said it was baloney. But others saw the chance of a quick quid. 'Now,' said Joe, 'there's one condition. Just one." He paused.

'What was it?' someone asked.

'Joe's one condition was that the rider on the horse had to drink a cup of tea after the start. Joe had to make it and the rider had to swallow it all before he could start the race. One of the patrons thought it might be a trick. He said, 'What about the temperature of the tea? Will it be boiling hot, straight out of the pot?' 'Not at all,' said Joe. 'I wouldn't trick you like that. Don't you trust me?' Then he said he'd taste the tea himself first, to prove he hadn't tampered with it.'

'What was the trick? There's gotta be a trick.'

'Wait,' said Don. 'Anyway, next thing they're outside the pub getting ready to race. They appointed a judge to make sure the rules were followed. They signed a bond with the rules in it and the judge was given the wager money. Well, just before the race is due to start, Joe Riley goes off to prepare the tea. Butter wouldn't melt in his mouth. He hands the tea to the judge to check it. It's covered over with a saucer so no one else can see it.

'What was in it?'

Don ignored the interjection. 'The judge lifts the saucer. He looks at the tea. Then he reads the rules carefully. He can't find a flaw. So he tells Joe to go ahead. Joe walks over to the rider waiting to race against him and hands him the cup. There's a big crowd watching by now.' He paused for another drink, swallowing slowly and wiping his mouth before going on.

'What happened?' someone asked impatiently.

'Quiet. Let him finish.'

Don continued. 'Joe really was a top foot racer. Next thing he takes off in a flash. The rider on the horse just sat there. The crowd went wild.' He paused again.

'What happened? Tell us what happened?'

'What was the trick?'

'Y'know what?' said Don. 'The rider had a cup full of tea – but it was a cup full of dry tea leaves! You could eat it but you couldn't drink it!'

There was a second of silence before the punchline sank in. Then the crowd clapped and cheered. Don sat back and smiled.

'That deserves a drink,' shouted someone.

'Get the bloke a drink,' said another.

'That's a good one, Don,' said Tim. 'I'd never have guessed.'

'Y'know,' said Don, when the noise had died down. 'The crowd didn't think much of Joe Riley's sense of humour.'

'You bet not!' shouted someone.

'But he took their money,' said Don. 'There's a lesson to learn from that.'

'Sure is. Don't trust a Pom!' said someone.

Barcroft hadn't guessed the ending. It was a good story. He liked what it said about human nature. People were so gullible when they saw a chance for easy money. He thought about it as he rode home in the rain later that afternoon. It was only light rain – not cold – just damp, and not unpleasant to ride through.

Barcroft felt unsettled. He didn't like surveying. It was boring. He didn't want to end up doing it for the rest of his life. It was harder to decide what he did want to do. He enjoyed going out and doing things. But he also enjoyed books and reading. He wondered if he could write. It would be good to be able to tell stories to people. But it would be hard to make a living out of it, he thought.

The people in the kitchen at Rocklands that evening irritated him. They were noisy. They talked even when they had nothing to say. They prattled on just to listen to the sound of their own voices.

Barcroft took his pipe outside onto the veranda. He looked out through the misty rain to the hills beyond. May was over there. Just over the other side of those hills. He liked imagining May. He loved those freckles of hers. He loved the way she wrinkled her nose. He pictured her face, with her coy smile. He smiled back.

Thinking about May improved his mood. It made him feel comfortable inside. He went to his quarters and lay in bed with his eyes shut. There she was, smiling and tossing her head. He went through all her gestures, the way she moved, the way she sat. He pictured the shape of her arms, her legs and her breasts. He loved all of her.

When he rode over to Rosedale on Sunday, it was Jean, not May, who met him. He said hello and asked her where May was.

'Why? Isn't my company good enough for you?' she replied, smiling wryly.

Barcroft was caught off guard. 'It's not that,' he stammered.

'You'll have to make do with me today,' she said. 'Are you sure you want to stay?' She seemed to enjoy putting him on the spot.

'Yes, of course,' he said, and he did mean it.

'May's in Sydney,' said Jean. 'A schoolfriend invited her. She's at a wedding.'

'Is her friend getting married?' asked Barcroft.

'No, she's a bridesmaid. It's a big society wedding. Sir Eric Wainwright's son is getting married. There'll be lots of rich people there.'

'I've heard about him. Sir Eric, I mean,' said Barcroft. 'His company owns lots of stations. I've heard people say that all he cares about is money. They say his company doesn't pay a fair wage, and they've got to work in bad conditions. If they get sick, he gets rid of them. They say he exploits people.'

'You'd better not say that sort of thing when Father's around,' said Jean.

'I'm only saying what I've been told.'

'Who by?'

'The shearers at the hotel. They said they were trying to get the stockmen and shearers on his stations to join the union.'

'For goodness' sake, don't mention any of that to Father. He'd have a fit. You know what he thinks about unions.'

'I wasn't going to. But don't you think it's unfair that some people should have all the wealth and others have to work for a pittance? I don't mean me, or the hands at Rocklands or Rosedale. We're all well enough looked after. But there's a lot of injustice the way the system of capital works. I've been reading about it in *The Bulletin*.'

'You'd better not mention that to Father either,' Jean said.

'I'm not that silly. But what do you think?'

'Lets go somewhere more private and I'll tell you. Why don't we go for a walk down by the river?' Jean said.

Barcroft agreed. He followed her round the side of the house towards the river. As they walked side by side, he wanted to hold her hand. He wasn't brave enough, and the moment passed. Jean looked at him and smiled. He smiled back. He felt a surge of friendliness towards her.

They followed an avenue of newly planted trees down to the river's edge. Late summer was a pleasant time of the year at Rosedale. The recent rain had brought a touch of green to the river meadows. Beyond the green river flats, the soft grassy contours of Bolaro Hill looked so smooth and gentle he was almost tempted to reach out and stroke its sides.

He and Jean stood looking down at the water as it gurgled and swirled its way past. The surface ripples sparkled in the sun. They could see right down to the pebbles on the bottom, where little fish hovered and darted amongst the shadows.

'I'm with you,' said Jean, taking up their conversation again. 'I can see there's unfairness. Father doesn't see it the same way. He's not a bad man. He always treats our workers fairly. No one could say he doesn't work hard himself. But he only sees what's immediately round him.'

'So what do you think is wrong?' Barcroft asked as they sat down on the grassy bank.

'I don't know,' said Jean. 'Maybe there's too much reliance on goodwill. That's fine when there's employers like Father. But there's nothing to stop bad people exploiting their workers. Then I can see why workers might want to join together – so as to stop being treated badly.'

'So you're in favour of unions?' Barcroft was surprised.

'I didn't say that. I just think people shouldn't be exploited. But they shouldn't be lazy either. Some so-called unionists are troublemakers. They just want to get paid for doing nothing. We had some of them here. They weren't shearers. All they wanted to do was cause trouble. They didn't want to work.'

'What happened?'

'Father got rid of them. It was nasty, though. They threatened to come back and burn our place down. That's why Father can't stand unions.'

'Now I understand.'

'What Father can't see is the underlying problem.'

'What's that?'

'It's the whole system of capital and labour. It sets people up against each other. It's like they say: money is the root of all evil. Money corrupts people. It makes them do bad things to each other. It would be so good if we could get rid of money. In an ideal world, every person would work to their ability and be rewarded according to their needs.'

Jean spoke quietly and earnestly. Barcroft agreed with her in theory. In practice, he knew it could never happen.

'All right,' said Jean. 'I know what you're thinking: it'll never happen. I've read about political theory so I understand it can't be like that – human nature being the way it is.'

'When did you learn about political theory?' asked Barcroft. 'That's unusual – for a girl.'

'Careful,' said Jean. 'You don't think I'm a second-class citizen because I'm a girl, do you?' She was smiling but there was a serious tone in her voice.

'Of course not. I just...'

'I'm sick and tired of being told do this, do that, don't question that, and having my opinions ignored – just because I'm a girl. Girls can think too, you know.'

'Jean, I never said you couldn't,' Barcroft protested.

'All right, I'm sensitive,' she said, calming down. 'It's because Father never listens to me.'

'Well, I do,' said Barcroft.

'I know you do. That's something I like about you. We can talk about things. I'm not sure what else I like about you,' she said, laughing.

'When did you start being interested in political theory? What sort of things have you read?'

'I've read John Stuart Mill, and Bentham and the Utilitarians. Freedom is a noble ideal. But you can't have unrestricted freedom. If you have no rules, there's no protection. We have to have some laws. In any case, all laws are restrictions on freedom in some way.'

Barcroft was impressed. She had obviously thought seriously about things. 'When did you learn all this?' he asked.

'I've been interested since I was at school. I wanted to go to university – but Father said no. We probably couldn't have afforded it, anyway. Mother needed help with the younger children, so I came home. Now they want me to marry into one of the local families round here.' She looked thoughtful as she picked a long grass stalk and trailed it in the water.

'Will you?'

'Not if I have my way. The men here are so boring. They're only interested in their horses.' She laughed. 'They should marry them!'

Barcroft thought for a moment then said, 'But I like horses. Should I marry mine?'

'If you like,' said Jean, smiling at him.

He didn't know how to take her answer. Jean's comments seemed deliberately ambiguous at times.

As they walked back to the house, Barcroft remembered it was her birthday. He asked if he could borrow her scrapbook. She brought it to him in the drawing room. He asked to be left alone so he could write her a birthday message. Then he took some notes out of his pocket and began to write.

A Few Verses

Miss Jean I've commanded
        My faltering Muse
To write you some verses;
        She dare not refuse

It's your birthday and what's
        More appropriate on it

Than I should sit down
        And write you a sonnet

I've sat down and now
        I don't know what to say
Oh! I know 'Many happy
        Returns of the day

I must not pay compliments
        More is the pity
I know you'd object to be
        Told that you're pretty

Shall I tell you you're plain
        No! my pen wouldn't write it
Besides there's your anger
        I dare not excite it

Miss Jean do you know
        That my poor feeble brain
I fear will succumb
        To this horrible strain

You'll be sorry, I know
        Some day when you find
That writing to you
        Drove me out of my mind

When you find (to use Scotch)
        'I've a bee in my bonnet'
The horrid result of this
        Broken backed Sonnet

Miss Jean I fear these scanty lines
        Your anger may provoke
Deal gently with me for I sign
        Yours humbly B.H. Boake

He illustrated the margins with some pen and ink drawings,

borrowing from the cartoon style of the day. When he'd finished, he found Jean and handed her the scrapbook. He waited while she read it.

When she'd finished, she looked up. 'Thank you, Bartie. You're a sweetie.' Her voice was softer than usual. She didn't often call him Bartie and had never called him a sweetie before. 'But you do make me sound rather fearsome. I'm a tad embarrassed.'

'I didn't mean to offend.'

'It's all right. I'm not really offended. Don't worry.' She looked at him reassuringly. 'Thank you for thinking of me. I'll keep it somewhere safe. You know, you're the first person to ever write me a poem.'

'I probably won't be the last.' He added, with a twinkle in his eye, 'There's sure to be heaps of odes dedicated to you.'

'Yes, from all of my many suitors!'

They both laughed.

Next weekend, May was back from Sydney. Barcroft met her and Charlie Mac in Adaminaby on Saturday morning. They had ridden into town together. Charlie had come to look at some horses from the Snowy Plains. May had joined him for company.

'Hey, Boakie,' Charlie said. 'Can you do me a favour? I need to check out these brumbies. They've been yarded but it turns out they're being held over Jindaboine way. It'll take me a while. Will you ride back to Rosedale with May?'

'So long as Miss May doesn't object,' Barcroft said quickly, with mock formality. He needed little encouragement.

'I'd be most agreeable if Mr Boake would accompany me,' said May, continuing the pretence.

'Thank you most kindly, ma'am.'

Charlie said a quick goodbye and cantered off.

'Why don't you take me to Rocklands on the way?' said May. 'I haven't been there for a long while. We could take the Cooma road to get home. The one that goes across Dry Plain.'

'I'd love to, so long as you're sure it won't take too long.'

'That's no problem. They're not expecting me home till evening.

Daisy here won't mind. Will you?' she said, patting her horse.

They set off at a leisurely pace, past the cemetery on the hill, then up through the flat grassy valleys towards Frying Pan Creek. Sheep dotted the landscape. Some were startled as they rode nearby, rushing off in a mob to join their friends, leaving a cloud of dust hanging in the air. High in the sky, a pair of eagles circled effortlessly on the shimmering updrafts.

'Did you enjoy your time in Sydney, May?'

'It was interesting. Sydney is very different, isn't it?'

'How do you mean?'

'The crowds, the colours, the action. It's so much busier than here.'

'I prefer it here,' said Barcroft.

'I don't know. The clothes were amazing. They have so many different styles. And the food was scrumptious. I've never eaten anything like it before.'

'You mean at the wedding?'

'Yes. They said it was a banquet fit for a king. I'm sure I'm no judge, but I think they were right. The Governor was there. All the best people in Sydney were there. They were all dressed up. Everyone looked so handsome.'

'You liked them, did you?'

'Not really. You wouldn't be a bit jealous would you, Bartie?' she said with a coy smile. 'It's all right. No one was too interested in me. Not when they found out where I came from. But Sydney's so rich!'

'There's dirt and poverty too. Didn't you see the beggars? Did you go down by the wharves?'

'No,' said May.

'Just as well. It's no place for you. It's dirty and it's grimy. And it's crowded with unpleasant people, spivs, painted women and drunks. Barcroft shuddered. 'I used to have to go past them every day when I worked in the city. The drunks outside the pubs would grab at your sleeve begging for money. I was so glad to leave.'

'I never saw any of that,' said May.

They rode on for a while without talking, watching the eagles circling.

'It's so peaceful and quiet here,' said May. 'Sometimes I feel we're missing out on something. Then at other times I think we're not. It's very different here. There's a good feeling about the land. I really liked it on the way back when I saw the Monaro bush country again.'

'I'm glad you're back.'

'I'm glad to be back too.'

At Rocklands, they gave the horses a feed and a spell. Barcroft quickly showed May his quarters. Luckily, he'd made his bed that morning. After eating a snack in the kitchen, they collected some food to take with them and set off again in the direction of Dry Plain.

'When I was riding this way before, I followed the creek downstream,' said Barcroft. 'Further down, there's a gorge, with a waterfall and a rock pool. It's quite interesting.'

'I think I've heard about it. The blacks used to say it was a special place. I remember one of them telling me something about it when I was young.'

'Really? That's interesting.'

'Why don't we go there? It could be fun to explore.'

'If you'd like to,' replied Barcroft. He felt a strange sense of excitement at the prospect.

After reaching Dry Plain, they followed the creek downstream past Long Lake. The country became increasingly rugged as grassland gave way to bush. They had to pick their way through jagged outcrops of lichen covered rocks. Twisted white-trunked gum trees clung to the steep valley sides with gnarled feet. Overhead, a solitary eagle soared on the updrafts.

'Isn't it pretty there!' said May, pointing at some tiny ferns hiding in the shade of overhanging rocks near the creek.

Further on, they came to a little waterfall. Here, the creek splashed into a small rock pool before continuing its journey. Green moss cushions hid between the smooth rocks on the bank of the creek.

'Let's stop here,' said May. 'Look,' she said as they dismounted. 'Isn't this the kind of place you'd find fairies?'

'Do you believe in fairies?'

'No, not now I don't. But I did when I was a little girl. Didn't you?'

'Not really. Well, maybe. I can't remember.'

'See, there's the fairy writing,' she said, pointing to the scribbles on the white bark of an old gum tree. 'The elves do that at night. That's why you never see them doing it. It's written in their secret language. Did you know that?' She smiled in a way that left him unsure if she was serious.

'No, I never heard that,' said Barcroft.

'It's not long since we used to show Lem where the fairies played. We had such fun. She's too old now. I miss it now she's grown-up. I guess I'll have to wait till I've got children of my own.'

Barcroft looked at her in surprise. It was the way she said it that surprised him. 'Are you thinking of that soon?'

'Perhaps not yet,' said May. Then she added with a smile, 'I'd have to get married first.'

He didn't know if she expected an answer. He returned her smile instead.

From the rock pool, they followed the creek downstream. As the river bed narrowed and the sides became steeper and rockier, they had to dismount and walk their horses. Suddenly, the creek disappeared. Ahead was a sheer cliff. The water tumbled over the cliff's edge down into a rock pool far below.

They stood beside the quietly flowing stream, where only seconds later it threw itself down the cliff face in a white torrent. In front of them, the valley opened out into a deep gorge cut out of the primeval rock. Around the edge of the gorge, the distant gum trees glistened and sparkled in the sun as they rustled gently in the warm breeze.

'What a magic place!' said May.

'It is pretty amazing, isn't it.'

'Can we get down there?' she asked, pointing at the rock pool below.

'Yes, but we'll need to go back and round.' He led the way along an animal track that eventually took them to the floor of the gorge. Here, the grass was fresh and green under the trees.

After splashing headlong into the pool at the base of the waterfall, the creek flowed amongst smooth-faced boulders through a series of channels carved out of the rocky floor of the valley.

They hobbled their horses and sat on the smooth rocks below the pool, polished by centuries of tumbling and washing.

It was warm at the bottom of the gorge, as it was sheltered from the wind and the northern sun shone directly onto the rocks. For a few moments, they sat watching the water splashing into the pool, listening to its busy conversation.

'This place makes me feel quite strange,' said May. After sitting a little longer, she said, 'I'm hot. Why don't we take a dip in the pool to cool off?'

Barcroft looked at her as if he was in a dream.

'We'll need to be modest,' May added quickly. 'You must promise not to look when we're getting undressed. Will you promise?'

'Yes,' he said. His heart was beating faster. 'Are you sure it's all right?'

'Of course,' she said. 'I can trust you, can't I? When we were little we used to go swimming in the river in summer all the time.'

'What about getting dry?' he asked in a daze.

'We'll just get dressed. If you wait a bit, you dry off quickly. Specially when it's warm like now.'

Barcroft felt nervous.

May seemed more at ease. 'Here, I'll put my clothes on this rock. You put yours there. You let me get into the water first. Remember, you're not allowed to look.'

He nodded.

They turned away from each other and took off their clothes.

Barcroft waited till he heard splashing then said, 'Is it all right for me to come in now?'

'Yes, I won't look,' said May, turning away.

Barcroft got into the water gingerly. He was worried he would embarrass himself by appearing aroused. But he was nervous and the water was cool.

'Isn't it good?' said May, as she ducked under the water.

'Yes,' he replied. He felt more relaxed now they were in the pool.

'Let's swim over to the waterfall.' When there, May sat on a rock ledge at its base, letting the water cascade over her shoulders.

Barcroft looked at her small firm breasts with their cute pointed nipples. He tried not to stare. He thought she looked so beautiful. He sat on the ledge beside her.

She put her hands out and caught the falling water, then splashed him with it. 'Come on. Let's swim to the other side,' she said, launching herself back into the pool.

He followed.

They swam across the pool before resting on the far side, half out of the water. Barcroft kept looking at her sideways, trying not to stare, but fascinated, almost fixated, by what he could now see of her. He felt tense – but very happy.

In the middle of the pool there was a smooth boulder just poking out of the water. May swam over to it. Barcroft watched as she climbed out of the water and sat on it, tucking her legs sideways under her. She tilted her head and shoulders back. For a moment, she shut her eyes as she faced into the warm sun.

When she opened them again, she turned to Barcroft. 'Do you think I look like a mermaid?'

He took a moment to reply. Then he blurted out, 'You look beautiful.'

'Come now, Bartie,' she said. 'No compliments, or I'll be embarrassed. Do you think I look like a mermaid, though?'

'Yes, you do.' He couldn't stop looking at her. At her soft pale skin. At her smooth round breasts with their pert little nipples. At her shapely waist and below it her dark brown pubic hair, just showing between her legs. It was darker than he'd expected, but it looked just right. It took his breath away. She was so beautiful!

'It's all right. I trust you now. You can look at me now,' she said.

From then on, she was uninhibited in front of him, standing up and diving into the pool without a sign of shyness. He was much less relaxed.

They swam backwards and forwards across the pool and played in the water for a while longer. Then they got out and dried themselves on the rocks in the sun.

It was mid-afternoon by the time they dressed and collected the horses. As they walked the horses up the far side of the gorge, they disturbed a mob of grey kangaroos. Off they went, bouncing their way noisily through the bush. Once clear of the gorge, the trees and rocks gave way to grassland and they were able to ride again.

'I don't know what came over me down there,' May said as they rode along. 'The spirits must've taken over. Promise you won't tell anyone?'

'I promise,' said Barcroft. He wouldn't tell anyone, but he knew he'd never forget it.

When they arrived at Rosedale, May had to help her mother. She said a quick goodbye. 'Thank you, specially for showing me the waterfall,' she said as she hurried off.

Barcroft didn't forget. But May never mentioned it again. When he saw her next Sunday, it was as though nothing had ever happened. She joined him as he was smoking on the Rosedale veranda.

'My, my, Mr Boake. You do smoke so much. I could never marry a man who smokes so much,' she said with a cheeky grin.

He couldn't decide if she was serious or not. Since their swim together he was almost certain it was May he loved absolutely. But she still remained a tantalising enigma to him. It was impossible for him to decide if she felt the same way as he felt about her.

9

Adaminaby Racecourse, 1888

On a summer race day, Adaminaby filled with people. Squatters, cockies and shearers came from all around. They came from Bredbo, Cooma and Queanbeyan to the north, from Cathcart and the coast, from Jindaboine, and from Kiandra and the mountains to the west. They brought with them the finest horses the Monaro and the mountains could breed.

The crowd gathered at the racecourse down on the Eucumbene Flats. Bookmakers shouted odds, jockeys fidgeted and fussed, while owners and trainers led frisky horses back and forth. Splashes of colour from the jockeys' costumes and the women's outfits gave the meeting a carnival atmosphere.

All the locals had come. The surveyors and station hands from Rocklands were there, as were the McKeahnies. Other local families included the Lettes, the Lockers, the Chalkers, the Cosgroves, the Balls, the Westermans, the Byrnes and the Yorks, to mention only some.

Ned Malone from Gegederick was there. He fancied his chances on his big bay, old Gaylad. Although the horse was getting on, he'd been a champion stayer in his day. Ned was beside the rails with Gaylad, all saddled up and ready for the next race, when Charlie Mac and Barcroft walked by.

Charlie knew Ned as a gun shearer. He also knew Gaylad's past form as stayer so he'd wagered ten pounds on him. 'Fancy your chances in the next one, you reckon?' he asked Ned.

Ned looked coy. 'Maybe,' he said, with a wry smile. 'I shouldn't be last.'

His wife and his baby son were with him at the rails.

'Give Dad a kiss for luck,' said Mrs Malone, holding up the baby.

The toddler stretched out his arms. 'Please, Dad, give Babs a ride,' the baby said.

Ned lifted the youngster up and sat him in the saddle.

'Be careful, Ned,' said Mrs Malone, with an agitated look.

Ned shortened the stirrups and adjusted them for the youngster. 'There. That's what it's like to be a jockey.'

Babs grabbed hold of the horse's mane with one hand and his Dad's whip in the other. He shouted in high-pitched excitement.

Just then the handicap field came racing round the bend, hooves drumming and shaking the ground. Gaylad snorted – then stamped.

'Take him off!' shrieked Mrs Malone.

It was too late. Gaylad saw the other horses racing towards him. He leaped forward. As they charged by, he joined the tail of the field out wide. Babs never let go of the horse's mane. Hanging on tightly and still shouting with excitement, his golden curly locks streamed behind him as the veteran horse galloped after the field.

Gaylad had given the leaders a start. But with his jockey only a featherweight he soon began to catch the others. The riders stared in amazement to see this baby go pounding by on his big bay, with a look of sheer excitement on his face.

'Oh, hell!' said Bob Murphy, checking his horse in her stride as the bay went past.

Gaylad never faltered. With the experience of an old hand, he let the others make the running round the bend. Then the leaders were in sight, only a couple of lengths ahead.

Down the straight to the finish, he gained on them every stride. Just as he was moving to take the lead, he started to falter. The crowd was cheering and shouting by now. Mrs Malone was going spare. Babs still clutched his Dad's whip in his tiny hand. Seeing the other jockeys using theirs, he copied them and gave it to Gaylad. Amazingly, the old bay responded and surged to the front.

With only fifty yards to go, Gaylad started to fade again. The jockey behind saw the old horse was gone but, in a split second, he pulled back at the finish line and let the baby win.

The crowd went wild.

Ned had grabbed a stockhorse to chase after his son. As the field slowed past the finish, he galloped past Gaylad and snatched his son from the saddle, unhurt.

'Amazing! Absolutely amazing!' said Charlie Mac, turning to Barcroft. 'You won't ever see that again!'

Barcroft shook his head. He was astonished.

When the excitement settled down, they ran the next race. Not surprisingly, Gaylad was a scratching. Charlie Mac got his money back.

'Just as well the nag never ran,' he said to Barcroft. 'You saw the way he faded at the end.'

At the race presentation, the president of the Turf Club announced the winner of the handicap as 'Old Gaylad, unofficial entry, ridden by Babs Malone.' The crowd cheered, banged and whistled in appreciation. A special toast followed to Babs Malone, the youngest ever winner of the handicap.

That signalled the start of celebrations for the day. The committed drinkers adjourned to the town hotels. Mr and Mrs McKeahnie took their daughters home. Charlie Mac, Tim and Barcroft joined the crowd at the Commercial Hotel.

'What a surprise!' said Tim with exaggerated astonishment as he walked into the bar. 'Fancy finding you here, Jimmy!'

Jimmy Wood was standing at the corner of the bar. He'd only been in town a few weeks but he'd already made the corner his own. He always dressed in formal attire, with a button-up waistcoat, a white shirt and a black tie. But his eyes were watery, and the red flush in his cheeks suggested a more than passing acquaintance with alcohol.

Barcroft smiled. He'd heard about Jimmy Wood. Mr Wood, as he preferred to be addressed, was the new sales clerk in the stock and station store. He was true-blue British in speech – and he had the ingrained manners of the old country.

'Good day to you, Mr Boyd,' he said, tilting his glass in Tim's direction. He was always polite.

'What's that you're drinking?' said Tim. He knew the answer. It was unsweetened gin, moderately watered.

'My usual, thank you,' replied Wood.

'Like us to get you one?' said Tim, with a wink at the others.

'No, thank you, Mr Boyd. I'll manage well enough alone.'

Tim and the others found a table. When it was his turn to shout, he said to the others, 'Watch this.' He bought a gin in his round and placed it on the bar in front of Jimmy Wood.

Wood looked askance at it. 'I'm sure your intentions are kind, Mr Boyd,' he said, speaking slowly and carefully. 'But I can't accept this drink from you.'

'Don't worry,' said Tim. 'You can shout the next round.'

'I much regret I cannot oblige. I do not hold with this shouting mania. 'Tis but generosity perverted.'

'Why not?' asked Tim in mock surprise.

'There's no doubt that drink's a curse. It latches onto men like a leech.' He spoke slowly and with a slight slur. Then he added, 'That said, it's an indisputable fact that man was meant to drink alone.'

'How so?' said Tim.

'I will never pay for others. Nor will I take drink from them.' He paused before continuing. 'And I always practise what I preach.' He hiccupped. 'One day I hope all good men should follow my example.'

'I don't know about your example,' said Tim, with a wink at the others. 'Looks to me like you don't need our help with drinking anyway.'

Jimmy frowned. He started to reply but Tim cut him off.

'Only stirring, Jimmy. Don't excite yourself. That's the trouble with you Poms. You've got no sense of humour.' He turned to the others. 'Here's a toast to Jimmy. To Jimmy Wood. They say he who drinks alone drinks a toast to Jimmy Wood. Let's all join him this time.'

The crowd at the table lifted their glasses and gave a cheer.

'Good on ya, Jimmy! We'll have one with ya.'

'No need to drink alone here, pal!'

Barcroft decided it was time he left for home. Sweetbriar also seemed keen to get home. Without encouragement, she galloped most of the way back to Rocklands.

She was less eager on Sunday morning when they set off for

Rosedale. She kept trying to stop and have a feed. As soon as they arrived, Barcroft let her loose in the home paddock.

From the stables, he could see Jean in the distance. She was standing at the far rails, with her back to him, looking out towards the hillside. Her body was pressed hard up against the rails.

As Barcroft approached, he saw what she was looking at. One of the stallions was playfully courting a mare. His long member dangled down as he nudged the mare's hindquarters with his head. Then he became fully erect and climbed onto her back, thrusting into her from behind.

Jean didn't hear Barcroft coming.

He stopped momentarily and watched as she stood there, pressing herself forwards against the rails, moving slightly from side to side. He started to get aroused himself as he watched her.

She suddenly noticed him and turned round. Her face went bright red. 'Mr Boake! Where did you come from?' she blurted out.

He didn't answer.

She quickly regained her composure. 'Don't let that give you any ideas, Mr Boake,' she said, looking at the horses. 'Women have to be married before they can let men do that to them.'

He stood there feeling awkward as she stared at him. Slowly, her eyes looked him up and down. Now it was his turn to feel embarrassed.

She noticed. Looking again towards the horses, she said, 'She does seem to like it, doesn't she.' It wasn't a question.

As she turned her head back, he saw a fleeting animal like look in her eyes – a look he'd never seen before. It quickly passed.

'We should join the others,' she said firmly. 'There's no prospect for us here now.'

Barcroft didn't know what to make of her remark. As he walked beside her to the house, he noticed she kept looking at him in a strange way.

Nothing further came of the incident that day. Barcroft was left wondering what her words had meant. He went over it again in his mind that evening but without conclusion. Jean never mentioned it again.

Autumn came to the Monaro with a chill wind. The kind of wind that blew through your clothes and through your skin right to your bones. The horses and the cattle turned their backs stoically to the wind and huddled together for shelter. It didn't seem to worry the sheep. Autumn leaves from the few English trees at Rocklands blew untidily across the yard.

Field work for the season was coming to an end. Barcroft had a feeling of apprehension. His two-year engagement with Commins would soon be over. He wasn't sure he wanted to continue with surveying. He liked it here on the Monaro but he needed to make a living. Aside from surveying, there was little work for him here, other than as a station hand. That didn't attract him. The pay was poor and the duties unexciting. His father wouldn't like it either, as it would be a waste of his training.

While he was out surveying, he had plenty of time to look about and let his mind wander. Jean and May were never far from his thoughts. He'd often think of them when he was in the field. He'd think of the little things they'd done, and he'd picture them in his mind. He liked the way May sat on her horse. She sat straight upright, with her shoulders back and her breasts pushing forward against her shirt. It wasn't posed, it was just the way she held herself. Her back curved down to the firm rounded outline of her hips. She looked so confident and in control. He liked the way she held the reins, and the little flick she gave them to prompt her horse. He also liked the way she sat on a chair. She looked so attractive. She sat upright, almost on the edge of the chair, with her legs tucked underneath but with her hips angled forward, emphasising the bend between her thighs and her waist.

Sometimes, he'd think of Gran and Addie. He still missed them. He wondered how they were doing. Addie's last letter said Gran hadn't been well recently. He hoped she was going to be okay. Then he thought of his father. He missed him too. They had never talked much. But that was fine. Often you didn't need to talk.

He knew his father meant well – and that he was probably right. It probably would be best if he qualified as a surveyor. The pay would be good, and the prospects for work much more dependable than something like photography. But the problem was that he didn't like surveying. There wasn't enough action or excitement. Much of it involved tedious work – being accurate with dimensions, checking calculations, carefully checking dimensions, then checking them again. Imagine having to do that for the rest of your life, he thought.

About one thing Barcroft was certain. Whatever he did with his life, it would need to be in the bush. He could never go back to Sydney now. The free and open life in the bush so much better suited him. Cities were too crowded, too dirty and too noisy, he decided. They were too full of false, unpleasant people being nasty to each other.

Out here in the bush you were close to nature. Out here you could feel nature's every whim. You felt the dampness of the misty rain, the force of the gales as they whipped the trees, the cold chill of a frosty dawn in winter, and the shimmering heat of noon on a still summer's day. And you could see nature's beauty.

He'd always remember the Monaro for its pastel pinks and faint blues, and for the way you could see so clearly right to the edge of the horizon. The coast was so heavy and so intense by comparison. Even the bush was crowded there.

There was a special beauty in autumn sunsets on the Monaro. He watched as, late in the day, the wooded hillsides were bathed briefly in the gentle glow of the setting sun. Touched by its fading warmth, their slopes glowed briefly pink and gold. As the sun dipped to the horizon, the undersides of the wispy bands of cloud turned a delicate shade of pastel pink. He'd only ever seen such colours here. For that brief moment, the countryside had a magical quality.

He liked the Monaro's distinct seasons. The crispness of autumn that gave way to the ice-cold nights of winter. Then came the mountain mists. They descended eerily in the night, lying in the low places, hovering above the creeks and marshes. Drifting through the trees, they left a light sprinkling of fine dew on leaves and rocks. In the early morning, like ghosts they disappeared into nothingness as the sun slowly warmed the day. There had to be poetry in the Monaro landscape, he thought. If only he could capture it.

It was late in autumn when May found the baby possum in the stable. It had fallen from the rafters and lost its mother. She saw it in the corner, amongst the hay, all curled up and quivering when she and Barcroft returned from their Sunday morning ride.

'Bartie,' she said, 'come and see what I've found.'

He liked the way she said his name. He specially liked it when she called him Bartie.

'Isn't it cute?'

He came closer to look.

She was holding the little creature in her hands, with its tiny face poking out between her fingers. 'The poor little thing. I wonder where its mother could be?'

'I'll take a look.' He climbed up on the stable rails to look between the rafters. 'I can't see anything. It's daytime, anyway. She's probably well and truly gone by now. It's lucky you found it. There's a good chance the horses would've trampled it.'

'Poor little thing,' said May, holding it close to her chest.

Barcroft moved closer to her. He almost put his arm around her, but held back at the last moment. He was so close as she bent forward over the baby possum he felt her hair brush against the side of his face.

'Would you like to hold it?' she asked, looking up at him wide-eyed.

'No, thanks. You're doing a much better job than I ever could.'

'It's so helpless, just like a little baby.'

He noticed a motherly tone in her voice he hadn't heard before.

'Do you like babies?' she asked, looking him directly in the eye.

He could see her eye lashes quivering slightly. He wasn't sure what to say. 'I don't know,' he said eventually. 'I can't say I've given it much thought.'

'I do,' she said, dreamily. 'They're really nice. I can't wait till I can have one of my own.' She bent over the baby possum, stroking it gently and comforting it.

He watched her quietly and silently. This was a side of her he hadn't seen before. She was a little mother, absorbed in giving all her love and affection to her little charge. It stirred his emotions. Again, he felt an urge to put his arm around her, to hold her gently. But he was too shy. In the end, he did nothing.

'Let's take it inside,' she said. 'Can you help me make a little nest for it?'

'All right.'

She led the way towards the main buildings.

'What've you got there?' asked Charlie Mac.

'May's found a baby possum,' said Barcroft.

'That'd be right. She's always finding lost animals. Where's it going?'

'We're going to make a nest for it,' said May.

'Not with my hat again you're not!' said Charlie.

'Out of the way, please. I need to feed it first,' she said, pushing past him.

'You do that,' said Charlie. 'Feed it well so it grows up nice and quick. It's getting so cold I could do with another possum-skin rug.'

'Charlie! Stop it! You're so horrid. I hate you at times!'

'Come on, May. I was only kidding,' said Charlie. He looked at Barcroft. 'She's so touchy, y'know. You've really got to watch out.'

Barcroft rode home in the moonlight that evening. The frost was already creeping across the hills and down into the gullies. By the time he got to Rocklands, there was a soft white dusting over the tops of the rails in the yard.

The ice was thick on the puddles the next morning.

'Look at those blasted crows,' said Commins as they got ready to saddle up. A flock of the jet-black birds had settled on the trees and fences around the Rocklands stables.

'They're a bad omen,' said Old Jack the stockman. 'No good'll come of it.'

'Nonsense,' said Commins. 'They're just a nuisance, what with their cawking and scavenging. It's just a sign of winter. They come down from the hills in winter.

'I don't like 'em,' said Jack. 'They look like a pestilence.'

'How come there's so many of them?' asked Barcroft. He didn't like them either. They chased away his friends the magpies, who stayed loyally at Rosedale all through the year.

'Probably because there's scant pickings elsewhere,' said Commins.

Ted threw a rock at the ones closest on the fence. They jumped up, squawking and flapping their wings, but didn't move far away. Their blackness looked out of place in the pale bleached colours of their surroundings. They were too black, thought Barcroft, and too shiny. They didn't fit in. Jack might be right. There was something uneasy about them.

The coming of the crows may well have been an omen. The weather worsened after their arrival. During the next week, it started snowing. It snowed on and off for most of the week after that. To pass the time while they were snowed in, he and Tim made some snowshoes.

Barcroft remembered Jean's interest in snowshoes last winter and decided he should take them to Rosedale next weekend. He was sure the other McKeahnies would be interested too. He and Charlie Mac might even be able to make some better ones. Tim said he didn't mind if Barcroft took them over to Rosedale.

Something disturbing happened before he could get there.

Rocklands, Adaminaby

16 July 1888

Dear Father

It is some time since I let you hear how I was getting on, though I wrote to Grannie and Addie not so long since but I have not heard from them for some time. As usual the weather is the all engrossing topic, we have had one very heavy fall of snow and numerous light ones, the snow was on the ground for four days before it began to thaw, and our poor horses got a starving I can assure you. We made a pair of snow shoes and tried our hands at snow shoeing, it must be a grand sport from what I can see of it. We got some awful spills – you will be going along fine, and suddenly your feet will give a jump and shoot straight from under you leaving you on the broad of your back. It is extremely amusing for the bystanders.

Things are very dull now, just the same old routine of work during the week and spending the Sunday at Rosedale.

Last Saturday night we had a high tragedy, when, through a piece of silly foolishness, I was with within an ace of losing my life. It has been a bit of a lesson for me not to indulge in foolish practical jokes. Boydie and I were in the kitchen talking and fooling with Miss Brooks and young Ted the Roustabout; and I forget what started it, but we said we would both hang ourselves. There was a gamble that they hung the sheep on hanging to a beam with a loose end of rope. I, like a fool, made a slip-knot in it, and, tieing a handkerchief over my face, said goodbye to them all and put the noose round my neck (Boydie was hanging himself with his handkerchief) and let the noose tighten round my throat. Miss Brooks ran out of the kitchen round to her room. I was swinging, as I said, with the rope pretty tight round my neck, with my weight on my hands; and the last I remember is Miss Brooks leaving the room.

Then I lost all consciousness of the outer world, but seemed to be dreaming. I felt no pain, but seemed to be pondering on the strangeness of this world and the people, and what a wonderful thing science was. But gradually I seemed to get a feeling of irritation and tried not to think, but I had to; thoughts seemed to crowd before my eyes like the passing of a train, so quickly that it was a pain to watch them. Then, I suppose, there was a blank; and the next thing I thought of was the Milson's Point boat. I could hear water splashing, and felt her gradually slow off as she drew alongside the wharf. Then I knew something had happened to me. I could see people all round me, and I knew at once I was on the boat and had been struck down by heart disease (Dr Cox told me that I had a weak heart) and I dreamily thought, Well, I am going to die at last; and then the boat seemed to be sinking down, and

I could feel the water rush over me and feel it wet on my cheek. There seemed to be some fearful weight crushing my chest in. It got worse and worse, and gradually I woke to the reality that I was lying on the floor with everyone round me bathing my hands and temples, while I was having a mortal struggle for breath.

Oh! It was an awful struggle – ten times worse than the hanging. I would sink back on the floor, and then suddenly be convulsed and nearly sit up in my struggle to breathe; and they told me the sounds I made were something sickening. I felt as if my chest was smashed in with a blow and would not expand – I never want to go through it again. At last I got better, and was able to swallow a little brandy; and got all right after a time – but my neck! I have a rope mark now all round it, and the next day (yesterday, that is) the muscles were swollen like great ropes, and the headache I had Saturday night and yesterday was enough to drive me mad.

After Miss Brooks went out of the kitchen Boydie took the handkerchief off his neck, and he and young Ted sat laughing at me. Neither of them knew I had been holding onto the rope with my hands; they both thought I had it tied round my shoulders. When they saw me my hands were stretched by my sides, the fingers just moving convulsively. It was very dark, so they could not see that I was hanging by my neck. A last Ted said, 'Come on, we'll cut him down,' and was very nearly letting me down whop. They made some delay, and Miss Brooks came back and said, 'This is beyond a joke Mr Boake,' and still they thought I was shamming; so they cut me down, and it was not till they took the handkerchief off and found I was black in the face, and blood oozing from the mouth, that they found out it was no joke, but real earnest.

I can tell you I gave them a fright. It took nearly half an hour to bring me to. I think a very few seconds would have cooked me. Of course, I suppose I was a dumb fool to put the rope round my neck, but still a fellow often does things without thinking, but they don't always have such awful consequences. I am as right as the bank now, barring a red ring round my neck and a big splotch under my left ear where the knot came – so you need not be frightened; but my sensations were so curious that I wish I could explain them to you more accurately.

Give my love to Granny and Addie, and write soon. I have not heard from you for a long time.

Your loving son, Bartie.

10

Rosedale, 1888

It snowed again during the week. Before setting off for Rosedale on Sunday, Barcroft strapped the snowshoes behind his saddle. He had to tie them across each other, sticking upwards in a criss-cross shape. The ground had frozen overnight, so Sweetbriar had to tread carefully on the frosty track. Although no snow had fallen since Friday, the drifts were still deep on the sheltered slopes and in the hollows. Ice crackled as they crossed the creeks and the marshes. In the steeper gullies, tiny waterfalls were frozen delicately in mid-fall.

By the Rosedale plain, they were able to gallop freely. It was a sharp winter's morning without a cloud in the pale blue sky. Barcroft could feel the rush of the crisp cold air on his cheeks. At the river crossing, the water was high from snow melt. Fast flowing eddies swirled past beneath the shade of the white-frosted tussocks on the banks. He was glad it was Sweetbriar who had to splash through the icy water.

Jean was at the stables when he arrived at Rosedale. 'What's that mark on your neck?' she asked.

'I did a silly thing last week,' he replied. He felt uncomfortable having to explain it. 'I was fooling around. We were pretending to be hanged. Then it went a bit wrong for me.'

'Let me see,' she said, pulling down his collar to inspect his neck. 'Keep still,' she ordered in a no-nonsense tone. 'This is serious,' she said. 'It doesn't look like a joke. What happened? How could you do something like this?'

'I don't know, really. I was just fooling round and it went wrong.'

'It certainly did. You could've killed yourself!' she said angrily.

'I know,' he replied sheepishly.

'So that's why you didn't come over last Sunday?'

'Yes. I had a terrible headache.'

'I can imagine! How could you do something like that? You disappoint me, Mr Boake.' She shook her head. 'I thought you'd be more sensible than that.'

'I didn't mean it to happen.'

She frowned at him. Then she noticed the snowshoes still strapped to Sweetbriar's saddle. 'Are those snowshoes?' she asked, changing her tone.

'Yes.'

'Can we try them out?'

'Yes, if you like. That's why I brought them over.'

'At least you can do something useful,' she said. Then she added in a more friendly tone, 'Here, I'll take them off. You go in and have a cup of tea. It's just being served. You must be cold from riding. I'll be with you in a minute.'

Barcroft was glad to accept a hot mug of tea in the kitchen. He was sitting at the table warming his hands around the mug when May came in. She immediately noticed his neck.

'What on earth have you done to yourself?' she asked in a concerned voice.

'It's nothing, really. It was just some fooling round gone wrong.'

'It looks horrid. What happened?' she said, sounding upset.

'I was pretending to hang myself, and it went a bit wrong.'

'Bartie! You could've hurt yourself really badly,' she said. 'You could even have killed yourself.' She looked most concerned.

'I won't do it again, I can tell you.'

'I'm so upset at the thought. How could you do something so silly? Didn't you think of me? Did you even think of the consequences?'

'I won't do it again,' he replied.

'Will you truly promise me?' she asked, looking at him pleadingly.

'Yes.'

'Really and truly?'

'Yes, I promise,' he said.

'Don't ever do anything like that again – or I won't have anything to do with you.'

'I won't. You can be certain of that.'

Just then, Charlie Mac came banging into the kitchen followed by Jean.

'Boakie's brought some snowshoes over. Let's go and try them out,' said Charlie.

'Did you really?' said May, looking at Barcroft. He thought she had such pretty eyes.

'Yes, but there's only two pairs.'

'We can share them,' said Jean. 'It'll be fun.'

'Let's go,' said Charlie.

First, they tried them on the hill behind the stables. There wasn't much snow and they didn't work very well. Then Charlie said he knew a spot where there'd still be lots of snow left. They climbed over the hill to the far side of the ridge, taking turns to carry the snowshoes. It was hard work trudging through the snow.

When they got there, it was worth it. Barcroft was surprised at how good Jean and May were at balancing on the snowshoes. Charlie and Barcroft were faster, but had more spills. Jean said girls were better at balancing because they were closer to the ground and had wider hips. In any case, girls were better at lots of things, she said. They laughed a lot at each other as they struggled to stay upright sliding down the slope. It was always amusing to see someone else take a tumble. Barcroft liked the determined look Jean and May had on their faces as they focused their attention on keeping balance. It reminded him of how much he liked them.

After an hour or so, they were all worn out. And they were soaked through. There was a marshy creek at the bottom of the slope. That was where they ended many of their runs, if they made it that far.

As they trudged back to the homestead, Barcroft explained how he and Boydie had copied the snowshoes they'd seen at Kiandra. Theirs weren't perfect, he admitted. The front ends weren't turned up as much as they should be. That's why they kept falling off when they ran into bumps in the snow, he explained.

'We can make some better ones next year,' said Charlie. 'What d'you say, Boakie?'

'I probably won't be here.'

'Of course not. I forgot,' said Charlie. 'You're leaving soon, aren't you?'

'Yes. In a few weeks' time.'

'Do you have to go?' asked May. 'We'll miss you.'

'I don't have a choice. My employment here with Mr Commins is finishing.'

'What are you going to do?' asked Jean.

'Boydie says there's a mint to be made up north. He was talking to this drover at the Commercial the other day. He said they're desperate for stockmen up Trangie way – and they pay top money. Boydie's going to check it out for us.'

'You won't be surveying, then?' said Jean.

'Not if I can help it.'

'Why not?' asked Jean.

'It's so tedious. You've no idea. I'd go crazy if I stayed surveying. I really don't like it.'

'Are we so boring here, then?' asked May.

'Of course not. I'd love to stay here. And I would if I could get the right work.'

'I don't think we could afford to take you on here at present,' said Charlie. 'We've had a few lean seasons lately. We could ask Father, though.'

'I wouldn't ask for that,' said Barcroft. 'Don't worry about me. I'll go off and make my fortune. Then I'll come back – rich or something.' He tried to sound positive. Underneath, he felt sad and hollow.

'It's a pity you have to go,' said May.

'You'll write to us, won't you?' said Jean.

'Of course I will.'

Back at the homestead, they changed out of their wet clothes and stoked up the fire in the living room. Charlie lent Barcroft some of his riding breeches while Barcroft's wet ones dried. Then they all sat in front of the roaring flames to warm up. The cook brought them hot mugs of soup. That warmed them even better than the flames.

Lunch at Rosedale that Sunday was a roast. Even better, it was roast beef. After the meal, Mr McKeahnie invited Barcroft and Charlie for a smoke in the drawing room. The girls were excluded. Sometimes, men needed time to themselves – without women, McKeahnie explained to the girls. Jean was obviously put out. Barcroft thought she seemed a bit crabby that afternoon.

'You're such a girl, Mr Boake,' she said when he spilt the milk at afternoon teatime.

By next Sunday, all the snow had melted. It was so warm it could almost have been spring.

Not long after Barcroft arrived at Rosedale, Mr McKeahnie took him aside. McKeahnie didn't talk a lot. Barcroft liked him but he wasn't someone to take liberties with.

'Come along with me, young fellow,' he said, ushering Barcroft into the drawing room. 'I thought we'd better have a talk before you leave.'

'Yes?' said Barcroft, feeling a little apprehensive.

'You've spent a fair bit of time with us over the last year or so.' McKeahnie's tone was reassuringly friendly. 'That's been good. Don't get me wrong. I've been happy to have you here. You've been good company for the others. Now they tell me you're leaving soon – to head up north, I understand.'

'Yes, in a couple of weeks.'

'I'd like to give you some advice before you go.'

'Yes?'

'I'm not blind. I can see you've got a fair interest in some of my daughters. That's so, isn't it?'

Barcroft felt himself going red.

'There's nothing wrong with that,' said McKeahnie quickly, to reassure him. 'There's no need to be shy about it. I'm sure your intentions are honourable. As far as I'm concerned, it doesn't even matter which of my daughters you have an interest in. My advice would be the same.' He paused.

To Barcroft it seemed a long pause.

'My advice to any young fellas interested in my daughters is this: my daughters deserve a good life. I've worked hard to provide for them and I want to be sure they'll be looked after properly when they leave here. Anyone who wants to marry my daughters needs to have some substance. They need to be able to look after them well.' He paused again.

Barcroft wanted to tell him it wasn't like that. He didn't even know if McKeahnie's daughters were interested in him.

'I didn't really want this to be a lecture. What I'm trying to say is, you need to make something of yourself. You're still young. You've got talent. And you've got opportunity. Don't waste it. I've worked damned hard to establish this place here. I know what it takes. It takes hard work.' He paused. 'I do wish you the best. And I hope to see you again.'

Barcroft didn't know what to say.

'It's all right. You don't need to say anything. I've said all I wanted. Don't worry, you'll always be welcome here. I'm sure you'll do well.'

'Thank you,' said Barcroft. 'I've liked it here. You've all been very kind to me. I will try my best.'

'That's it, young fella.' McKeahnie put his hand on Barcroft's shoulder.

That evening, Barcroft felt very sad. He had desperately wanted to tell May how he felt before he left. But every time an opportunity presented, he had misgivings about her feelings towards him. He also feared he would make a fool of himself, and embarrass her as well. So he said nothing. Then he hated himself for being cowardly.

It wasn't straightforward. He also wanted to tell Jean how much he really cared for her. Perhaps not as much as May. Except that wasn't right. It was just different. His feelings for Jean were very powerful too. But he wasn't sure of her feelings either. Jean was so touchy at times. He feared her reaction if he'd misjudged the situation. It was safer to do nothing. But then he felt bad.

The night before his last Sunday at Rosedale, Barcroft made a resolution. He would definitely tell May and Jean how he felt towards them. He just had to overcome his shyness. He wouldn't be seeing them again for a long time, maybe ever, so it wouldn't matter if he embarrassed himself. It would be worth the risk, he told himself before he went to sleep.

His resolve evaporated in the cold light of day. Jean and May seemed distant that morning. Their attitude gave him no encouragement to speak freely to them about his feelings. As time passed, he gave up the idea.

The evening before, he'd prepared some lines to bid them all farewell. With mixed feelings, he copied them into Jean's scrapbook that afternoon.

Good-bye.   12th August 1888

Rosedale, my other home, to you I bid
Regretfully one lingering, sad farewell.
We two have met as on that mountain stream
Which, clearly flowing, bathes your furrowed fields,
Two leaflets meet and gently glide along
In friendly company, linked side by side,
When, lo – an eddy from a hidden rock
Remorselessly doth tear them far apart.
Perchance it leaves one stranded on the bank
To shrivel up and wither in the sun,
And bears the other on its widening stream
To fate unknown.

So Rosedale, you remain, while I go on
Launched on that treacherous stream that men call life,
Which bears them helpless over spray wrapt falls,
O'er sparkling shallows and deep gloomy pools,
To strand them in oblivion whence they sprung.

It may be that life's stream, by some strange freak,

May turn and bring me back to clasp again
Your hands outstretched to welcome my return;
To see once more the crossing at the stream,
The green of drooping willows and the plain
Fringed by its border of bold wooded hills.

–

Once more at early morn to see the mist
Drawn from the river's bosom by the sun
Lift up to heaven and vanish like a dream.
Or in the evening by the genial fire,
In merry cadence hear your voices rise,
Telling of pleasures past and joys to come.

But if I come not – in some idle hour
You may with loit'ring finger turn this page
Then pause awhile, and give one kindly thought
To him who writes at parting his last prayer -
        God guard you – and – good-bye.

In his first draft, he had the leaflets meeting again later in life. When rewriting them, he recast the lines to make their reunion less certain.

Jean read the verses and looked at him. 'So we're to shrivel and wither in the sun here, are we?' she said, somewhat querulously.

He felt he'd upset her in some way. 'I didn't mean that. I had to say something in that line. It's just a poem,' he replied defensively. 'Later on, it says we might meet again.'

'Hmm,' she said, as if she wasn't entirely convinced.

He wished he'd written it differently.

May read it next. 'There's no mention of me in it,' she said, also sounding miffed.

'I was thinking of you when I wrote it,' he said, lamely.

She didn't look reassured. He wished he'd put her in it. Jean and May's reactions added to his already depressed mood.

The atmosphere at dinner was better. Mrs McKeahnie encouraged everyone to talk about the good times they'd all had together. After dinner, Barcroft read to the youngest children for the last time. Polly and Lem gave him a hug and said they'd miss him. He was moved.

When it was time for him to leave, Jean surprised him by giving him a kiss on the cheek. May was even bolder. She gave him a hug as well as a kiss. Then she quickly left the room. Jean made him promise to write to them. He said he would.

As he rode home across the river flats, his heart was heavy.

After Barcroft left Rosedale, Jean found May in her bedroom looking upset.

'You've been crying,' Jean said. 'You really care about him, don't you?'

'Not really. I'm just tired. I don't like partings. They make me sad.'

Jean didn't believe her. She was sad herself but she wasn't about to show it. She had hoped Barcroft would say something to her. At one point, she thought he might. She was cross with him for not doing so. She wanted him to say who he liked out of her and May. If it was really May, then she could try and get him out of her mind. Now it would remain unresolved. He made her so cross at times. Why couldn't he have been more positive, she asked herself, almost out loud.

May spent the rest of the evening in her bedroom. She told the others she was tired. When she was alone, she lay on her bed and cried. She had hoped Barcroft would say something special to her. He should have talked to her, she said to herself. He should have said something special to her. It was so unfair that he had to leave. And he didn't really seem to care.

11

On the Road to Naromine, 1888

Barcroft had been torn between wanting to stay and needing to leave. Now he was on the road, the excitement of starting a new adventure took over. He was riding Sweetbriar and Tim was on Dancer, his favourite. They'd bought the horses with their paid-out earnings. They intended travelling light, so all they carried was a rolled-up swag, their stockwhips and some provisions slung behind them in their saddlebags.

Barcroft couldn't remember when he'd felt so good. At last he was free of surveying! With some money in his pocket, his own horse and Tim for company, what more could he want? He had no idea what the future held in store but he was facing it with high spirits. He hoped there'd be adventures to be had, stories to tell and a fortune to be made. He pictured himself riding across the Rosedale river flats in a few years' time – a 'man of substance'.

It was still winter. Dark grey clouds hung menacingly over the ranges as they rode out of Cooma. The weather worsened as they headed north past the Squatter's Arms at Bunyan. By the time they got to Bredbo, the rain was driving at them horizontally in squalls, doing its best to unseat them. Sleet stung their hands and their faces as they hunched over their horses.

'This ain't much fun,' shouted Tim through the rain. 'How 'bout we stay the night at the Bredbo Hotel? No chance of getting a fire going tonight.'

'Okay,' Barcroft shouted back, the wind tearing the words out of his mouth.

This was a change of plan. Their initial intention had been sleep out along the way to save on costs. With this in mind, they'd packed basic supplies of flour, bully beef, tea and sugar.

Jack Goggin, the publican at the Bredbo Hotel, was pleased to see them. He knew Tim. On talking to Jack, they discovered he knew most of the people in the district. When they told him their plans, he offered them a cheap room out the back. After eating a wholesome meal and warming themselves in front of the fire, they turned in for the night.

Fortunately, the storm blew itself out overnight. In the morning, they headed north through Michalago towards Queanbeyan. They left the mountains behind after the Limestone Plains. The rugged mountain ridges that had flanked them as they followed the Murrumbidgee River from Bredbo gave way to rolling hills as they rode on towards Yass.

Feed became sparser. There'd been a dry winter in these parts. Both horses and their riders started to tire. The novelty of travelling began to wear off. By the time they got to Ann's Vale, they were ready to take a break.

Barcroft was glad Tim was travelling with him. He found Tim good company. He never let things get him down. He always had a positive word to say. Barcroft knew his own temperament was less robust. He let little things worry him too easily. If it hadn't been for Tim, he would have lost heart when their bedding got wet, when they took the wrong track and ended in a marsh full of snakes! – and when the flour bag broke and left a trail of white behind them.

Tim just made light of these things. 'It's only flour,' he said when they discovered the broken flour bag. 'Plenty more where that came from. Look on the positive side. At least we can't get lost again. We've marked our own trail – just like Hansel and Gretel!'

After a spell at Ann's Vale, they set off north again. From Adaminaby to Trangie was roughly three hundred miles. Neither Tim nor Barcroft had ever been this way before. They had to find their own way. This led to some interesting experiences on the way as they headed through Burrowa, Molong and Naromine. Barcroft wrote to the McKeahnies about their adventures.

To My Friends at Rosedale

We left Ann's Vale two Sundays after we left you. It was a great 'chuck in' for us stopping there; it did our horses a lot of good. In fact if it had not been for that we would never have seen Trangie. Besides, Boydie and I were both getting full of travelling: it is not much of a lark, I can assure you.

We got on very well after we left Burrowa, till we got to Molong, where we were going to turn off to go to Dubbo. I knew there must be some shorter road, but did not know where to find it out. Just by the merest chance I went into a bakers for some bread, and happened to ask the man: and by good luck, he told us he had been up there and knew all the country. So he directed us how to go a back road which cut off a day's journey; but the country was awfully dry – not a blade of grass and our last day before getting to Naromine we rode the whole day and never saw a blade the whole twenty miles – nothing but the bare ground covered with leaves.

To crown it all, we pushed on to get to Naromine for a camp, and got there just at dark, having to turn out at the first place we came to – and in the morning our horses were gone! Well, I sent Boydie one way to inquire if they had gone back through the town, and I went the other way. I walked from eight o'clock till eleven; came back and saw Boydie; no news. I started straight away again and walked till three o'clock, when I came home and had some dinner; and by Jove! wasn't I tired! Well I had a rest till four, and started again, and did not get back till eight o'clock. It took me two hours to come the last two miles. I was never so knocked up in my life. I did not seem to care whether I ever got back. I felt I would have gladly died straight away. Besides I felt so miserable. To get on so well till just within twenty miles of our destination, and then to meet with a knock like that! If you could have seen me crawling along, hardly able to drag one foot after another. I am sure you would have pitied me. I can assure you I pitied myself.

Well, next day I started out again, but I was so stiff it was misery to walk. Boydie went out to Trangie by rail to see if he could get the loan of a horse from Mr Chapman. This was on Wednesday. I was just mooching back with some water for tea when I met Boydie with a smile all over his face, and he told me he had not been able to get a horse, but had heard of ours – they had been seen seven miles back on the road we had come, and were going straight away.

Well, we could not get a horse high or low, so the lad started after them on foot. He did not start till after dark, and got five miles on the road and turned back. He had my heavy boots on, and they blistered his feet, so he took them off and footed it back barefoot. By George! he was about full of it when he got back.

The next day I started at daylight, and, as luck would have it, found them just where Boydie had turned back. I could hardly believe my eyes when I saw them feeding towards me. I fetched them back quick, and we packed up and shook the dust of Naromine off our feet; and I hope I never set eyes on it again.

Your true friend, BHB

Their destination was Mullah Station, just past Trangie. They arrived just in time for the spring muster.

'What took you so long?' said Will Chapman. He was the overseer they were contracted to work for. 'We ain't a benevolent institution y'know.' He was big, hairy and ugly.

They explained how they'd lost their horses, which had delayed them unexpectedly.

'Lost your horses, eh? You'd be a right pair of dills, wouldn't you! Wait till I tell the other boys that one!' He spat on the ground strategically. 'Listen here. You lose any of our horses here, an' you pay for 'em. Got that?'

'It wasn't our fault,' said Tim. 'The hobbles must've broke.'

'I don't care what happens. What goes missing here gets paid for. That's company policy. Now get your kits into the quarters. We've got work to do.'

He wasn't joking. The pay might be all right, said Tim later, but you sure had to work for it.

They were woken at dawn the next morning. Within the hour, they were on their way to the outstation.

At the outstation, their life was reduced to the basics: work, eat, sleep. They had no time to dwell on things. By the evenings, Barcroft was so dog-tired it was all he could do to collapse into bed. Rosedale became a distant memory.

Life at the camp had its moments. Except for Bully Chapman, as the others called him, the stockmen at the camp were a good bunch to work with. Out here, you had to rely on each other. You had to work as a team. Barcroft enjoyed it. There was satisfaction to be had from chalking up a tally at the end of the day, knowing you'd done it together. Some days, they'd really get humming along. The only thing that ever stopped them was the way the sheep behaved.

'Sheep have gotta be God's most stupid creatures,' said Tim. 'He must've run out of brains when He got to them.'

Barcroft agreed. Up till now he hadn't thought much about them. Working closely with animals usually gave you respect for them, people said. Working with sheep was the opposite. They were totally stupid. They had no redeeming features. They got themselves stuck in dams, snared themselves on fences and panicked at imaginary dangers. Then, when you got one of them to go through the race, the others followed mindlessly, even if they were off to be butchered. As for their tails, they had to be the most useless piece of equipment ever seen on an animal. No wonder they needed to be taken off. Then there was the way they looked at you. Hundreds of eyes staring at you, watching your every move. Barcroft felt like shouting at them, 'Hey! What d'you lot think you're staring at! Get lost!'

By the end of November, the temperature started to rise. The bush became tinder dry. The horizon shimmered. The dust and heat became oppressive.

Barcroft wrote to the McKeahnies again. He also wrote to his father.

November 1888

Dear Father

For the last three weeks we have been camped out lamb-marking and mustering, and I have not been in at the station once during that time except one day to get a fresh horse. We are working very hard at the camp from four o'clock in the morning to dark. I shall be glad when it is over and we can settle down again.

Boydie went to Sydney last Monday. He was very glad to get out of the dust and heat. My word! it is getting hot now. Last Sunday, at four in the afternoon, it was 98 degrees in the shade. It is a terror working in the yards now, but it is nothing to what we got putting out a bush fire the other day. We were all drafting when Will Chapman came galloping up to tell us there was a fire coming across the paddock about a mile away. We all made a rush for horses, and galloped off like mad along a swamp where the grass is four or five feet high and as dry as a bone. There was a wall of fire coming across like the side of a house. You could not get near the front of it, so we had to start at the sides, and one would rush in with a bush and beat it out till the smoke drove him back, and then another would take his place. After about half an hour I was nearly dead. It was a boiling hot day to start with; and what with the heat of the fire, and smoke, and no water, it was worse than anything I ever experienced before. We stopped the fire by lighting another one in front, and letting it burn back.

Have a stiff neck from sleeping in the veranda last night. I always sleep there now, so as to get up early. One does not want bed-clothes. I just chuck a rug down and a pillow, and camp on that; and as the day breaks I saddle my horse and off. The only things that disturb me are the 'possums. They run up and down the veranda and squeak the whole night. One ran up and sat on the eave of the house, and incautiously let his tail dangle over the edge, and I sneaked up and caught of it – and didn't he jump! He must be going yet.

Your affectionate son, Bartie

A month later, he still hadn't received a reply from either the McKeahnies or his father. It didn't surprise him greatly, as he'd been told the mail was unreliable out west. Since it was possible some of his letters might have got lost, he wrote to his father again.

Mullah, Trangie

10 December 1888

Dear Father

It seems very strange that you have not answered my last letter, so as there is a chance you have not received it I write this. I have nothing new to tell.- we are still anxiously waiting for the breaking of the drought which continues with great severity. It is getting very hot now, it is 100 and over nearly every day. It has been up to 114 in the shade, the other night it was 96 in the evening at bed time in the sitting room.

I don't feel the heat nearly so much as I expected: in fact, I can stand it with much less inconvenience than I could the cold of the Monaro. The only thing I feel is the thirst: I never seem to be satisfied.

Times are pretty easy now. Most of the work is over among the sheep, and all I have to do is ride round about twenty miles of the boundary to see that no sheep are getting bogged at the water. I generally make a start at about four in the morning, when it is cool, and get back about ten o'clock. After that, as a rule, I have nothing to do for the rest of the day except pass the time reading, unless I feel inclined to take a ride round the lagoon about sundown...

As soon as we get rain though there will be plenty of work as the sheep are all mixed up any how on account of having to let them go anywhere they like for water. The losses are very heavy among the stock, I am glad to say they have been very small comparatively speaking on the run but on others thousands of sheep have become food for the crows. In a month's time Mr

Chapman's brother on the Brogan will not have a single sheep alive on his run if we don't have rain.

How is Addie, give my love to Granny,

Your affectionate son, Bartie.

He wanted to write to the McKeahnies as well but he felt inhibited. He worried they might have lost interest in him now he'd been gone so long. He knew that times changed and life moved on. It was hard being such a distance away and not knowing if his letters had been received.

Now there was less work to occupy him, he often thought about the people who mattered in his life. Although he was often alone, he wasn't lonely. He couldn't be lonely when there were always lots of people in his head. He thought about May and Jean; and Addie, Clare and Evie; and Gran and his father. He hoped May and Jean hadn't forgotten him. He wished he could write to them privately. But imagine the talk in the McKeahnie household if he ever did that!

With little to do at the station, tensions flared in the heat. Rusty, one of the older stockmen, had a stand-up fight with Bully Chapman. It started over some imagined slight, though in truth it had been brewing for weeks. Rusty was a lot smaller than the overseer, but he gave a good account of himself. Not surprisingly, he was sacked on the spot and sent packing without his outstanding bonus. Barcroft thought that was unfair.

The fight between Rusty and Bully Chapman was the chief excitement for that week. Most days, it was a case of sitting around in the shade watching what was happening. Generally, that was nothing much, except for the odd territorial squabble between roosters.

One afternoon, Barcroft and Tim sat watching Gramps, the station dog trying to chase chickens. He was called Gramps because of his age. He would have to be at least eighty in dog years, thought Barcroft. His fur was going grey and it was a long time since he'd been any use as a working dog. No doubt he'd lived a full dog's life. Now he had trouble moving.

He was a sight to watch. You could see all the old urges were there but he just wasn't up to it any more. The chickens could tell. They came right up close, just to annoy him. He barked and lifted himself half up. But he was too slow. They just hopped sideways and kept pecking at the ground. When he finally got to his feet and lunged at them unsteadily, they hardly bothered getting out of his way. A couple more barks and he gave up and lay down again.

'You gotta shoot me before I get like that,' said Tim.

'I don't know,' said Barcroft. Who's to say he isn't happy with his life. Maybe a life lived to the full could give you the comfort to deal with the trials of old age.

Christmas at Mullah was a quiet affair for Barcroft. He ate Christmas dinner on the veranda of the main house with the Chinese cook and the serving maids. Tim and the other stockmen went to Trangie to celebrate the occasion. Barcroft was glad he didn't go. By all accounts they had an eventful time, drinking and gambling. They were a sorry looking lot as they straggled back to the station on Boxing Day nursing their hangovers.

The Christmas mail included a letter from his father. It was no surprise to Barcroft that his father pressed Barcroft to reconsider a career in surveying. He offered to help Barcroft get his qualification to practise as a surveyor. Barcroft wrote back.

29 December 1888

Dear Father

Your last letter must assuredly have miscarried, as it is two months or more since I heard from you. From the tone of your letter I should say the world is treating you better than hitherto. It is about time too.

So there is another inhabitant added to this continent. Poor little beggar! I wonder if he will ever wish he had never been born, like most of us do. I think it is a natural consequence of being face to face with nature so continually but the great mystery of human nature often comes before me as I ride about. It seems to me so sad and disheartening – to toil, with the knowledge of the vanity of it all in our hearts. Civilisation is a dead failure: it only brings these truths more forcibly before us: a savage never thinks of these things.

I have very easy times now – far too easy, in fact. The less I have to do the more time I have to grumble. Good hard work – physical labour – is the best panacea imaginable for a discontented mind. When I used to be in the yards in the heat and dust all I would think of was how to do the work well and expeditiously and have done with it; but now, from eleven o'clock in the morning I have absolutely nothing to do but kill time. I am up early, and my riding is done by ten or eleven; and I find it very hard to pass the time away; but I believe this will be all over soon, as the stock out back will be in great straights for water soon, and then our joy begins.

I have read your advice and I wish for your sake and Grannie's I could bring myself to follow it. But oh! I should smother if I were to go back to Sydney again: I should have no heart. There is a curious phenomenon in stock-breeding called 'throwing back'. After years and years of careful breeding, you will sometimes find a beast born with all the characteristics of the original stock. In the same way, I believe some of the wild blood of our savage Irish ancestors has been transmitted to me. At any rate, my home is in the bush; and as no good is to be done but on the confines of the settled country, that is where I hope to go within the next year.

I had just finished a letter to Grannie this afternoon just before finishing this of yours. I enclose a slip of paper for her in this. Give my love to all.

Your affectionate son, Bartie

Barcroft became increasingly restless at Mullah. Passing stockmen told stories of the good money to be had further north. They told tales of life on the road with thousands of cattle. They talked of the endless plains of the Diamantina. They spoke of huge mobs of cattle mustered from as far away as the Gulf country in the far north of Queensland – and of driving them all the way down to Victoria.

These stockmen were tough, wiry-looking characters. Hardbitten, dusty men, burnt red and brown from the fierce outback sun. They spoke casually about injury and death out on the wastes of the Never Never. No chance of a doctor out there. If a beast crushed a man's leg out there, he just had to grit his teeth and bear it. No chance of a fancy funeral if you died. They buried you where you lay. A dusty mound beside a stock route is all that would mark your grave. There were plenty of graves like that out west, the stockmen said, out on the edges of the settled country.

These were the real men of the bush, thought Barcroft. They were really living life to the full. Facing death and danger without flinching. Knowing the risks and taking the consequences without a murmur.

Barcroft felt he was ready for that kind of life. As Tim was of a similar mind, together they decided to set off north when the worst of the summer heat was over. Tim's younger brother was visiting and asked if he could come along. They agreed. His nickname was Half Pint. Barcroft asked why.

'He was such a tiny kid when he was little – only pint-sized. We called him Half Pint to tease him. The name stuck. He's so big now we should call him Quart Pot!'

Tim and Barcroft struck a problem when they went to collect their payouts from Chapman. He wouldn't pay their bonuses in full. Half of the amount was taken off for 'deductions'.

'What's this deductions business?' said Tim, getting excited. 'We only signed up because of the size of the bonus. How come you won't give it to us?'

'You should've checked the wording of the contract, sonny boy,' said Chapman. 'It says deductions will be made for wear and tear. I've been generous to you. I could've taken off more. I never charged you for the broken stockwhip, or the saddle cloths.'

'We've been dudded,' said Tim. 'The base rate's only ordinary. It was the bonus what got us here.'

'I don't make company policy, sonny. That's for Sir Eric. He's told me to make sure I take all the deductions off.'

'I've a mind to bring the union in on this,' said Tim, getting steamed up.

'You better not be threatening me, sonny.' Chapman took a step forward and leaned over Tim. He was a big man. He didn't get his nickname for nothing. 'We don't have no truck with unions here! Best you take what I've given you and get out of here,' he threatened.

For a moment, Tim looked as though he mightn't back down. Then he thought better of it. 'Come on, let's go,' he said to Barcroft. He was furious. As they rode off he said, 'Now I know what that union bloke was on about. Now I understand why they call that Sir Eric bastard Moneygrub. I didn't reckon there was any need for unions before. This has sure changed my mind!'

Barcroft said nothing. He wasn't proud of himself. He should have backed Tim up but he'd said nothing. It was the same as always. He had no trouble facing physical danger. He even had a reputation for bravery. It was a different matter when it came to dealing with people.

'I should've jobbed him,' said Tim, as they cantered out of the yard.

'I was ready,' said his brother. 'I would've backed you.' He almost sounded disappointed.

'Don't worry, Half Pint,' said Tim. 'Let's get out of here. We've got better things to do.'

12

Droving, 1889

As they put distance between themselves and Mullah, the dispute over the deductions was soon forgotten. Barcroft's spirits lifted as they rode along. Once again he was setting out on an adventure. He had no idea what the future would bring but for now his expectations were high.

They made a point of travelling in a leisurely fashion, taking time to spell the horses regularly. They'd learnt from their earlier travelling that it was important to keep something in reserve. When they reached Brewarrina, they stopped for a few days. They were now on the main stock route from Queensland – the cattle highway from the Gulf to Victoria. Their plan was to follow it north to Barringun on the Queensland border to see if they could pick up work with the travelling stock parties.

Barcroft wrote to his father from their river side camp.

Brewarrina

10 May 1889

Dear Father

You will see from the above address that I have shifted my quarters at last. I am two hundred miles away from Mullah now, this place is on the Barwon River on the main stock road to Queensland. I left Mullah in company with the two Boyds last Monday week. We have had a very good trip so far, the country looks splendid. I never saw such grass as there is in some places. We had beautiful weather too, only one wet camp which was last Sunday.

At the crossing of the Womerah River we had been told to cross in a certain place by an old sheep bridge. I did not like the look of it at all, but as there were dray tracks both in and out the other side I supposed it could not be very bad, so I rode in leading a packhorse, but had not gone three paces when my horse went down to the saddle flaps in mud. I let the packhhorse go and jumped off and when he was relieved of my weight my old horse managed to struggle through and go accross – to let him go straight ahead was the only chance as you could not turn around in the mud. There were we on this side of the river and my horse on the other. However I found a place where I could wade across, so I got my horse and waited till the others crossed higher up at a dam.

I was a nice state I can assure you – pants and leggings all covered with thick mud. My old horse was the one though, he was pure white when he went in but after he got out he was a sight - the mud is not all off him yet and it is nearly a week.

I don't think there is any use your answering this as I don't know what address will find me. Give my love to Granny and the girls.

Your affectionate son, Bartie.

PS I am writing this on the river bank where we are camped, on the stump of a tree which has been sawn.

After a night at the river camp, they indulged themselves by booking in for a couple of days' accommodation at the main hotel. Barcroft enjoyed sleeping in a bed. The meals at the pub were also a welcome change. The horses got a good feed too.

'We're not so broke we can't afford a bit of luxury now and then,' said Tim.

'Yeah. Bully beef and damper's fine when you're hungry,' said Half Pint. 'But it don't beat a good feed at a pub.' He had a reputation as an eater. Barcroft had noticed that he really wolfed his food down.

'Can't see as you'd notice the difference,' said Tim pointedly. 'I reckon you'd eat anything they put on a plate. Do you ever look at it?'

'Why waste time looking at it?' said his brother. 'That'd only slow you down.'

That evening they had a drink in the bar. It was full of travelling stockmen.

Harry and Brian introduced themselves as regulars. 'Lookin' for work, are yer?' said Brian. 'Don't ever take a job with Danny O'Hare. He's a right mongrel.'

'Sure youse young blokes from down south are up to it?' stirred Harry.

'Come on. Give the young fellas a break,' said Old Mick. He shouted them a drink. It was obvious he'd already had a fair number himself. He wouldn't hear of taking one in return.

They told him their plans.

'I'm only an old bloke, but I can tell youse a few things,' he said.

'Don't listen to him,' said Harry. 'He wouldn't know. The old fella's past it.'

'That's not true,' said Old Mick. 'Sure I'm getting old. Sure I mightn't be as quick as you young fellas.' He took a swig from his beer. 'But that don't matter nothing. He paused again. 'Let me give youse youngsters some advice.' He steadied himself against the table. 'Life's not about the 'ere an' now. That's rubbish. Look around. It's not about this. Life's about the future. It's about dreams. It's not about what you are, or what you're doing now. It's about hope.' He stopped again. 'Remember this,' he said leaning forward. 'As long as there's hope, there's life. When there's no hope, there's no future. There's no point in livin' when there's no hope.' He swayed slightly and looked at them blurrily.

'Is that all?' said Harry. 'There's nothing new in that. We've heard all that before.'

Old Mick looked at him. He was about to say something then turned away, with a look of disgust on his face. 'You heard me,' he said to Tim and Barcroft. 'That's all I've got to say.'

'He's got a point there,' Tim said to Barcroft.

Barcroft wondered what lay behind the old man's outburst. He'd spoken with such passion.

The next morning, the local stock agent told Tim and Barcroft that Cobb and Co. were looking for stockmen. Drovers were needed to bring a mob of cattle down from the Diamantina River. They signed up on the spot.

They set off from Brewarrina the next day in the company of another drover they'd seen in the bar the night before. He was off to the same job. He wasn't much of a talker. He told them his name was Jack, and that his horse was Vanity. No one seemed to know his second name. He was just known as Jack.

'Maybe he's forgotten it,' the publican said the night before. 'He don't talk enough to remember it.'

Jack mightn't talk much but he sure knew how to ride. He also knew the bush like the back of his hand. When the track disappeared into featureless dust, Jack knew exactly where to go.

'It's damned lucky we're with Jack,' said Tim as they surveyed the endlessly stretching scrub.

Barcroft agreed. With Jack leading the way, they made good time to the Diamantina.

After a few weeks mustering, it was as though they'd never done anything else. Barcroft wrote to his father from Currawilla.

11 August 1889

Dear Father

We are kept going so continually that it is with great difficulty I can snatch these few minutes to let you know I am alive. We are on the road now with eleven hundred head of cattle for Cunnamulla, from Devonport Downs, Diamantina river. We were five weeks mustering on the station.

The cattle have to be watched all night. I am lucky, and have the first shift – from six to eight. Still, as we are going from before daylight of a morning, it makes the hours pretty long. Fourteen hours a day I reckon I have in the saddle straight off.

Still, this is the only life worth living that I see. No more New South Wales for me, except for a visit. This is the only place where a poor man can get a cheque together in a short time.

Love to Grannie and the girls.

Your affectionate son, Bartie

Barcroft was surprised to receive a letter from his father when they reached Windorah in late August. He wanted to know if Barcroft had received the letters of introduction he had sent to Mullah. Barcroft replied.

29 August 1889

Dear Father

Enclosed you will find a note in pencil. I don't know if you will be able to decipher it. The day I wrote it I was very sick, and was bad for three days with a touch of the fever they get out here. At present I have very bad eyes from the flies and dust: everyone gets it.

This is a regular dog's life. Breakfast by starlight; with the cattle till dark; then get up in the night to do two hours' watch. Still it has its charms. As a song of ours says –

Still his wild roving life with its hardships is dear

To the heart of each wandering bush cavalier.

About those letters of intro. It was very good of you to go to so much trouble about me. I don't deserve it, really. I am very sorry I never got them.

Give my love to Grannie and the girls. I often think of you on watch. I am getting good wages; and with a bit of luck, if I get in so far this trip, will see you for a few days somewhere after Xmas.

Your affectionate son, Bartie

The mob was destined for the Cobb and Co. station at Burrembilla, near Cummamulla. Barcroft wrote to his father again when he arrived there.

21 October 1889

Dear Father

We let the bullocks go yesterday; and went to bed last night with the strange feeling that we had no watch to do. However, it won't be for long; for we start tomorrow for the Yowah, another of Cobb's stations about 80 miles from here, to bring in a mob of fat cows, which will be drafted here, and then go on to Bathurst. In all probability I shall go with them, so that is four months of the future mapped out. I have a new boss now: the man I came in from the Diamantina with is not going to get any more cattle to drove – he loses too many.

Before he could finish writing, he got called to go after the horses. He put the letter aside to finish later.

Barcroft said goodbye to Tim and his brother at Burrembilla. Tim had a call from home telling him their mother was ill. Barcroft was sad to see them go. They'd been good company. They'd had some good times together. Tim wrote down his home address and gave it to Barcroft. He said to drop by sometime.

Barcroft watched their horses kicking up the dust as they wheeled out of the yard. He still had some company for the ride to Yowah. Jack had also signed up for the job.

When he and Jack arrived at Yowah, the manager was just about to leave for the musterers' camp. He told them to join him.

On 2 November, Barcroft finished writing the letter he'd started on 21 October.

I had to leave this to go after horses, and we have not had time to continue until today. We are out at the Yowah now, very busy mustering; and hope to be away next week some time. They had to knock off today to shoe horses, as they are nearly all footsore from the stones. It is very rough country here – nothing but stones and scrub – a bit different to the Diamantina, where it is nothing but plains. The cattle here are as wild as hawks, and we are galloping all day long.

The first day we went out to camp about ten miles away. We just took pack horses, and, as it was very hot, only a blanket apiece. In the middle of the night it started to rain hard, and I lay in two inches of water till morning. Nobody had any coats, only shirts and pants on. We were quite unprepared for any bad weather. We had a job to light a fire, and it was infernally cold; but it cleared up after breakfast. Anthony Trollope, in one of his books about Australia, says: 'The life of the Australian bushman is one of continual picnic.' He would not have said so if he had put in that night alongside me.

Oh, well! I suppose a man reaps as he sows. I often grumble at these sorts of things, but at the same time console myself by the thought that it is my own choosing. I might have been jogging along in monotonous respectability as a civil servant; but they don't live, these men – they only vegetate. We have a pleasure and excitement in our work that they never feel. Every day brings something new: no two are alike. There is a charm about this life always in the saddle only those can appreciate who have lived it.

I got dear Grannie's letter. This must do for her and Addie as well as for you, for I have to go up to the station presently. I am afraid Grannie must be getting very feeble. Dear old lady! won't she be glad to see her good-for-nought grandson again! I often think about my prospective trip to Sydney when between the blankets, with the mosquitoes singing a sweet lullaby round my head. I have not decided yet whether I am going to surprise you at Croydon or in town. Don't be surprised if you see a lanky young man with a cabbage tree hat on walk into the office and say 'Hello Dad!' for that will be me. I have not altered a bit in appearance – at least, not that I can see. Some time in February we hope to be in Bathurst, when I may be able to run down for a few days.

I got a letter from Addie telling me about her little girl Doris. It is a pretty name. Fancy those two girls married and mothers! It will be right enough as long as they stop at one; but I have seen too many when I was in the Survey with big families and small salaries. Better to keep single than to drag your wife down to the level of a household drudge as many do. Well, my dear Dad, I must say Goodbye. I have a little while yet, but I must devote that to a letter to Mrs McKeahnie, as they have not heard from me for a long time. Give my love to Grannie and Addie and the girls.

Hoping to see you all in a few month's time.

Your affectionate son, Bartie

Barcroft took a break for a cup of tea and a smoke before starting the letter to Mrs McKeahnie. He had only written a few sentences when he got a call to help with the horses. He didn't get a chance to write any more for the rest of the week.

Barcroft was woken at first light on 12 November. The camp manager was shouting at the hands to get the horses. Barcroft could hear the jingle of hobble chains as the horses were rounded up. He rubbed his eyes and stumbled out onto the veranda. The sun had not yet risen.

Jack was having an argument over the age of one of the mares, the young grey one. Barcroft thought it odd for Jack to be saying so much. As Jack was arguing, Tomboy and Vanity took off, kicking their tales in the air. Tomboy was Barcroft's new horse since Sweetbriar had got lame on the Diamantina. Barcroft and Jack had a devil of a job chasing after them. Eventually, they managed to herd them back to the main mob and get their saddles on.

A dusty cloud hung over the cattle as they were drafted. Stock whips cracked, cattle bayed and hooves thundered till the ground shook.

Barcroft and Jack were soon amongst the action. Jack rode straight at the mob. Cracking his whip, he cut out a big curly horned bullock. No sooner was the animal separated from the mob than he wheeled around in a cloud of dust and rejoined them. Jack cut out the beast again.

Barcroft watched as Jack chased after the bullock. He was about to give him a hand when a little white calf trotted out from the herd. It must have missed its mother or something. It ran straight across Jack's path. Barcroft shouted. Vanity tried to swerve, changed her mind and tried to jump. It was too late! She and her rider crashed headlong into the calf – with a sickening bone-crunching thud.

Barcroft jumped off his horse. He ran over to the heap of jangled limbs and knelt beside Jack, lying pinned beneath his fallen horse. There was nothing he could do.

'The mare,' whispered Jack. 'Is she dead?' He reached out and stroked Vanity's smooth lean head. She looked up at him with her big soft eyes. As he watched, her eyes slowly glazed over. She whinnied quietly, then lay down, dead.

The other stockmen crowded round. Barcroft gently cradled Jack's head. He dared not move him. He could see his body was crushed under the horse. As he nursed him, Jack's breathing got shorter and shallower. He looked up at Barcroft and tried to say something. Instead he coughed feebly. Then he died.

Barcroft wanted to cry. But he couldn't.

They buried Jack at Yowah Station.

Life went on. The cattle were brought to Burrenbilla to rest for a few weeks. It would improve their condition before starting the journey to Bathurst. The manager told Barcroft he could take a break in Cunnamulla while they were waiting. He said he'd make sure Barcroft got work taking them to Bathurst.

In Cunnamulla, Barcroft took the opportunity to catch up on his correspondence. He wrote to his grandmother.

18 November 1889

Dear Grannie

I have not heard from any of my girls for a long time now; but I told them not to write, as I did not know where I might be. I am staying in this town for a fortnight until Mr Leeds comes back to start a mob of cattle away to Bathurst. I hope to go with them. It is getting very hot and dry here now, and the sooner I turn my back on Banana-land for a few months the better I will be pleased.

I am enjoying the unaccustomed luxuries of clean sheets and mosquito curtains. I seems quite strange to sleep in a bed once more; but I wish I was on the road again. Lying about doing nothing but smoke does not suit me at all.

Your loving grandson, Bartie

The time alone in Cunnamulla began to weigh heavily on him. Despite his natural inclination to be a loner, his happiest times had often been with others. Even Jack's non-communicative company had improved his outlook. Now he was on his own. Jim and his brother had gone. Jack had gone. Sweetbriar had gone. He hadn't heard from the McKeahnies for a long time, nor from his sisters. The only person he had regular contact with was his father.

20 November 1889

Dear Father

I feel very lonely here – a stranger in a far land; and the time hangs very heavy.

It is strange how easily the current of our life is turned. I don't think in Sydney I could have found the pleasure in life that exists for me here – that is at times: oftener I feel sick of the whole thing and long for some other country and a more stirring life.

There is a pleasure in a mad gallop; or in watching the dawn of day on a cattle camp – to see the beasts take shape, and change from an indistinguishable mass of white and black into their natural colours; in the dead of night to find yourself alone with the cattle – all the camp asleep, perhaps only a red spark betokening the camp. I always when I think of it, find something unearthly in this assemblage of huge animals ready at any moment to burst forth like a pent-up torrent, and equally irresistible in their force. When every beast is down, asleep or resting, just pull up and listen. You will hear a low moaning sound rising to a roar, then subsiding to a murmur like distant surf – or, as I fancy, the cry of the dammed in Dante's 'Inferno'. When the cattle are like that it is a good sign. But in the moonlight this strange noise, the dark mass of cattle with the occasional flash of an eye or a polished horn catching the light – it always conjures up strange fancies in me: I seem to be in some other world.

If only I could write it, there is a poem to be made out of the back country. Some man will come yet who will be able to grasp the romance of Western Queensland and all that equally mysterious country in Central and Northern Australia. For there is a romance, though a grim one – a story of drought and flood, fever and famine, murder and suicide, courage and endurance.

And who reaps the benefit? Not the poor bushman; but Messrs So and So, merchant, of Sydney or Melbourne – or the Mutual Consolidated Cut-down-the drovers' wages Company, Limited – or some other capitalist. If you showed them the map half of them could not point out the position of their runs. All they know is that their cheques come in regularly from the buyers; and if the expenses pass the limit they in their ignorance place, they sack the manager and get another easy enough.

I often wonder if a day will come when these men will rise up – when the wealthy man, perhaps renowned on the coast for his benevolence, shall see pass before him a band of men – all of whom died in his service, and whose unhallowed graves dot his run – the greater portion hollow, shrunken, burning with the pangs of thirst – others covered with the evil slime of the Diamantina, Cooper, and those far western rivers – burnt unrecognisably in bush fires, struck down by sunstroke, ripped up by cattle, dashed against some tree by their horses, killed in a dozen different ways – and what for? A few shillings a week; and these are begrudged them. While their employer travels the Continent, and lives in all the luxury his wealth can command, they are sweating out their lives under a tropic sun on damper and beef.

This is no exaggerated picture, I can assure you. Marcus Clarke has grasped the meaning of Australia's mountains and forests in his eloquent preface to Gordon's poems; but neither he nor Gordon has written about the plains and sandhills of the far west – it remains for some future poet to do that.

Your loving son, Bartie

As he was walking back to the hotel after posting the letter, Barcroft met Mr Sullivan. Sullivan was the new drover in charge of the cattle to be taken to Bathurst. He told Barcroft to get ready to leave for Burrenbilla the next morning. The cattle were ready to be collected for the trip.

Barcroft was glad. He now had four months on the road to Bathurst to look forward to. But it wasn't the same without Jack or the Boyd brothers. The other drovers were a reasonable bunch but he felt distant from them. Then there was Sullivan. The man had a drinking problem – a serious drinking problem. He started each day with a swig of spirits. You could smell him from yards away. By the afternoon, it was a wonder he stayed on his horse. All the drovers knew to keep well clear of him in the evening.

The journey to Bathurst was uneventful. The cattle were delivered to the agent in March. Unfortunately, they'd lost a fair amount of condition while on the road. This caused a problem with payment. The agent and Sullivan couldn't agree on an amount. The agent said it would take time to sort out as he'd have to take instruction from his principal.

Barcroft was keen to see his family, so he came to an agreement with Sullivan that he'd spend a week in Sydney before returning to pick up his payment cheque. Sullivan promised to look after his horse and offered Barcroft work on his next assignment, driving a mob from Bathurst to Victoria.

Barcroft caught the train to Sydney. He walked up to his father's studio in George Street just as he'd promised, wearing his cabbage tree hat and with his belongings in a swag slung over his shoulder. The studio was shut. A note on the door in his father's writing said he was on assignment at Hunter's Hill.

Barcroft was disappointed. He felt let down. He'd been looking forward to surprising his father. He walked down George Street to the ferry terminal to catch the ferry to Milson's Point. Sydney hadn't changed. It was still crowded and grimy. The people in the street hurried by, avoiding looking each other in the eye.

At least Gran was pleased to see him. When she opened the door, he was shocked at how frail she looked. He noticed she was leaning on a walking stick. Her skin was pale and blotchy and hung loosely on her arms. Her veins stood out. He followed her as she hobbled slowly down the corridor and into the kitchen.

'I don't go in the garden much these days,' she said as she sat down, out of breath. 'It's too much trouble with those stairs.'

He wished he could do something to help her. 'Where's Addie?'

'She and her little baby are over with Gregory's parents.'

'How come? Don't they have a place of their own?'

'It's better that way for a while. Gregory doesn't have regular work at present. I couldn't cope with them here, what with her new baby and all. It's all I can do to help your father look after Clare and Evie.'

'And Violet, where's she?'

'Now she's married, they're living out near Parramatta. George is such a nice boy.'

Clare and Evie were pleased to see Barcroft when they arrived home from school. Clare said she couldn't spend much time talking. She had an exam to prepare for. Evie had homework too.

His father was surprised but pleased to see Barcroft that evening. Barcroft told him he would only be staying a week in Sydney before heading back to Bathurst to collect his cheque.

'Are you sure you can trust this Sullivan?' his father asked. 'I'm not sure I'd want him looking after my money, from what you say.'

'It'll be all right,' said Barcroft. 'A man's word is his bond in the bush. It's not like the city.'

'If you say so. I still think you'd be better off with a profession like surveying, instead of this casual droving work.'

'I know that's what you think, Father. But I'm grown-up now. I have to make my own decisions. I really don't like surveying,' Barcroft replied.

'All right. I won't press you any more. It's your decision.'

The following day, Barcroft visited Addie. Mrs Kerr, Gregory's mother, answered the door. She told Barcroft that Addie was busy with her baby. She invited him into the kitchen until she was free. He could hear a baby crying in the background. While waiting in the kitchen, he made polite conversation with Mrs Kerr. She took the opportunity to tell him at length, and in some detail, all about her ailments.

Addie finally managed to settle little Doris. Then she and Barcroft escaped to the back veranda, where they had a cup of tea.

'Where's Gregory?' Barcroft asked.

'He had to attend to business at the club.'

Barcroft thought he knew the sort of business that meant. He'd known Gregory from his time working in the city. Gregory was a nice enough fellow. He was talented in many ways, but a dilettante and a dreamer, and something of a soak. 'Is he looking after you well?'

'Why do you ask that?' Addie said quickly.

'Just wondering.'

'We're doing well enough. I'm fortunate Mrs Kerr can help look after Doris. That way I can get some of my work done.'

'You're working? What work are you doing?'

'I'm colouring in photographs for Father. He pays me for it. It helps us get by.'

'So Gregory doesn't have regular work?' He knew the answer. Gregory always had plans. Nothing ever came of them. It had worried him when he heard Addie was planning to marry Gregory. He said nothing at the time. Now he wondered if he should have.

'Gregory's a gentleman. He always treats Doris and me well.'

'I was only asking.' He could hear the defensive tone in her voice so he decided to say no more. She looked tired, even worn out. She wasn't the carefree Addie he'd known before. 'You look tired, are you all right?'

'I don't know. Honestly, Bartie, I never thought having a baby would be this hard. It really wears me out. Some days it's so hard. I do everything I can, but Doris just won't behave. I hardly had any sleep last night.' She looked as if she might cry.

Barcroft felt embarrassed. Hesitantly he put his hand on her arm.

'I'm sorry, Bartie. I shouldn't trouble you with this,' she said, sounding upset.

'It's all right.'

They sat there for a while, without saying anything. They didn't need to.

On his way home on the train, Barcroft felt sad. He knew it could never be the same between him and Addie. He still loved her dearly – and he could tell she cared for him. But there had been a change. They had gone their different paths in life. Something had changed forever.

By the end of his week in Sydney, Barcroft was keen to return to Bathurst and the bush. On arriving in Bathurst, he discovered that Sullivan was no longer there.

The publican at the hotel where Sullivan had been staying had a strong opinion about what he'd do with him if he ever found him. Apparently he had left without settling his account. 'The bastard sneaked away in the night. Are you a friend of his?' he asked Barcroft.

'No, certainly not,' Barcroft said quickly. 'I was working for him. He owes me wages. He was going to pay me when he got the droving cheque. There was some problem with the payment when we got here.'

'Would that be a cheque from Cobb and Co.?'

'Yes, probably.'

'Don't like your chances of seeing that money.'

'Why's that?'

'Because I cashed it for him on Thursday. I took out what he owed me for drink first. Then he went and blew the lot at the races yesterday – before I could get the rest of my payment out of him.'

'So when did he leave? He's got my horse.'

'Not now he ain't. He sold all his horses on Wednesday – to pay for the women. I should've got in then,' the publican said, shaking his head.

Barcroft had a sinking feeling. 'Have you any idea where he's gone?'

'Like I told you at the start,' the publican said testily, 'if I knew, I'd be there to thump the Bejesus out of him.'

Barcroft realised there was no more to be discovered. He thanked the publican for his trouble and returned to the train station. By now he was furious. He spent his last pennies on the train fare.

By the time he reached Sydney, his anger had turned to depression. He had to explain to his father what had happened. His father didn't say I told you so. He didn't need to.

For the next month, he helped his father out in the studio. Then he had little choice but to go along with his father's advice that he return to surveying.

In April, he commenced service as a surveyor's assistant with Mr Lipscomb in the New South Wales Riverina. Lipscomb had a government contract to prepare plans for the lease and sale of Crown land in the districts of Wagga Wagga, Urana, Tarcutta and Tumbarumba. Barcroft's father was pleased with the outcome. At least you can depend on work for the government, he told Barcroft.

13
Riverina, 1891

Barcroft couldn't remember when he started writing poetry. At first it was to no great purpose. He did it to pass the time when he was out surveying. He had a volume of Gordon's works that became his bedside companion, so he used Gordon's lines as a model, putting his own words in place. It wasn't long before he was making up his own verses.

Mostly, the ideas for his poems came to him while he was in the field. Survey fieldwork involved a lot of waiting. There was plenty of time to play around with the words in his head before he had something he could jot down.

He wrote some satirical lines about certain local Wagga identities. At Raymond's suggestion, he sent them to the *Advertiser*. He was surprised when they were published and the editor asked him for more. He sent the editor some of his bush poetry.

In what seemed no time to Barcroft, word got around that he had talent as a bush poet. In January, when he was reading a copy of the *Bulletin* he saw a 'Notice to Artistic and Literary Contributors.' It said,

STRICTLY ORIGINAL matter contributed to THE BULLETIN will be paid for. The Editor will be glad to receive and consider contributions.

He read on. The notice invited 'humorous poems (from eight to forty eight lines preferred)' – 'serious poems, of similar or greater length' and 'short Australian or other stories.' The notice specified,

All contributions must be WRITTEN LEGIBLY on ONE SIDE ONLY of the paper, and folded, not rolled… The Editor does not undertake to enter into any correspondence respecting rejected manuscripts.

The notice gave him enough encouragement to submit some of his work to *The Bulletin*. At first he was daunted at the thought, but he eventually plucked up courage and posted off a letter enclosing his latest efforts. He remembered not to roll it.

In February, he wrote to Addie from his survey camp at Carabost.

16 February 1891

Dear Addie

Tonight is the proudest moment of my life. I feel that at last I have my foot on the first rung of the ladder that leads to fame. I have just got a letter from the editor of The Bulletin, acknowledging some verses. This is what he says: it is short but very sweet –

Dear Sir, – Shall be glad to publish your pretty and melodious verses: they may be kept for Xmas and illustrated. Cheque will follow in due course. Hoping to hear from you shortly. Yours etc J.F. Archibald.

I nearly jumped out of my skin when I got it – I was so surprised. This letter is rather egotistical; but I felt I must write to some one or die –

Your loving Bartie

The initial excitement of being a published poet didn't last long. Barcroft still had to get up each morning and go out surveying. In some ways, his acceptance as a poet made it harder to endure the monotony of surveying. A window had opened on another possibility, yet he was still stuck in his old routine.

There was a darker side to his poetry. His mind would race when he was creating a new work. Later, after the work was complete, he'd get a feeling of emptiness. He'd feel let down, drained and purposeless. The depressions he'd experienced when younger began to return. He wrote in his diary on 12 March 1891, 'I do myself believe with Tolstoi that the sooner the race dies out the better for all concerned.'

Barcroft welcomed the opportunity when Lipscomb asked him to travel to Lockhart to get supplies for the survey camp. When the supplies didn't turn up, he had to stay overnight in the local hotel.

In the morning, he went outside for a smoke on the hotel front veranda. The landlord, Mr Hartigan, joined him. Hartigan looked just the way you'd expect a landlord to look – round and friendly, with bushy whiskers and ruddy cheeks.

'Any chance of the mail coach getting in early?' Barcroft asked.

'Not likely. Lucky if we see it before lunch.'

Barcroft looked down the dusty street. 'Not much happening,' he said. His comment was as much to make conversation as out of interest. 'Is it usually this quiet?'

'It usually is this time of day,' replied Hartigan. 'The shearers won't be up till after lunch. Then it'll be on again.' He sat beside Barcroft. 'You said you'd been droving up north?'

'Yes. Before I started surveying here in the Riverina.'

'Any chance you might've bumped into Billy Scott up there?'

Barcroft was surprised. 'Yes, I know Billy,' he said. 'Not well, but I know him. Billy was up the Diamantina the same time as me. I doubt he'd know me, though.'

'What d'you know about him?'

'Not a lot,' said Barcroft. 'He's pretty well known up north. Got a reputation for being a bit wild. They say he's one of the best horsemen up north – so long as he stays off the grog. He likes his drink and his women they say. Why d'you ask?'

'I was afraid you'd say that. If you've got some time, I'll tell you a story. If that's all right with you.'

'Sure, go ahead.'

'Would you like a drink?'

'No, thanks.'

'What about a cup of tea?'

'Yes, that'd be good.'

'I'll just duck inside and get the wife to fix it for us.'

'Thanks.'

While Hartigan was gone, Barcroft watched a solitary horse and rider clump slowly past along the dusty street.

'We used to have this young barmaid here,' said Hartigan on his return. 'Skeeta was her name. A great little girl she was – full of life. I'd known her since she was so high.' He gestured at chair height. 'The bar crowd loved her. She was beaut for business. She could've had the pick of any of 'em for her man. Fact is, she'd get an offer a night – includin' from them that was already married.' He smiled wryly.

'Anyway, this Billy character, he drifted by one time. He was a real ladies' man – a ladykiller, good lookin', with the gift of the gab. Smooth as they come. Even my missus reckoned he was somethin'. He was full of stories of the wild north – of things he'd seen and done out on the Never Never. Silly young Skeeta, she fell for 'im. She took it all in. Swallowed it all – hook line and sinker.'

Mrs Hartigan brought the tea. Barcroft thanked her. She didn't stay.

'They got married and he took her off to Warren,' continued Hartigan. No sooner was they there than he was makin' plans to be off droving again. I was in Warren at the time. I saw 'im leave. It fair broke her little heart to see 'im go. Hardly a goodbye from 'im. He just rode off and left her with nowhere to stay.' Hartigan paused to sip his tea.

Barcroft sipped his own.

'That wasn't the end of it,' Hartigan continued. 'I brung her back 'ere. I gave her a job back at the bar. But it wasn't the same. He'd left her with child. She wasn't well. Then she got sick and the baby was still born. We buried it down the cemetery. It's in the far corner if you're going past.' He paused.

'The story gets worse. You see, our Skeeta, she just couldn't get over that cad. She'd always be askin' the drovers comin' through if they'd seen her man. None of 'em ever had. Least, that's what they told her. It really cut me up to see the look of disappointment in her sad little face. In the end, one of the drovers said he had seen 'im – this man of hers. Except they let on he'd been off drinkin' an' carryin' on with the gins. That was the end for her.'

Hartigan took out a cloth and wiped his face. 'The poor thing had been sick ever since her little babe died. After hearin' that news about her man carryin' on, she just wasted away. She wouldn't eat. We got the doc in but it did no good. She died last week.' He stopped. His voice trembled slightly as he went on. 'She's buried down there, next to her babe.'

Barcroft felt for Hartigan. He tried to think of something to say that might help. 'I'm sorry to hear it ended so badly,' he eventually said, rather lamely.

'I guess life goes on,' said Hartigan, standing up. 'I'd better get busy then.'

The mail coach turned up after lunch. Fortunately, the supplies were on board. Barcroft loaded his horse and said thank you, and goodbye, to Hartigan.

On his way out of town, he had to ride past the cemetery. He slowed down as he approached the graveyard fence. As he did, he noticed a man kneeling in the far corner. The man stood up and slouched his hat over his eyes. Barcroft immediately recognised him. It was Billy Scott. Barcroft watched as Billy slowly mounted his waiting horse and left. He didn't notice Barcroft, even though he rode straight past him.

On his way back to camp, Barcroft thought about the events he'd just witnessed. There could be such sadness in the bush.

In June 1891, the survey camp moved to Mundawaddrah, near Brookong Station. Soon after they arrived, it started raining. The rain came down as Barcroft had never seen before.

25 July 1891

Dear Father

I suppose you saw by the paper that the floods in this part of the country have been without precedent in the recollection of the oldest settlers. We arrived at Brookong and camped there on the Thursday before the memorable 12th July. It began to rain on

Friday, and that night 120 points fell. All day Saturday it poured, and the lamb markers were working all through it. On Saturday night Mr Dixon, the sheep overseer, came in from the camp at Green's Gunyah, and told us that they had been up to the waist in water all that day crossing sheep, and that the creek was rising very fast.

The buildings at Brookong are scattered all over the place; the manager's house, bachelors' quarters, men's huts, and kitchens being down near the creek, while Mr Halliday's house and garden, the stables, and the office and store, are a couple of hundred yards away. Raymond and I were installed in the old schoolroom, which stands away by itself from the store. We used it for an office, and slept in the bedroom adjoining. Mr Lipscomb had a room in the big house across the garden from us. He used to walk over to Mr Grierson's (the manager's) house for meals while we used to go to the barracks.

On Saturday night the water was up in Grierson's back yard: but we never expected to see it as it was on Sunday morning. Staines, the storekeeper, whose room was just opposite the schoolroom, accompanied us down to look for breakfast. In order to get to the barracks we had a hundred yards of water up to our knees. When we got down, there was six inches of water on the kitchen floor, and it was just commencing to ooze into the dining room. It was running like a mill race in the passage between the two houses.

After breakfast Syd, Wellman, Staines and I got the boat out and started to take the letters out to the mail. The mail change is about a mile away, but the water was right over the plain. Syd and I took the oars, and away we went. All the time it was pouring in torrents and blowing half a gale. It was great fun pulling over the tops of fences and dams in and out among the trees, but we could not get right over the road. We got the boat stuck, and had to get out and pull her along. Now and again we'd come to a deep gutter, and down one of us would go over his head. It was beginning to get rather chilly by the time the coach came along. It would have made a striking picture: the boat in the foreground and the scarlet coach with its four horses coming towards us – sometimes with the water over the wheels and the horses almost swimming – and then, as far as the eye could reach, the plain one sheet of water. We were wishing we could have a photo of the scene.

I tell you, when we got back to Brookong we were glad to get dry things on. We three started a fire in the school room and stayed there. The water rose all day, and at night they were rowing between Grierson's house and our residence. At eight o'clock Sunday night it was into the store, and we had to shift two tons of flour and one of sugar into a place of safety. The lamb markers had all come into the station, and everything seemed pretty safe as far as the men were concerned.

We went to bed on Sunday night with three inches of water in our rooms. It never rose any higher, and on Monday was beginning to fall. Then the bad news came. A man coming in from Green's Gunyah hotel, where the lamb markers had been camped, reported finding two of them dead on the main road about two miles from Brookong. Some of them had left the public house to come in on Sunday in a wagonette. They were all drunk and these two unfortunates had dropped out of the cart and lain there and perished – how, can never be ascertained. The coroner would not come out: he was afraid of the creek. He wired to bury them, and held an enquiry a week afterwards; but their comrades swore they were all so drunk they remembered nothing. Yet they were able to drive ten miles in that fearful storm, and never hit a tree or a gate.

On Monday night news came in from the out station that a young fellow named Arthur Biscay was missing. They had been scouring the country, but it was not until Tuesday that they found him, also lying dead in the bush. They had all left the Gunyah together, but Arthur had slipped away from them and was never missed. He was riding a young thing, and the general opinion is that he got off and it pulled away from him; for they found a lot of hoof marks of a struggling horse, and also Arthur's hat. When it got away he walked on and on until he got exhausted and fell down. He then dragged himself along on his stomach for about a hundred yards, then burying his face in his hands, lay to sleep – and never woke. He was a fine young fellow, a great horseman, and the most popular man on the station.

They would not bury him until the parson could come out, which was Wednesday. Every man on the station was at the funeral. Including visitors, there were ninety men followed his body to its grave at the wool wash. We drove; but all who had no horses had to wade through mud and water up to their knees. It was a most impressive ceremony, rendered so by the earnestness of Arthur's comrades, who had worked with him, played with him, and whose rough hands fashioned the coffin and dug his grave, and who now followed him to it in the silence of the brilliant morning, broken only by the shrill tolling of the bell which had rung him and them out to work so many times. They put the coffin in a low waggonette: one of them perched himself on the side and drove the horses. Two poor little wreaths of jonquils and geraniums, twined with the lustrous leaves of the kurrajong – all the flowers afforded by the garden reposed on the shell. The buggies fell into line, the horsemen and footmen four deep, and the cortege moved off down the creek. The most pathetic touch in the whole thing was that one of the boundary riders led Arthur's horse immediately behind the remains of its master, saddled, with the stirrups crossed dejectedly over its back. Its presence brought sharply home the fact of its one time rider's absence. We take Death as a matter of course, and a slight thing such as that serves to remind us of its awful reality.

Every body was very much affected at the grave. I saw one young fellow crying manfully: I, for one, was not very far off it. The three victims of that awful night lie side by side in the little knot of graves on Brookong Creek; but I think it will be many a long day before the recollection of the 12th July,1891, fades from the minds of the dwellers in Riverina. I have only spoken of what came within my own experience; but every station was flooded, and lives lost besides those at Brookong.

He had to stop writing. It was getting late and he needed to be up early the next morning. Two days later, he finished the letter.

I was very pleased to hear of Evie's success. I suppose the scholarship entitles her to go to the High School for a certain period, and prepare for University. I wish to God I could change places with her.

I have very little time at present for writing – I do long sometimes to be able to sit down quietly and write, but everything I do is done in snatches. To have a quiet room with an easy chair and a desk, and no one to disturb me, is the height of my never to be gratified ambition.

I ought to have written to dear Grannie, but I have spun this out so long there is no time. You must give this to her to read instead. Give my love to Addie and the girls –

Yours affectionately, Bartie

On the afternoon of the funeral, he was inspired to write some lines in memoriam of Arthur, and sent them off to the *Albury Banner*. They were published in its 24th July edition.

IN MEMORIAM

There's a stockwhip hanging idle,
There's a saddle on the floor,
And the dust has gathered thick upon its pads.
There's a broken trailing bridle
That he'll buckle on no more:
There's sorrow and there's grief among the lads.

There's a mare without a rider
Standing lonely in the stall,
And glancing vainly at the stable door;
Ne'er again will he bestride her,

And she listens for the call
And the step of one who'll saddle her no more.

Listen! his dog is whining
And struggling to be free,
It yelps aloud and rattles at the chain,
Poor creature, it is pining
For what can never be,
The touch of one who'll never come again.

Although his absence grieves us,
Not a man amongst us knows
The wherefore and the why of Arthur's fate.
Shall we mourn because he leaves us?
Shall we sorrow that he goes
Where all of us must follow soon or late?

The next letter he wrote he addressed to Mrs McKeahnie. But he made it clear it was for all in the family who might be interested. His news was mostly about where he'd been and where he would be surveying next. He didn't mention why he was no longer droving. He finished by mentioning that some of his poems had been published. He tried not to sound as though he was singing his own praises.

He received a reply from Mrs McKeahnie a few weeks later. Jean and May had also signed it. His heart quickened as he looked at their signatures. It brought back memories. He pictured them drawing the delicate lines on the page with their own pretty little hands.

The news in the letter was mostly unremarkable. It had snowed little this year. Prices for stock were very poor. Charlie had been up the mountains mustering brumbies. Some new people had moved into town. It was news from such a distance. It hadn't come from far as the crow flies. After all, the Monaro was only over the other side of the mountains. But it was news from a different world. It was a world he'd left behind so long ago. He wondered now if he could ever return to it.

Memories of Rosedale gave him the idea for a poem. He set it in a 'garden fair' where 'He loved her, but she did not care.'

A Memory

I held her hand that I might trace
    Her fortune in its palm:
A bolder moonbeam than the rest
    Crept up and kissed her arm,
And, kissing once, was loth to leave,
So hid himself within the sleeve
That clasped the lithe arm, white and bare,
All in that garden fair.

I traced her fortune: love and wealth –
    Though life, alas! was short.
But will that wealth be bought with love?
    Or love with wealth be bought?
I know not: knowing only this –
Her hand seemed waiting for a kiss:
I longed to, but I did not dare,
All in that garden fair.

But she, alas! is not for me,
    And I am not for her;
Yet ever deep within my heart
    A faint regret must stir –
A thrill of longing that among
Those moonlit paths with lover's tongue
I might return, and woo her there
All in that garden fair.

If only, he thought, if only he could return and recapture the happiness he'd experienced at Rosedale. At times, these memories seemed the only thing that kept him going. The only thing that gave him hope in his present dull existence.

He wasn't always in such a depressed state of mind. Sometimes his outlook was more positive. Sometimes for weeks at a time the depressions would leave him alone. Occasionally, he even had moments when he felt on top of the world. He wrote to his father from his camp at The Rock.

19 October 1891

My Dear Father

Did you ever lie on your back in the sun and have beautiful thoughts, that you can't put into words, come to you? That is what I was doing this evening. You just lie down and fix your eyes on the red crest of the old rock and wait. Presently you feel yourself melting away, and then the body stops behind you and away you go – somewhere – I don't know where – fairy land, I suppose – that's where all the lovely things come from. Some men go and bring back beautiful stories; others poetry: some men only wake up with a sigh and have the recollection. I was thinking how nice it would be if one could always stay young, and not have too much work to do, and just lie in the sun. But then the sun doesn't always shine: besides, it would get monotonous. This is apropos of nothing at all; only I have just been musing under the stars while I waited for one gentleman named Achenar to come to his East elongation. We are having the most perfect weather possible. It is simply joy to be alive. If it would only always be spring!

Fond greetings from your affectionate son, Bartie

Barcroft posted the letter on his way to Brookong. Lipscomb had noticed a problem with some of the field readings, so he asked Barcroft to ride back and check them. Luckily, it was Raymond who'd got them wrong. Barcroft didn't mind making the journey alone. It gave him a break from the camp for a few days.

On his way to Brookong, he had to ride past Jim's place. He remembered Jim and Sally for their hospitality whenever he and Raymond had visited them. He looked forward to meeting Jim again.

As he approached the homestead, there was no sign of Jim. Instead, he noticed some of the yard railings had fallen down. Odd, he thought.

Sally must have heard him coming. She came out onto the front veranda as he dismounted. He saw she was cradling a baby.

'It's good to see you,' she said. 'Please come in.' She ushered him into the kitchen. 'If you give me a minute, I'll put this little one down. He's just gone to sleep.'

Barcroft took off his hat and sat at the table. Sally put the baby to bed in the next door room, behind the hessian curtain.

Barcroft looked around. Jim's whip was hanging on the wall. Jim can't be far away, he thought.

'It's really nice to see you,' Sally said as she returned from behind the curtain. 'I don't often get company these days – now Jim's gone.'

'Why? Where's he gone?' asked Barcroft.

'You haven't you heard?'

'No,' said Barcroft, apprehensively.

'Jim was killed in June.' Sally looked as if she was about to cry.

Barcroft was shocked. 'I'm so sorry. Why? What happened?'

'I found him dead up the far paddock. He must've taken a fall, or something. His horse came back alone. That's how I knew there was something wrong.' She pulled out a handkerchief to wipe a tear from her eyes. 'I found him lying under a tree.' She swallowed and wiped her eyes again.

Barcroft didn't know what to say. So many people had died lately. Each death hit him like a blow to the chest. It didn't get any easier. He never knew what to say. With Jim, it was even harder. He had really liked Jim.

'I'm awfully sorry.'

'It's all right. I'm glad you came. It helps to talk about it. It really does.'

'How are you managing? Are you out here all alone now?'

'Jim's brother comes by every few days. He's just over the way. He helps me out. He cuts the wood and brings me stores.'

She poured Barcroft a mug of tea and put a plate of cakes on the table in front of him. 'Here, I've just made a pot of tea and some hot cakes. They're not very fancy but they're fresh-cooked. Please have some.'

Barcroft was reluctant to do so, but to refuse would have been rude. He worried he would be depleting her scarce stores. Sally poured herself a tea and sat down opposite him.

'I'm coming back this way in a couple of days,' Barcroft said as he sipped his hot tea. 'Is there anything I can bring you?'

'No, I think I'll be all right.'

'Are you sure?' he pressed.

'Perhaps a little more sugar. I am running a bit low.' She started rummaging around in a bag hanging on the wall. 'I'll see if I can find some pennies to give you.'

'Don't worry about that,' he said quickly.

'Are you sure?'

'Absolutely. I insist. You and Jim have given me more hospitality than could ever be repaid by a little sugar.'

'Thank you very much. You're so kind,' she said, wiping her eyes again.

Barcroft finished his tea and accepted a second cup. 'I see you've kept Jim's whip on the wall.'

'Yes. I like to keep it there. It reminds me of Jim. I don't ever want to forget him. Every time I look at it, I can see him again. Somehow, if it's there, he can't be far away. He'll always be near me.'

Barcroft finished his second cup of tea. Then he apologised that he had to leave so as to get to Brookong before nightfall. He thanked her for her hospitality.

As he rode into the setting sun, he thought how brave she was, out in the bush all alone. The clouds on the skyline were touched with gold and orange hues, surrounding him with an illuminated amphitheatre. Such beauty and yet such sadness, he thought. It was hard to fathom. What deeper meaning could there be that allowed things like this to happen?

On his return journey from Brookong, he carried as much flour, sugar and tea as he could load onto his horse. He refused to let Sally pay for them. He had to be quite insistent on this point.

Barcroft's engagement with Lipscomb was due to end in December 1891. In November, they moved camp to near Tumbarumba. This was the last district requiring survey. The new location gave Barcroft a chance to visit the local township.

Now he was taking his poetry more seriously, Barcroft was always on the lookout for material for his poems. He did a lot of listening, often in the local pub. Before going to sleep, he'd make some notes if he heard something interesting.

On the first Saturday after their arrival in the district, Raymond and Barcroft visited the Tumbarumba Hotel.

The Cobb and Co. coach manager was holding forth when they arrived. He was a big man with a loud voice. It was impossible to ignore him as he addressed his lunch companions. 'Do I know Polly Brown? You ask me if I know Polly Brown? The young slip of a girl that saved the Carabost Mail? Do I know her? My good wife and me, we brung her up,' boomed the manager in a voice more suited to shouting at stage grooms than the lunch table.

The man sitting next to the manager asked a question. Barcroft couldn't hear what he said.

'Well, let me tell you what really happened,' the manager replied. 'My wife was on the coach. She and Polly Brown. There's no doubt Polly saved her life.' He paused, but only briefly.

'See, Polly was Sammy's little girl. Sammy was me mate from the Crackenback claim. It was me what taught her how to handle coach horses. Damned glad I did, now. I'd have her up high on the driver's seat when she was too small to even walk. The little tot loved it up there. Polly's mum, old Mother Brown, she liked a drop of rum. It was the death of her. We found her down a mineshaft after a night on the horrors. That's how me wife and me ended up looking after Polly. Sammy asked us to.'

The manager paused while the serving maid took orders. Raymond and Barcroft caught her attention and ordered as well. They listened as the coach manager continued.

'If it wasn't for Jimmy Maloney Polly'd be with us still. You know, Jimmy, the gun shearer from down Paddlesack Run? Well, our Polly — she's Mrs Maloney now.'

Someone at the table asked a question.

'Yes, I was getting to that,' the manager said. 'It was like this. My wife's here in Tumbarumba and I'm down Germanton way after some coach horses. Polly sends me a wire that my good wife's fallen down and broken a leg. There's no doctor closer than Tumut so the blacksmith's set it best as he can. I tells Polly to get them both on the morning coach down to me and I'll warn the doctor to be ready when they arrive.

'Well, the coach driver, he's my deputy, he's one of the best. But, sad to say, like most of them he's a terrible soak. The stupid man, he chose that morning of all mornings to get a skinful. He loaded up the coach – with my wife and Polly on board – and started the journey – dead drunk! It might've been all right if he'd left it at that, but the skunk pulled up at Rosewood for another nip. That finished him off. Polly said she saw him half asleep on the driver's box after the stop. He didn't last long. At the first bend he fell right off. Polly and the others saw him go.

'Imagine! Here's the coach with four horses, thundering downhill with no driver, heading to certain disaster. The passengers saw him fall. So out they bailed after him – all except Polly and my injured wife. Do you think that's the end of it? No! Polly never faltered. She gathered up her skirts and climbed up onto the driver's box. She had one of those flimsy little parasols they use in the city. She used that to reach down and collect the reins.' He paused to take breath and wipe his forehead with his handkerchief.

'Yes, it was amazing. It was one of those frail little things, all lace and whathaveyou from the city. Never dreamed it could be useful like that in the bush. Now here's where my teaching bore fruit. Polly pulled hard on the blocks and reined those charging horses in as they bolted down the hill. They were heading for the Carabost break. You know, the narrow opening in the fence line before the horse change? She got them under control just before the break. Then she steered them clean through the gap, still at top speed. She wheeled them round on the flat and brought them back to the startled coach change groom. I taught her how to do that. Though I say it myself, I'm told it was the best bit of driving ever done this side of the range.'

Someone asked what happened to the driver.

'Well you might ask,' replied the manager. 'No, I didn't have to summons him. The coroner found he died from a serious abrasion. Both wheels of the coach went over his head.'

That evening, Barcroft made some notes and started writing a poem based on the coach manager's story. He called it 'How Polly Paid for her Keep'.

The final weeks working for Mr Lipscomb dragged for Barcroft. There was little fieldwork, and the monotony of camp life did not suit him. He made an offhand remark to Raymond to the effect there had to be more to life than what they had to put up with.

'Why?' asked Raymond.

'Don't you worry there's got to be more meaning to life than this?'

'What do you mean?'

'That there's got to be more than this boring day-to-day routine we have to follow.'

'Why does there need to be?'

'It just seems without any purpose,' said Barcroft.

'The trouble with you, Boakie, is you think too much. And what good does it do you? Life's for living, not for worrying about. If you do too much thinking, it just makes you unhappy. There's no need to be searching for a deeper meaning for life. You make it so hard for yourself. It's really easy. Just get on with it. Take what's there and enjoy it.'

Barcroft didn't reply. Raymond found life so easy. He wished he could take the same casual approach. But it wasn't possible – and he couldn't work out why.

At the start of the first week in December, Barcroft wrote to his father. He told him they would soon be breaking up camp and he'd be back in Sydney. Later that week, Lipscomb told Barcroft he wasn't sure if he would be getting any further government work. He offered to provide Barcroft with a letter of recommendation for his next position. Barcroft thanked him but said he wasn't sure yet what he would be doing next.

14

Sydney, 1891

Mr Boake picked up the newspaper. 'Disastrous Times Ahead,' trumpeted the headline. He skimmed the text. There would be hard times for business in the coming year, it said. Banks were under pressure from panicky customers, creditors were calling in debts. Australia was no longer attractive to capital. It was going to get worse before it got better, the article claimed. Already, some prominent businesses in Melbourne had been declared bankrupt.

He idly tossed the paper onto a table at the back of the studio. He felt uneasy. It reminded him about his loan from Sir Eric. He had yet to accumulate sufficient profit to offset it. The money side of business was not his strong point. His wife had looked after the finances for him initially. She was the daughter of an accountant. Since her death, he'd found it hard to account for where the money was going to or coming from, let alone balance the books. Somehow, he'd muddled through. He comforted himself with the thought that at least he produced high-quality photographs. There should always be a market for quality, he said to himself.

A week after he'd read the article, a man in a suit knocked on the studio door. Boake let him in.

'Sir Eric has sent me,' the man said, holding out a piece of paper.

Boake saw it had been signed by Sir Eric.

'I have authority to act for Sir Eric over the money you've borrowed from him.'

Boake felt a sinking feeling.

'Sir Eric regrets any inconvenience it may cause you,' said the man. 'But his business affairs require that you repay the loan forthwith.'

Boake felt flushed. 'But he said I didn't have to pay it back for five years – or even longer,' he stammered.

'I'm sorry, but Sir Eric requires you repay it now.'

'What d'you mean, now? I don't have any money here. I can't find that sort of money – just like that!' said Boake, becoming agitated.

'It's not Sir Eric's concern how you find it. That's for you to work out.'

'But Sir Eric said – I mean, he said it was a five-year loan. He said I wouldn't have to pay anything for five years at least.'

'Do you have that written down?' the man asked tersely.

'No. We discussed it like gentlemen. He offered it to me. It was an agreement.'

'If there's no written contract, you have no grounds for delaying repayment.'

'I told you. I simply don't have the money,' said Boake, becoming increasingly frustrated.

'You have possessions, though, don't you?'

'What do you mean?'

'This studio, do you own it?'

'No, I only rent it.'

'What about this equipment here?'

'Yes, I own the equipment. That's what the loan was used to purchase.'

'What about your house? Do you own your house?'

'Yes? But...'

'Well, there you are. You have possessions. You can sell them.'

'But if I sell the equipment I won't have any means to make a living,' said Boake agitatedly.

'That's not my concern. You hear all sorts of hard luck stories in my business. I could never do my job if I paid any attention to them.'

'Could I have some time to think about this?'

'All right. I'll give you a week,' said the man. 'You should consider yourself lucky. I see there's no interest payable on this loan. Sir Eric has been generous to you so far. I'll be back in a week's time. Good day to you.'

The man left. Boake closed the door after him. He sat down. He was stunned. He had no idea what he should do.

A week later, the man returned. Boake had spent the week worrying but could think of no easy way out. 'I don't know how I can find the money,' Boake told the man.

'If you don't want to cooperate, I can put the matter before the court.'

'Couldn't there be some other way of resolving this? Could I have some more time? I'm sure business will pick up in the new year. Perhaps I could pay it back a little at a time.'

'Let me think about that,' said the man. He thought for a minute. 'All right. How much cash do you have now?'

'What do you mean?'

'Just what I said. Do you have money in the bank?'

'Yes.'

'How much?'

'I've got around two hundred and fifty pounds.' Boake paused to think. 'Then there's three outstanding commission payments. One's due next week. That's a total of around three hundred pounds.'

'Give that to me next week as a first instalment and I'll hold off court action.'

'If I pay you all that, I won't have any money to pay the studio rent. It's due next week as well.'

'Like I said before, that's your problem, not mine.' The man's tone hardened. 'Give me the cash or I'll have no choice but to put the matter before the court. I'll be back here next Tuesday – at ten a.m. sharp. Make sure you have the cash. We'll discuss repayment of the balance then. Good day to you.' The man left.

When he was gone, Boake noticed his hand wouldn't stop shaking. He wished there was someone he could turn to for advice. He was at his wit's end. He'd have to tell the girls now. He couldn't keep it a secret from them any more. It was the worst time for this to happen. Grannie was sick and Evie needed extra money next year to qualify for university.

To make matters worse, when he arrived home that evening Evie handed him a letter from Barcroft. His heart sank when he read it.

Barcroft wrote that he would soon be returning home to Sydney. Boake feared the worst. He wished something would happen to deter him. He desperately feared the effect of his own worries on Barcroft's sensitive nature. He worried that Barcroft would come home full of high spirits only to be met by a house of gloom.

Barcroft walked into his father's studio at 330 George Street a week later. All he carried was a light suitcase and a possum-skin swag. In the swag were a few small articles, including the lash of his stockwhip.

His father tried to greet Barcroft cheerfully. Afterwards, he worried that Barcroft had noticed something was wrong. He didn't have the heart to tell him about his financial woes immediately, though he knew it wouldn't be possible to keep it secret for long.

The day after his arrival, Barcroft joined his father on the veranda. 'Addie tells me things are not very blooming with you, Dad. Well, I've got fifty pounds, and that will square off the household debts at all events.'

After some half-hearted protests, his father accepted the money. He felt vaguely conscious it was the wrong thing to do. Barcroft paid the money into his father's account the next day.

For the next few days, Barcroft seemed alert, cheerful and happy. He now had what he'd said he always wanted, 'a quiet room with an easy chair and a desk, and no-one to disturb him.' He began writing.

It wasn't so easy. Some days, ideas came reasonably easily. On other days, they seemed to dry up. His poems developed best if he left them to sit for a while before reworking them. What was he to do in the meantime? He used to get ideas while he was doing other things. Sitting in front of a blank piece of paper gave him no prompts. There was nothing to start a train of thought.

He began to doubt his commitment to being a writer. Sometimes he didn't feel like writing anything.

His father's financial circumstances worried him. He wished he could do something to help. Gran's illness worried him even more. She was so weak she could barely get out of bed now.

The Monday after his return, he took breakfast in to her.

She stared at him as if he were a stranger. 'Who are you?' she said, sitting bolt upright in bed.

'What – ' he faltered, taken aback. He nearly dropped the breakfast tray.

'Who are you? What do you want?' she demanded.

'I'm Bartie. You know me, Gran. I've brought your breakfast.'

'All right, put it there,' she ordered, pointing to the beside table.

He put the tray on the table.

'You can go now,' she said, curtly.

'But, Gran – '

'Don't argue with me, young fellow. Off you go.'

She sounded quite determined. He decided it was best to leave.

The incident upset him badly. He felt he'd lost something important from his life. He told Addie what had happened. She said the same thing had happened to her recently.

'It's a worry. But it'll pass. She'll remember you again,' she said, as comfortingly as she could.

He didn't feel reassured. It was most unsettling.

Gran did remember him again. Before lunch she called out to him to come and get her tray.

'Gran,' he asked. 'Did you know that you didn't recognise me this morning?'

'No, I don't remember,' she replied, looking puzzled.

'It was rather disturbing,' he said. 'It rather upset me. I hope it doesn't happen again.'

'Sit down, Bartie,' she said, patting the bed covers. 'There's something you need to know.'

'What's that?'

'Bartie,' she said, looking him directly in the eyes, 'I'm going to die soon.'

The words shocked him. 'No, Gran,' he said, leaning forward.

'It's no good pretending,' she said firmly. 'You need to prepare yourself. I'll be gone soon. I won't be a burden to you much longer.'

'But, Gran, you're no burden to us.'

'Of course I am. Look at me. I can't even feed myself properly. And I know the troubles your father is having.'

'We don't mind looking after you.'

'You need to get on with your own lives. I've lived mine. Truly, Bartie, I'll be glad when this is all over.'

'Gran, don't say that.'

'It's true. Now that's enough. I won't discuss it further. Just make sure you don't fuss about me. I hate fuss. Promise you won't fuss.'

'But, Gran – '

'No ifs or buts. Promise you won't fuss.'

Reluctantly, Barcroft agreed. 'All right, I promise.'

'Good. Now off you go. Go and enjoy yourself. Get on with your life.'

Barcroft took the tray and left the room. He was even more unsettled now. Her failure to recognise him earlier in the morning had been bad enough. Now she was preparing for her death and saying goodbye. She was almost willing death to come and take her. It made him feel so lonely.

Mr Boake's financial difficulties had a devastating effect on the family. After Christmas, so as to ease the burden on the family finances, both Addie and Violet moved permanently to live with their in-laws, while Clare and Evie went to stay with friends. Only Gran, Barcroft and his father were left in the house.

Barcroft decided he had to try to find some employment. He wrote to the Government Survey Office inquiring whether there was any prospect of a position. Late in January he received a reply. The letter said there was no immediate requirement for either qualified or unqualified surveyors, nor was the situation likely to change in the foreseeable future. The answer didn't greatly surprise him, as he'd read about the retrenchments sweeping through the New South Wales Civil Service.

He also wrote to Mr Lipscomb. Lipscomb replied that he was

unaware of any suitable opportunities. What Lipscomb didn't mention was that Barcroft was now well known in surveying circles as a poet, rather than as a surveyor. A number of Lipscomb's colleagues had made it clear to him they would be less than keen to employ someone like Barcroft, whose main ambition clearly lay outside surveying. They had arrived at this view as a result of discussions with Lipscomb.

Barcroft felt increasingly useless. He now had no income, apart from the few payments he received for the publication of an occasional piece of poetry or prose. His meagre savings were almost all gone. His efforts to gain employment seemed doomed. Soon he would have difficulty even finding enough money to buy tobacco.

He wasn't the only one in financial difficulty. The arrangement finally settled on for the repayment of Mr Boake's debt to Sir Eric involved the loss of Boake's financial independence. It was agreed the loan need not be repaid immediately. Instead, all of Boake's income from his business, except for a small allowance, was to be paid to Sir Eric as an interest repayment on the loan. This left Boake with no capacity to repay the principal or improve his financial position – and still with the threat of foreclosure hanging over his head.

His father's unhappiness affected Barcroft strongly. He desperately wanted to help. As he sat smoking on the veranda, he remembered Mr Nugent. He shuddered involuntarily. But Nugent was comfortably off, he recalled. Perhaps he could help. He knew his father would be too proud to ask for help. So it was no good suggesting it to him. He would have to approach Nugent himself. He didn't want to. For the moment, he decided to put off thinking about it.

The next day, he decided he had to try – much as he didn't want to. He walked to the station and caught a train. While on the train, he mentally rehearsed what he'd say to Nugent. He'd keep it short and simple. It wouldn't be pleading. If the man showed reluctance, he wouldn't press him.

Nugent lived at the end of a leafy green street, shaded by large spreading plane trees. Barcroft stopped in front of the entrance driveway. It was flanked by two sandstone gateway towers. Heavy wrought-iron gates swung inwards. Barcroft walked up the gravel driveway, treading as quietly as he could. He wiped his feet before entering the portico that framed the imposing front entrance door.

He rang the large brass doorbell knob beside the front door. He rang it again and waited. Nothing happened. He rang once more. He could hear it ringing inside the house. He waited again.

After a while, a young face peered at him from a side window. The door then opened slightly.

A young boy, perhaps ten or eleven years old, looked out at him. 'Mr Nugent asked me to tell you the tradesman's entrance is at the side.'

'I'm not a tradesman,' said Barcroft.

'Oh.'

'I'm a friend of Mr Nugent's. I've come to see him.'

'I'll tell him,' said the boy. He shut the door before Barcroft could give him his name. A few minutes later he came back. 'Mr Nugent said to tell you he's not disposed to meet visitors. He's not seeing anyone today.'

Barcroft didn't want his efforts to have been wasted. 'Could you please tell Mr Nugent that it's Mr Boake, Barcroft Henry Boake. I have some important business I'd like to discuss with him.'

The boy shut the door again. Barcroft waited.

After a long wait, the boy eventually returned. 'Mr Nugent is unable to see you. He said it would be best if you leave.'

Barcroft didn't know what to do. Before he could think of anything more to say, the boy said thank you and shut the door.

Barcroft was confused. He stood for a while, then turned and walked slowly down the driveway and back out into the street.

When he got home, he didn't mention where he'd been. For the rest of the day he sat smoking on the veranda. He didn't feel like writing. Yet another thing he'd tried had failed.

He wished he could talk to Addie, as they had in the past. But Addie had her own concerns these days. She now had two little babies to care for, and a husband to worry about. The last time they talked she spent most of the time telling him about Gregory's problems getting work. He listened out of politeness. It was harder for Gregory, Addie said, now that he had a family to support. Barcroft didn't have the heart to raise his own problems.

As for Gregory – why couldn't Addie see that all his troubles were of his own making? Couldn't she see the man was a waster – that he never did any of the things he talked about? That he was always full of excuses? Even Father could see that Gregory was a helpless creature – why else would he have been dismissed from the Railways Department? Why didn't she ask where he found the money for his drinking? Addie was way too good for him. Why were the good people in life treated so badly, he asked himself. Life was so unfair!

The increasingly straitened economic times affected Mr Boake's photography business. Bankruptcies of major businesses in Melbourne reverberated through the commercial community in Sydney as well. Boake's commissions dried up as the moneyed classes tightened their expenditure. Unwisely, he had invested his only savings in the Melbourne land boom. He received a letter telling him he had lost the lot.

Without commissions, he was left with little to do. He began staying at home so as to save the cost of train and ferry fares. On these days, he and Barcroft would sit at home, sometimes for hours at a time in the same room, without saying anything to each other. The atmosphere in the room could not have been gloomier.

His father wished he could say something cheerful to lift Barcroft's spirits. He tried occasionally but everything he said sounded so artificial and contrived. He himself was in no state to make anyone happy. He felt crushed by his own problems.

Late in March, as they were sitting in the kitchen, his father suggested to Barcroft they should take up a business somewhere in the country. As soon as he'd said it, he realised it was a silly suggestion. Neither of them had the wherewithal to start anything. Barcroft raised his head at the suggestion, but made no reply.

At the end of April, his father decided it would be better for both of them if they went to the studio each day. There was little for them to do at the studio but at least the travelling took them out of the house. He had given up any further attempts to suggest what Barcroft might do.

Barcroft could feel himself sliding into an abyss, a bottomless pit of depression and lethargy. Occasionally, he'd get a spark of motivation and begin writing. For a brief time when he completed a work, he would think positively about the future. Perhaps he could make a career in writing, he'd think. This positive feeling rarely lasted into the next day.

His thoughts often wandered back to his experiences in the bush. He'd think of the McKeahnies and the Monaro. Or he'd think of the drovers and the tough but rewarding life they lived. It was a stark contrast to the artificial city life he saw around him every day. He hardly dared think of the McKeahnies now. How hollow his promises sounded, made at the time of his leaving Rosedale. He was going to make his fortune and return 'a man of substance'. What a joke!

At Easter, he had a brief moment of inspiration. He wrote a poem in which he tried to capture how he felt about the city and the bush.

An Easter Rhyme

Easter Monday in the city –
    Rattle, rattle, rumble, rush;
Tom and Jerry, Nell and Kitty,
    All the down-the-harbour 'push,'
Little thought have they, or pity,
    For a wanderer from the bush.

Shuffle, feet, a merry measure,
    Hurry, Jack and find your Jill,
Let her – if it give her pleasure –
    Flaunt her furbelow and frill,   *furbelow: pleated border of*
Kiss her while you have the leisure,   *a gown*
    For tomorrow brings the mill.

Go ye down the harbour, winding
        'Mid the eucalypts and fern,
Respite from your troubles finding,
        Kiss her, till her pale cheeks burn,
For to-morrow will the grinding
        Mill-stones of the city turn.

Stunted figures, sallow faces,
        Sad girls striving to be gay
In their cheap sateens and laces.
        Ah! how different 'tis to-day
Where they're going to the races –
        Yonder – up Monaro way!

Light mist flecks the Murrumbidgee's
        Bosom with a silver stain,
On the trembling wire bridge is
        Perched a single long legged crane,
While the yellow, slaty ridges   *slaty: made of slate*
        Sweep up proudly from the plain.

Somebody is after horses –
        Donald, Charlie or young Mac –
Suddenly his arm he tosses,
        Presently you'll hear the crack,
As the symbol of the cross is
        Made on 'Possum's steaming back.

Stirling first! the Masher follows,
        Ly-ee-moon and old Trump Card,
Helter skelter through the shallows
        Of the willow-shaded ford,
Up the lane and past the 'gallows,'   *'gallows': where stock were
        Driven panting to the yard.   hung up after slaughtering*

In the homestead, what a clatter;
        Habits black and habits blue,
Full a dozen red lips patter:

'Who is going to ride with who?'
Mixing sandwiches and chatter,
   Gloves to button, hair to 'do',

Horses stamp and stirrups jingle,
   'Dash the filly! won't she wait?'
Voices, bass and treble, mingle,
   '*Look* sharp, May, or we'll be late;'
How the pulses leap and tingle
   As you lift her featherweight!

At the thought the heart beats quicker
   Than an old Bohemian's should,
Beating like my battered ticker   *ticker: watch*
   (Pawned this time, I fear, for good).
Bah! I'll go and have a liquor
   With the genial 'Jimmy Wood'.

When it was finished, he was pleased with it and sent it off for publication. He was certain it would be published. He knew when his poetry worked.

His inspiration wasn't sustained. As the rest of Sydney returned to work after Easter, his depression descended on him again like a suffocating blanket of gloom.

A week after Easter, he received a letter from Mrs McKeahnie. He quickly turned to the end. Neither Jean nor May had signed it. He sat down in the kitchen to read it. Mrs McKeahnie wrote about the weather. It had been a very wet autumn. Jimmy Wood had died – from too much drinking, Mrs McKeahnie was sure. Bill Sweetland was spending a lot of time with May. There was talk of them getting married. Mrs McKeahnie hoped they would be happy together.

A wave of emotion hit Barcroft. It came from nowhere. It gripped him and stopped him from breathing. He dropped the letter. Just then, Addie came into the room. She had come over to visit Gran who'd taken gravely ill.

'What's wrong?' she asked. 'Have you seen a ghost?'

Barcroft didn't reply.

'You look pale. What's happened?'

Barcroft stared at the table. 'I've had rather a knock today,' he said, without looking up. 'I hear my best girl is going to be married.' He said no more and hung his head.

Addie decided she'd better not say anything more. She put her hand on his shoulder. Then she left the kitchen quietly, so he could be alone.

Barcroft was shattered. The news from Rosedale completely destroyed his last spark of will. Nothing mattered any more. There was nothing left in his life.

He couldn't sleep that night. He lay awake tossing and turning. His mind raced endlessly. In the morning, he told his father he wouldn't be coming to the studio as he didn't feel well.

During the day, he started imagining things. He couldn't eat. He thought he could hear voices. Voices from dead people. He couldn't stop thinking about death – the deaths of others, his own death. He thought about all the people he knew of who were now dead: Jack, Jim, the Brookong stockhands, Jimmy Wood – and his mother. Then he thought of Gran, dying in the room next door. Gran didn't fear death. He remembered how he'd almost died himself, hanging from the beam at Rocklands. If death was like that, it would be painless.

All that day, the dead people in his head wouldn't leave him alone. He decided there really was nothing to fear from death. Perhaps death could be an escape, he thought, an escape from this tortured life. It hadn't hurt at Rocklands. There hadn't been any pain from dying then. The pain had come when he returned to living again. Why should he go on living? What was the purpose? There was nothing in the future he could see that made life worth living. He remembered the old drover's words. 'Life's about the future,' the drover had said. 'It's about hope. When there's no hope there's no future. There's no point living when there's no hope.'

The old drover was right. There was no point in living if there was no future. He could see no future for himself. There was no point in living.

On 2 May, after another sleepless night, Barcroft ate breakfast early. His father came into the kitchen as he was finishing. He looked furtively at Barcroft, hoping to see some improvement in his manner. Barcroft raised his head and their eyes met briefly. This was unusual. The impact of the glance remained with his father for a few moments. As he travelled to the studio, he wondered at the meaning.

After breakfast, Barcroft slung his possum swag over his shoulder and set off for Lavender Bay. It was where the family had lived when he was a little boy. Barcroft had fond memories of his mother there.

His family never saw Barcroft again. He was found eight days later, not far from Lavender Bay. A constable from the Water Police knocked on Mr Boake's studio door on 10 May. He told Boake his son's body had been found suspended by the lash of his stockwhip from the limb of a tree. A man clearing the bush for services to a new subdivision had found him. The place he'd chosen, on the shore of Long Bay, was so secluded he might otherwise have hung there for months, the constable said.

His father was stunned – but not surprised. When Barcroft didn't return home, he and the rest of his family had feared the worst. Now he knew that Barcroft's glance in the kitchen had been his last goodbye. If only he'd said something to him then, he desperately wished in hindsight.

Barcroft's death left Mr Boake a broken man. He may have guessed the outcome – but nothing had prepared him for the unbearable anguish of a father's grief at the loss of a son.

At the coroner's inquest, a verdict of suicide was returned. Mr Boake was required to identify the body. He was only able to do so by the letters, F.E.B., Barcroft's mother's initials, which were tattooed on his left arm by Assimul, a black boy from Noumea. The police handed Mr Boake two library tickets found in Barcroft's pocket. On the backs were written in pencil,

Dear Father, – Write to Miss McKeahnie. – Your loving son, Bartie.

Give 'Jack Corrigan' and 'Featherstonhaugh' to Mr Archibald; he will pay you for them.

His father did as he was asked. He had the body conveyed to North Sydney cemetery, where it was buried. The inscription on his grave read,

26th March 1866

BARCROFT HENRY BOAKE

2nd May 1892

The McKeahnies received a letter from Mr Boake three days after he posted it. It was addressed it to Mrs McKeahnie. The contents were brief. Mr Boake regretted to advise the sad news that his son, Barcroft, had taken his own life on 2 May 1892. He also advised that that a note found in Barcroft's pocket had particularly requested that he write to Miss McKeahnie. He did not specify which Miss McKeahnie.

Mrs McKeahnie opened the letter in the kitchen. She read it out loud to the rest of the family, who were sitting around the table. They sat in stunned silence as the news sank in. May got up from the table and left the room. Jean bit her lip.

'The stupid bastard,' said Charlie Mac, forgetting he was in company.

Mr McKeahnie shook his head.

'How sad,' said Mrs McKeahnie.

'How unnecessary,' said Mr McKeahnie.

May ran to her room and lay face down on her bed, crying. Why? Why did he do it? she sobbed to herself. She should have told Barcroft how she felt about him before he left – how she still felt. Ever since he'd gone, she'd been waiting for him. How could he do this?

May knew her mother wanted her to marry Bill Sweetland. She liked Bill, but not the way she felt for Barcroft. All this time, she'd been secretly hoping Barcroft would come back. Now he never would. He was her true love. He was the one who quickened her heart like no one else. Now he was dead. But why?

Jean went for a long ride by herself that afternoon. Out of sight of the homestead, her eyes filled with tears. She looked at the soft rolling hills, at their quiet beauty, and she cried.

Two days later, when the McKeahnies were eating their evening meal, Charlie mentioned Barcroft's death again. No one had spoken of it since Mrs McKeahnie had read out Mr Boake's letter.

'The talk round town is that Barcroft killed himself for the love of a girl,' said Charlie. 'They're saying he did himself in over one of the McKeahnie girls – one of my sisters!'

'Who's saying that?' asked Mrs McKeahnie.

'I heard people in the main street talking about it. It's all over town.'

'Really,' said Mrs McKeahnie. 'How embarrassing.'

'That means it's got to be one of you two,' said Charlie, looking at May and Jean. 'Was it you, May?' he asked. 'Did I miss something?'

'It wasn't me,' said May.

'Was it you, Jean?'

'It wasn't me,' said Jean.

'He was a nice boy,' said Mrs McKeahnie. 'It's a pity he was so sensitive.'

'Yes,' said Mr McKeahnie. 'It is a pity. He was a good lad. But you need to be a bit tough to make your way in this world. Could you please pass the butter.'

Postscript

Old Adaminaby is now drowned under the cold, clear waters of Lake Eucumbene. The Murrumbidgee still flows past Rosedale, but the willow-shaded ford has been replaced by a concrete bridge. A few forlorn old trees are all that remain of the plantings at Rocklands farm, where Barcroft once boarded.

There is no sound of the clatter and chatter of the McKeahnie girls at Rosedale. It is now called Bolaro Station and the imposing main residence bears little resemblance to the homestead of the McKeahnies' time.

All those who knew Barcroft are also long since dead.

On a cold still winter's night, Lake Eucumbene blankets Old Adaminaby in icy silence. Out on the wastes of the Never Never, a dusty quiet lies over the drovers' unmarked graves. If you listen carefully, you cannot hear the cries of the dead men. You cannot see their faces. Even if you knew where to look for them, they are not there.

Historical Facts

Charlie McKeahnie died in 1895 at the Bredbo Hotel as a result of a horse-riding accident.

May McKeahnie married Bill Sweetland in 1898.

Jean McKeahnie remained single until she was fifty years old, when, in 1913, she married Jack Cosgrove.

In 1895, a run of bad seasons led to Alex McKeahnie's downfall, and Rosedale Station passed into the hands of the banks.

Adaminaby was flooded following the creation of Lake Eucumbene in 1956. Some residents and their homes were relocated to a newly created township but many left the district never to return.

It is claimed that during a visit to the Bredbo Hotel Banjo Paterson told the publican that Charlie McKeahnie was one of the mountain horsemen on whom he based 'The Man from Snowy River'.

Locations

A number of Barcroft Boake's poems are set in the Monaro district of New South Wales, and the adjacent Snowy Mountains. At the time of his writing the principal towns in this area were Cooma, Jindabyne, Adaminaby and the gold mining town of Kiandra.

Kiandra is no longer populated and is now part of the Kosciuszko National Park. The former township sites of Jindabyne and Adaminaby were flooded by the creation of Lake Jindabyne and Lake Eucumbene – as a result of the damming the Snowy and Eucumbene rivers for the Snowy Mountains Hydro-Electric Scheme. In his work Barcroft refers to the Eucumbene River's golden sands. This was a reference to its sandy beaches as it flowed through granite country.

Barcroft's travels as a stockman and a drover took him to northern New South Wales (Narromine Trangie/Mullah Station, Brewarrina) and Queensland (Cunnamulla/Burrembilla Station, Windorah, Diamantina River) before returning to Bathurst. When surveying in the Wagga Wagga/Riverina district of New South Wales – to the west of the Snowy Mountains – places where he spent time included Brookong Station, near Boree Creek and Lockhart (then called Green's Gunyah), The Rock and Tumbarumba.

Barcroft Boake: Selected Works

In a memoir published in 1897 A.G. Stephens wrote,

> To Australians, lovers of letters, the brief and thwarted life of Barcroft
> Boake must always remain a theme of regret. By education he was
> poorly equipped for poetry. He found his talent late, and early made
> an end. His small performance was completed in a period of scarcely
> more than a year. Dying by his own hand at the age of twenty-six,
> he achieved little of all that his capacity promised. Yet, had fortune
> favoured, this ill-starred idealist might easily have won recognition as
> one of the foremost poets of Australia.
>
> For those who have learned to know him well, admiration of the
> poet may merge in admiration of the man. With many defects, Boake
> had no vices. From a hundred little sources flows evidence of his
> courage, of his generosity, of his unselfish affection, of his simplicity
> and worth. That shy, moody, dispirited bushman had a heart of gold.

The selection of his work in this appendix includes those poems most likely to be of general interest today.

A collection of twenty-one of Barcroft's published poems, including the works in this appendix, can be found at the Barcroft Boake Internet web site: www.boake.net

The web site collection does not include 'To a Hatpeg', which has not been previously published and for which copyright is still current.

The poems in this appendix and on the web site are in the form initially published in *The Bulletin* (or elsewhere). A more extensive collection of Barcroft's works (though not fully comprehensive) can be found in the collection of his poems *Where the Dead Men Lie*, edited by A.G. Stephens and published by Angus & Robertson in 1897. It was republished in 1913 with a revised memoir.

Stephens made significant punctuation amendments and some

other minor editorial changes; he said he 'strengthened a line or changed a word where the advantage seemed obvious or the necessity great'. Stephens loved exclamation marks and peppered Barcroft's text with them. Wherever possible, I have reverted to Barcroft's initially published text, notwithstanding any perceived faults.

Droving/Out West

Where the Dead Men Lie
(Banjo Paterson thought this was one of Barcroft's first-class works.)

Out on the wastes of the 'Never Never',
That's where the dead men lie,
There where the heat-waves dance forever,
That's where the dead men lie;
That's where the Earth's lov'd sons are keeping
endless tryst – not the west wind sweeping
feverish pinions, can wake their sleeping –
Out where the dead men lie!

Where brown Summer and Death have mated,
That's where the dead men lie,
Loving with fiery lust unsated,
That's where the dead men lie;
Out where the grinning skulls bleach whitely,
Under the saltbush sparkling brightly,
Out where the wild dogs chorus nightly,
That's where the dead men lie.

Deep in the yellow, flowing river,
That's where the dead men lie,
Under the banks where the shadows quiver,
That's where the dead men lie;
Where the platypus twists and doubles,
leaving a trail of tiny bubbles;
Rid at last of their earthly troubles,
That's where the dead men lie.

East and backward pale faces turning,
That's how the dead men lie;
Gaunt arms stretched with a voiceless yearning,
That's how the dead men lie;
Oft in the fragrant hush of nooning,
Hearing again their mother's crooning,
Wrapt for aye in a dreadful swooning,
That's how the dead men lie.

Nought but the hand of Night can free them;
That's when the dead men fly;
Only the frightened cattle see them –
See the dead men go by;
Cloven hoofs beating out one measure,
Bidding the stockman know no leisure,
That's when the dead men take their pleasure,
That's when the dead men fly.

Ask, too, the never-sleeping drover,
He sees the dead pass by,
Hearing them call to their friends – the plover,
Hearing the dead men cry.
Seeing their faces stealing, stealing,
Hearing their laughter pealing, pealing,
Watching their grey forms wheeling, wheeling
Round where the cattle lie.

Strangled by thirst and fierce privation –
That's how the dead men die
Out on 'Moneygrub's' furthest station,
That's how the dead men die;
Hardfaced greybeards, youngsters callow,
Some mounds cared for, some left fallow,
Some deep down, yet others shallow,
Some having but the sky.

'Moneygrub' as he sips his claret
Looks with complacent eye
Down at his watch-chain, eighteen-carat,
There in his club hard by:
Recks not that every link is stamped with
Names of the men whose limbs are cramped with
Too long lying in grave-mould, camped with
Death where the dead men lie.

Jim's Whip

Yes, there it hangs upon the wall
And never gives a sound,
The hand that trimmed its greenhide fall
Is hidden underground,
There, in that patch of sallee shade,
Beneath that grassy mound.

greenhide: leather strap at the end of a whip handle

sallee: wattle bush/small tree

I never take it from the wall,
That whip belonged to *him*,
The man I singled from them all,
He was my husband, Jim;
I see him now, so straight and tall,
So long and lithe of limb.

That whip was with him night and day
When he was on the track;
I've often heard him laugh, and say
That when they heard its crack,
After the breaking of the drought,
The cattle all came back.

And all the time that Jim was here,
A-working on the run,
I'd hear that whip ring sharp and clear
Just about the set of sun,
To let me know that he was near
And that his work was done.

I was away that afternoon,
Penning the calves, when, a bang!
I heard his whip, 'twas rather soon –
A thousand echoes rang
And died away among the hills,
As towards the hut I sprang.

I made the tea and waited, but,
Seized by a sudden whim,
I went and sat outside the hut
And watched the light grow dim –
I waited there till after dark,
But not a sign of Jim.

The evening air was damp with dew,
Just as the clock struck ten
His horse came riderless – I knew
What was the matter *then*.
Why should the Lord have singled out
My Jim from other men?

I took the horse and found him, where
He lay beneath the sky,
With blood all clotted on his hair;
I felt too dazed to cry –
I held him to me as I prayed
To God that I might die.

But sometimes now I seem to hear –
Just when the air grows chill –
A single whip-crack, sharp and clear;
Re-echo from the hill,
That's Jim, to let me know he's near
And thinking of me still.

On the Boundary

I love the ancient boundary-fence,
That mouldering chock-and-log.
When I go ride the boundary
I let the old horse jog
And take his pleasure in and out
Where the sandalwood grows dense,
And tender pines clasp hands across
The log that tops the fence.

'Tis pleasant on the boundary-fence,
These sultry summer days;
A mile away, outside the scrub,
The plain is all ablaze,
The sheep are panting on the camps,
The heat is so intense;
But here the shade is cool and sweet
Along the boundary-fence.

I love to loaf along the fence,
So does my collie dog,
He often finds a spotted cat
Hid in a hollow log;
He's very near as old as I
And ought to have more sense,
I've hammered him so many times
Along the boundary-fence.

My mother says that boundary fence
Must surely be bewitched;
The old man says that through that fence
The neighbours are enriched;
It's always down, and through the gaps
Our stock all get them hence,
It takes me half my time to watch
The doings of that fence.

chock-and-log: timber log fence

sandalwood: a shrubby bush

pines: native cypress pine trees; grow closely together in thickets; prevalent in dry and rocky areas

But should you seek the reason
You won't travel very far,
'Tis there a mile away among
The murmuring Belar:
The Jones's block joins on to ours,
And so, in consequence,
It's part of Polly's work to ride
Their side the boundary-fence.

Jack's Last Muster

Diamantina River, Western Queensland

The first flush of grey light, the herald of daylight,
Is dimly outlining the musterer's camp,
Where over the sleeping, the stealthily creeping
Breath of the morning lies chilly and damp,

As, blankets forsaking, 'twixt sleeping and waking,
The black-boys turn out to the manager's call;
Whose order, of course, is, 'Be after the horses,
And take all sorts of care you unhobble them all.'

Then, each with a bridle (provokingly idle)
They saunter away his commands to fulfil –
Where, cheerily chiming, the musical rhyming
From equine bell-ringers comes over the hill.

But now the dull dawning gives place to the morning,
The sun, springing up in a glorious flood
Of golden-shot fire, mounts higher and higher,
Till the crests of the sandhills are stained with his blood.

Now the hobble-chains' jingling, with the thud of hoofs mingling,
Though distant, sound near – the cool air is so still –
As, urged by their whooping, the horses come trooping
In front of the boys round the point of the hill.

What searching and rushing for bridles and brushing
Of saddle marks, tight'ning of breastplate and girth;
And what a strange jumble of laughter and grumble –
Some comrade's misfortune the subject of mirth.

I recollect well how that morning Jack Bell
Had an argument over the age of a mare,
That C.O.B. gray one, the dam of that bay one
Which Brown the storekeeper calls the young Lady Clare.

C.O.B.: Cobb & Co. cattle brand

How Tomboy and Vanity caused much profanity,
Scamping away with their tales in the air,
Till after a chase, at a deuce of a pace,
They ran back in the mob and we collared them there.

Then the laugh and the banter, as gaily we canter,
With a pause for the nags at a miniature lake,
Where the 'yellowtop' catches the sunlight in patches,
And lies like a mirror of gold in our wake.

'yellowtop': yellow-flowered perennial grass

Oh! the rush and the rattle of fast-fleeing cattle,
Whose hoofs beat a mad rataplan on the earth;
Their hot headed flight in! Who would not delight in
The gallop that seems to hold all that life is worth.

And over the rolling plains, slowly patrolling
To the sound of the cattle's monotonous tramp,
Till we hear the sharp pealing of stockwhips, revealing
The fact that our comrades have put on the camp.

From the spot where they're drafting the wind rises, wafting
The dust, till it hides man and beast from our gaze,
Till, suddenly lifting and easterly drifting,
We catch a short glimpse of the scene through the haze.

What a blending and blurring of swiftly recurring
Colour and movement, that pass on their way
An intricate weaving of sights and sounds, leaving
An eager desire to take part in the fray:

A dusty procession, in circling succession,
Of bullocks that bellow in impotent rage;
A bright panorama, a soul stirring drama,
The sky for its background, the earth for its stage.

How well I remember that twelfth of November,
When Jack and his little mare, Vanity, fell;
On the Diamantina there never was seen a
Pair who could cut out a beast half so well.

And yet in one second Death's finger had beckoned,
And horse and bold rider had answered the call
Brooking no hesitation, without preparation,
That sooner or later must come to us all.

Thrice a big curly horned Cobb bullock had scorned
To meekly acknowledge the ruling of fate;
Thrice Jack with a clout of his whip cut him out,
But each time the beast galloped back to his mate.

Once more, he came blund'ring along, with Jack thund'ring
Beside him, his spurs in poor Vanity's flanks,
As, from some cause or other forsaking its mother,
A little white calf trotted out from the ranks.

'Twas useless, I knew it, yet I turned to pursue it;
At the same time, I gave a loud warning to Jack:
It was all unavailing, I saw him come sailing
Along as the weaner ran into his track.

Little Vanity tried to turn off on one side,
Then altered her mind and attempted to leap;
The pace was too fast, that jump was her last,
For she and her rider fell all in a heap.

I was quickly down kneeling beside him, and feeling
With tremulous hand for the throb of his heart.
'The mare – is she dead?' were the first words he said,
As he suddenly opened his eyes with a start.

He spoke to the creature, his hand could just reach her,
Gently caressing her lean Arab head;
She acknowledged his praising with eyes quickly glazing,
A whinny, a struggle, and there she lay dead.

I sat there and nursed his head, for we durst
Not remove him, we knew where he fell he would die.
As I watched his life flicker, his breath growing thicker,
I'd have given the world to be able to cry.

Roughvoiced, sunburnt men, far away beyond ken
Of civilisation, our comrades, stood nigh,
All true hearted mourners, and sadly forlorn, as
He gave them a handshake and bade them goodbye.

In my loving embrace there he finished life's race,
And nobly and gamely that long course was run;
Though a man and a sinner he weighed out a winner,
And God, the Great Judge, will declare he has won.

'Twixt the Wings of the Yard

(Banjo Paterson thought this was one of Barcroft's first-class works.)

Hear the loud swell of it, mighty pell mell of it,
Thousands of voices all blent into one,
See 'hell for leather' now trooping together, now
Down the long slope of the range at a run;
Dust in the wake of 'em, see the wild break of 'em,
Spear-horned and curly, red, spotted and starred,
See the lads bringing 'em, blocking 'em, ringing 'em,
Fetching 'em up to the wings of the yard.

wings of the yard: side rails leading into the mustering yard

Mark that red leader now, what a fine bleeder now,
Twelve hundred at least if he weighs half a pound,
None go ahead of him, mark the proud tread of him,
See how he bellows and paws at the ground;
Watch the mad rush of 'em, raging and crush of 'em,
See when they struck how the corner post jarred,
What a mad chasing and wheeling and racing and
Turbulent talk 'twixt the wings of the yard.

Harry and Teddy, there, let them go steady there,
Some of you youngsters will surely get pinned,
What am I saying? I've had my last day in
The saddle, I might as well talk to the wind.
Why should I grieve at all? soon I must leave it all,
Leave it for ever, and yet it seems hard,
That I should be lingering here, 'stead of fingering
Handle of whip 'twixt the wings of the yard.

Hear the loud crack of the whips on the back of the
Obstinate weaners who will not go in,
Sharp fusilade of it till, half afraid of it,
Echo herself shuts her ears at the din,
They'll say when it's over now that I'm in clover now,
Happy old pensioner, yet it seems hard,
E'en on the brink of the grave, when I think of the
Times out of mind that I rode to that yard.

Hark to the row at the rails, there's a cow at the
Charge, how she laughs all their lashes to scorn,
Mark how she ran ag'in little Tom Flannagan.
Lucky for him that it wasn't her horn;
He'd make no joke of it had he a poke of it,
There she comes back, but he's put on his guard,
Greenhide descending now, sharp reports blending now,
Flogging her back up the wings of the yard.

The breeze brings their bellowing, soft'ning it, mellowing,
Till it sounds like a spent giant in pain,
Steals up the valley on, sounding a rally on
Sonorous hills that return it again,
Useless my whining now, useless repining now,
'Twon't make me any less battered and scarred,
Though I've grown grey at it, oh, for a day at it,
Oh, for an hour 'twixt the wings of the yard!

Oh, how I yearn for those times, how I burn for those
Days when my weapons, the whip and the spur,
The double reigned bridle, were not hanging idle,
But I'm old, and as useless as Stupmy, that cur,
He's no good for heeling now, yet he's a feeling now,
Not unlike mine, that it's woefully hard,
That we should be lying here, groaning and sighing here,
Watching the cattle come up to the yard.

Life has no salt in it, see how I halt in it,
I, who once rode with the first of the flight,
Watching and waiting now, feebly debating now
Whether the close will bring darkness or light;
Half my time pondering, back through life wandering,
Groaning to see how that life has been marred,
Seeing the blots in it, all the bad spots in it,
Mustering, bringing past sins to the yard.

***

Shall I be able to show a clean waybill to
God, when He rounds up and drafts off His own,
When, at the mustering, millions of clustering
Souls come to judgement before the white throne?
Is the Lord's hand on me? Have I His brand on me?
When I go up will the passage be barred?
Am I a chosen one? must the gates close on one?
Shall I be left 'twixt the wings of his yard?

At the 'J.C.'

(Banjo Paterson thought this was one of Barcroft's first-class works.)

None ever knew his name,
Honoured, or one of shame,
Highborn or lowly;
Only upon that tree
Two letters, J and C,
Carved by him, mark where he
Lay dying slowly.

Why came he to the West?
Had then the parent nest
Grown so distasteful?
What cause had he to shun
Life, ere 'twas well begun?
Was he that youngest son,
Of substance wasteful?

Were Fate and he at War?
Was it a penance, or
Renunciation?
Is it a glad release?
Has he at length found peace,
Now Death hath bid him cease
Peregrination?   *peregrination: travel*

Hands white, without a blot,
Told us that he was not
One of 'the vulgar'.
What can those cyphers be?
Two only, J and C,
Carved in his agony
Deep in the 'Mulga'?

Was there no woman's face
Whose sunny smile might chase
Clouds from above him?
No bosom white as snow?
No lips to whisper low,
'Why doth he seek to go?
Do *I* not love him.'

Haunted by flashing charms,
White bosoms, rounded arms,
Lips of fair ladies,
Striving to break some link,
Was't that which made him sink,
Dragged by the curse of drink
Deeper than Hades?

Now, the wind across the grave,
Tuning a sultry stave,
Drearily whistles,
Stirring those branches where
Two silent cyphers stare,
Two letters of a prayer,
God's Son's initials.

Snowy Mountains/Monaro

Kitty McCrae – A Galloping Rhyme

The Western sun, ere he sought his lair,
    Skimm'd the treetops, and glancing thence,
Rested awhile on the curling hair
    Of Kitty McCrae, by the boundary fence;
Her eyes looked anxious, her cheeks were pale,
For father was two hours late with the mail.

Never before had he been so late,
    And Kitty wondered and wished him back,
Leaning athwart the big swing gate
    That opens out on the bridle-track,
A tortuous path that sidled down
From the single street of a mining town.

With her raven curls and her saucy smile,
    Brown eyes that glow with a changeful light,
Tenderly trembling all the while
    Like a brace of stars on the breast of night,
Where could you find in the light of day
A bonnier lassie than Kitty McCrae?

Born in the saddle, this girl could ride
    Like the fearless queen of the silver bow;
And nothing that ever was lapped in hide
    Could frighten Kitty McCrae, I trow.
She would wheel a mob in the hour of need
If the Devil himself were in the lead.

But now, in the shadows' deepening
    When the last sun-spark had ceas'd to burn,
Afar she catches the sullen ring
    Of horse-hoofs swinging around the turn,
Then painfully down the narrow trail
Comes Alex McCrae with the Greytown mail.

*Greytown mail: gold
delivery from Kiandra*

'The fever-and-ague, my girl,' he said,
    ''Twas all I got on that northern trip,
When it left me then I was well-nigh dead,
Has got me fast in its iron grip;
And I'd rather rot in the nearest gaol
Than ride to-night with the Greytown mail.

'At Golden Gully they heard to-day –
    'Twas a common topic about the town –
That the Mulligan gang were around this way,
    So they wouldn't despatch the gold-dust down,
And Brown, the manager, said he thought
'Twere wise to wait for a strong escort.

'I rode the leaders, the other nags
    I left with the coach at the 'Travellers' Rest'. *Traveller's Rest: hotel in*
Kitty, my lass, you must take the bags – *Adaminaby*
    Postboy, I reckon's about the best;
'Tis dark, I know, but he'll never fail
To take you down with the Greytown mail.'

It needed no further voice to urge
    This dutiful daughter to eager haste;
She donned the habit, of rough blue serge,
    That hung in folds from her slender waist,
And Postboy stood by the stockyard rail,
While she mounted behind the Greytown mail.

Dark points, the rest of him iron-grey,
    Boasting no strain of expensive blood,
Down steepest hill he could pick his way,
    And never was baulked by a winter flood –
Strong as a lion, hard as a nail,
Was the horse that carried the Greytown mail;

A nag that really seemed to be
    Fit for a hundred miles at a push,
With the old Manaro pedigree,
    By 'Furious Rising', out of 'The Bush',
Run in when a colt from a mountain mob
By Brian O'Flynn and Dusty Bob.

And Postboy's bosom was filled with pride
    As he felt the form of his mistress sway,
In its easy grace, to his swinging stride
    As he dashed along down the narrow way.
No prettier Mercury, I'll go bail,
Than Kitty ere carried a Guv'nment mail.

Leaving the edge of O'Connor's Hill,
    They merrily scattered the drops of dew
In the spanning of many a tiny rill,
    Whose bubbling waters were hid from view:
In quick-step time to the curlew's wail
Rode Kitty McCrae, with the Greytown mail.

Sidling the Range, by a narrow path
    Where towering mountain ash-trees grow,
And a slip meant more than an icy bath
    In the tumbling waters that foamed below;
Through the white fog, filling each silent vale,
Rode Kitty McCrae, with the Greytown mail.

The forest shadows became less dense,
    They fairly flew down the river fall,
As out from the shade of an old brush-fence
    Stepped three armed men with a sudden call,
Sharp and stern came the well-known hail:
'Stand! for we want the Greytown mail!'

Postboy swerved with a mighty bound,
    As an outlaw clung to his bridle rein,
A hoof-stroke flattened him on the ground
    With a curse that was half a cry of pain,
While Kitty, trembling and rather pale,
Rode for life and the Greytown mail.

To save the bags was her only thought
    As she bent 'fore the whistle of angry lead
That follow'd the flash and the sharp report;
    But, 'Oh, you cowards!' was all she said.
Fast as fast as the leaden hail –
Kitty rode on with the Greytown mail.

Safe? ah, no, for a tiny stream
    On Postboy's coat left its crimson mark.
Still she rode on, but 'twas in a dream,
    Through lands where shadows fell drear and dark,
Like a wounded sea-bird before the gale
Fled Kitty McCrae with the Greytown mail.

And ever the crimson life-stream drips,
    For every hoof-stroke a drop of blood,
From feeble fingers the bridle slips
    As down the Warrigal Flat they scud,
And just where the Redbank workings lie,
She reels and falls with a feeble cry.

The old horse slacken'd his racing pace
    When he found the saddle his only load,
And nervously sniffed at the still, pure face
    That lay upturned in the dusty road;
Like a gathered rose in the heat of day,
She droop'd and faded, Kitty McCrae.

Did Postboy stay by the dead girl's side?
    Not he. Relieved of her feather-weight,
He woke the echoes with measured stride,
    Galloping up to the postal gate –
Blood, dust, and sweat from head to tail,
A riderless horse with the Greytown mail!

warrigal: wild horse, brumby

Redbank workings: former gold mine workings

postal gate: where the mail is delivered

And now a river-oak, drooping, weeps
　　In ceaseless sorrow above the grave
On the lush-green flat where Kitty sleeps,
　　Hush'd by the river's lapping wave –
That ever tells to the trees the tale
Of how she rode with the Greytown mail.

The Demon Show-Shoes

(A Legend of Kiandra)

The snow lies deep on hill and dale,
In rocky gulch and grassy vale,
The tiny, trickling, tumbling falls
Are frozen 'twixt their rocky walls
That grey and brown look silent down
Upon Kiandra's shrouded town.

The Eucumbene itself lies dead,
Fast frozen in its narrow bed,
And distant sounds ring out quite near,
The crystal air is froze so clear,
While to and fro the people go
In silent swiftness o'er the snow.

And, like a mighty gallows-frame,
The derrick in the New Chum claim
Hangs over where, despite the cold,
Strong miners seek the hidden gold,
And stiff and blue, half-frozen through,
The fickle dame of Fortune woo.

Far out, along a snow capped range,
There rose a sound which echoed strange,
Where snow-emburthen'd branches hang,
And flashing icicles, there rang
A gay refrain, as towards the plain
Sped swiftly downward Carl the Dane.

river-oak: she
oak (casuarina
cunninghamana

Eucumbene: river flowing
past Kiandra shortly
after it rises in the Snowy
Mountains

New Chum: gold mine
overlooking Kiandra

His long, lithe snow-shoes sped along
In easy rhythm to his song;
Now slowly circling round the hill,
Now speeding downward with a will;
The crystals crash and blaze and flash
As o'er the frozen crust they dash.

Among the hills the first he shone
Of all who buckled snow-shoe on,
For though the mountain lads were fleet,
But one bold rival dare compete,
To veer and steer, devoid of fear,
Beside this strong-limbed mountaineer.

'Twas Davy Eccleston who dared
To cast the challenge: If Carl cared
On shoes to try their mutual pace,
Then let him enter for the race,
Which might be run by anyone –
A would-be champion. Carl said 'Done.'

But not alone in point of speed
They sought to gain an equal meed,
For in the narrow lists of love,
Dave Eccleston had cast the glove:
Though both had prayed, the blushing maid
As yet no preference betrayed.

But played them off, as women will,
One 'gainst the other one, until
A day when she was sorely pressed
To loving neither youth confessed,
But did exclaim – the wily dame,
'Who wins this race, I'll bear his name!'

These words were running through Carl's head
As o'er the frozen crust he sped,
But suddenly became aware
That not alone he travelled there,
He sudden spied, with swinging stride,
A stranger speeding by his side;

The breezes o'er each shoulder toss'd
His beard, bediamonded with frost,
His eyes flashed strangely, bushy browed.
His breath hung round him like a shroud.
He never spoke, nor silence broke,
But by the Dane sped stroke for stroke.

'Old man! I neither know your name,
Nor what you are, nor whence you came:
But this, if I but had your shoes
This championship I ne'er could lose.
To call them mine, those shoes divine,
I'll gladly pay should you incline.

The stranger merely bowed his head –
'The shoes are yours,' he gruffly said;
'I change with you, though at a loss,
And in return I ask that cross
Which, while she sung, your mother hung
Around your neck when you were young.'

Carl hesitated when he heard
The price, but not for long demurred,
And gave the cross; the shoes were laced
Upon his feet in trembling haste,
So long and light, smooth polished, bright.
His heart beat gladly at the sight.

Now, on the morning of the race,
Expectancy on every face,
They come the programme to fulfil
Upon the slope of Township Hill;
With silent feet the people meet,
While youths and maidens laughing greet.

High-piled the flashing snowdrifts lie,
And laugh to scorn the sun's dull eye.
That, glistening feebly, seems to say –
'When Summer comes you'll melt away:
You'll change your song when I grow strong,
I think so, though I may be wrong.'

The pistol flashed, and off they went
Like lightning on the steep descent,
Resistlessly down-swooping, swift
O'er the smooth face of polished drift
The racers strain with might and main.
But in the lead flies Carl the Dane.

Behind him Davy did his best,
With hopeless eye and lip compressed:
Beat by a snow-shoe length at most,
They flash and pass the winning-post.
The maiden said, 'I'll gladly wed
The youth who in this race has led.'

But where was he? still speeding fast,
Over the frozen stream he pass'd,
They watched his flying form until
They lost it over Sawyer's Hill,
Nor saw it more, the people swore
The like they'd never seen before.

The way he scaled that steep ascent
Was quite against all precedent,
While others said he could but choose
To do it on those demon shoes;
They talked in vain, for Carl the Dane
Was never seen in flesh again.

But now the lonely diggers say
That sometimes at the close of day
They see a misty wraith flash by
With the faint echo of a cry,
It may be true; perhaps they do,
I doubt it much; but what say you?

How Babs Malone Cut Down the Field

Now the squatters and the 'cockies,'
Shearers, trainers and their jockeys
Had gathered them together for a meeting on the flat;
They had mustered all their forces,
Owners brought their fastest horses,
Monaro-bred – I couldn't give them greater praise than that.

'Twas a lovely day in Summer –
What the blacksmith called 'a hummer',
The swelling ears of wheat and oats had lost their tender green,
And breezes made them shiver,
Trending westward to the river –
The river of the golden sands, the moaning Eucumbene.

If you cared to take the trouble
You could watch the misty double,
The shadow of the flying clouds that skimmed the Boogong's brow,
Throwing light and shade incessant
On the Bull Peak's ragged crescent,
Upon whose gloomy forehead lay a patch of winter's snow.

Idly watching for the starting
Of the race that he had part in,
Old Gaylad stood and champed his bit, his weight about nine stone;
His owner stood beside him,
Who was also going to ride him,
A shearer from Gegederick, whose name was Ned Malone.

nine stone: horse's handicap weight for the race

Gegederick: district near Berridale in the Snowy Mountains

But Gaylad felt disgusted,
For his joints were fairly rusted,
He longed to feel the pressure of the jockey on his back,
And he felt that for a pin he'd
Join his mates, who loudly whinnied
For him to go and meet them at the post upon the track.

From among the waiting cattle
Came the sound of childish prattle,
And the wife brought up their babe to kiss his father for good luck;
Said Malone: 'When I am seated
On old Gaylad, and am treated
With fairish play, I'll bet we never finish in the ruck.'

But the babe was not contented,
Though his pinafore was scented
With oranges, and sticky from his lollies, for he cried,
This gallant little laddie,
As he toddled to his daddy,
And raised his arms imploringly – 'Please, dad, div Babs a wide.'

The father, how he chuckled
For the pride of it, and buckled
The surcingle, and placed the babe astride the racing pad;
He did it, though he oughtn't,
And by pure good luck he shortened
The stirrups, and adjusted them to suit the tiny lad,

surcingle: horse's outer girth strap

Who was seemingly delighted,
    Not a little bit affrighted,
He sat and twined a chubby hand among the horse's mane:
    His whip was in the other;
    But all suddenly the mother
Shrieked, 'Take him off!' and then 'the field'
came thund'ring down the plain.

    'Twas the Handicap was coming,
    And the music of their drumming
Beat dull upon the turf that in its summer coat was dressed,
    The racehorse reared and started,
    Then the flimsy bridle parted,
And Gaylad, bearing featherweight, was striding with the rest.

    That scene cannot be painted
    How the poor young mother fainted,
How the father drove his spurs into the nearest saddle-horse,
    What to do? he had no notion,
    For you'd easier turn the ocean
Than stop the Handicap that then was half-way round the course.

    On the 'bookies' at their yelling,
    On the cheap-jacks at their selling,
On the crowd there fell a silence as the squadron passed the stand;
    Gayest colours flashing brightly,
    And the baby clinging tightly,
A wisp of Gaylad's mane still twisted in his little hand.

    Not a thought had he of falling,
    Though his little legs were galling,
And the wind blew out his curls behind him in a golden stream;
    Though the motion made him dizzy,
    Yet his baby brain was busy,
For hadn't he at length attained the substance of his dream!

He was now a jockey *really*,
    And he saw his duty clearly
To do his best to win and justify his father's pride;
    So he clicked his tongue to Gaylad,
    Whispering softly, 'Get away lad;'
The old horse cocked an ear, and put six inches on his stride.

    Then, the jockeys who were tailing
    Saw the big bay horse come sailing
Through the midst of them with nothing but a baby on his back,
    And this startling apparition
    Coolly took up its position
With a view of making running on the inside of the track.

    Oh, Gaylad was a beauty,
    For he knew and did his duty;
Though his reins were flying loosely, strange to say he never fell,
    But held himself together,
    For his weight was but a feather;
Bob Murphy, when he saw him, murmured something like 'Oh, hell!'

    But Gaylad passed the filly;
    Passed Jack Costigan on 'Chilli,'
Cut down the coward 'Watakip' and challenged 'Guelder Rose';
    Here it was he showed his cunning,
    Let the mare make all the running,
They turned into the straight stride for stride and nose for nose.

    But Babs was just beginning
    To have fears about his winning,
In fact, to tell the truth, my hero felt inclined to cry,
    For the 'Rose' was still in blossom,
    And two lengths behind her 'Possum,'
And gallant little 'Sterling,' slow but sure, were drawing nigh.

Yes! Babsie's heart was failing,
For he felt old Gaylad ailing,
Another fifty yards to go, he felt his chance was gone.
Could he do it? much he doubted,
Then the crowd, oh, how they shouted,
For Babs had never dropped his whip, and now he laid it on!

Down the straight the leaders thundered
While people cheered and wondered,
For ne'er before had any seen the equal of that sight
And never will they, maybe,
See a flaxen-haired baby
Flog racehorse to the winning post with all his tiny might.

But Gaylad's strength is waning,
Gone in fact, beyond regaining,
Poor Babs is flogging helplessly, as pale as any ghost,
But he looks so brave and pretty
That the 'Rose's' jockey takes pity,
And, pulling back a trifle, lets the baby pass the post.

***

What cheering and tin-kettling
Had they after at the 'settling,'
And how they fought to see who'd hold the baby on his lap;
As President Montgom'ry,
With a brimming glass of 'Pomm'ry,'
Proposed the health of Babs Malone, who'd won the Handicap.

'settling': when the bets are settled

On the Range

On Nungar the mists of the morning hung low,   *Nungar: mountain range*
The beetle-browed hills brooded silent and black,   *near Kiandra*
Not yet warmed to life by the sun's loving glow,
As through the tall tussocks rode young Charlie Mac.
What cared he for mists at the dawning of day,
What cared he that over the valley stern 'Jack,'
The Monarch of frost, held his pitiless sway? –
A bold mountaineer born and bred was young Mac.
A galloping son of a galloping sire –
Stiffest fence, roughest ground, never took him aback;
With his father's cool judgement, his dash, and his fire,
The pick of Manaro rode young Charlie Mac.
And the pick of the stable the mare he bestrode –
Arab-grey, built to stay, lithe of limb, deep of chest,
She seemed to be happy to bear such a load
As she tossed the soft forelock that curled on her crest.
They crossed Nungar Creek where its span is but short
At its head, where together spring two mountain rills
When a mob of wild horses sprang up with a snort –
'By thunder!' quoth Mac, 'there's the Lord of the Hills.
Decoyed from her paddock, a Murray-bred mare
Had fled to the hills with a warrigal band;   *rills: mountain streams*
A pretty bay foal had been born to her there,
Whose veins held the very best blood in the land –
'The Lord of the Hills' as the bold mountain men
Whose courage and skill he was wont to defy
Had named him, they yarded him once, but since then
He held to the saying, 'Once bitten, twice shy.'

The scrubber, thus suddenly roused from his lair,   *scrubber: mountain horse*
Struck straight for the timber with fear in his heart;
As Charlie rose up in his stirrups, the mare
Sprang forward, no need to tell Empress to start.
She laid to the chase just as soon as she felt
Her rider's skill'd touch, light, yet firm, on the rein;

Stride for stride, lengthened wide, for the green timber belt,
The fastest half-mile ever done on the plain.
They reached the low sallee before he could wheel
The warrigal mob; up they dashed with a stir
Of low branches and undergrowth – Charlie could feel
His mare catch her breath on the side of the spur
That steeply slopes up till it meets the bald cone.
'Twas here on the range that the trouble began,
For a slip on the sidling, a loose rolling stone,
And the chase would be done; but the bay in the van
And the little grey mare were a sure-footed pair.
He looked once around as she crept to his heel,
And the swish that he gave his long tale in the air
Seemed to say, 'Here's a foeman well worthy my steel.'

They raced to within half a mile of the bluff
That drops to the river, the squadron strung out –
'I wonder,' quoth Mac, 'has the bay had enough,'
But he was not left very much longer in doubt,
For the Lord of the Hills struck a spur for the flat
And followed it, leaving his mob, mares and all,
While Empress, (brave heart, she could climb like a cat)
Down the stony descent raced with never a fall.
Once down on the level 'twas galloping ground,
For a while Charlie thought he might yard the big bay
At his uncle's out-station, but no! He wheeled round
And down the sharp dip to the Gulf made his way,

Betwixt those twin portals, that, towering high
And backwardly sloping in watchfulness, lift
Their smooth grassy summits to the far sky,
The course of the clear Murrumbidgee runs swift;
No time then to seek where the crossing might be,
It was in at the one side and out where you could
But fear never dwelt in the hearts of those three
Who emerged from the shade of the low muzzle-wood.
Once more did the Lord of the Hills strike a line

the Gulf: area near the present Tantangara Dam, where the Murrumbidgee River flows between two steep bluffs

muzzle-wood: small eucalyptus tree (stellulata), the wood of which was used to make muzzles for young calves so as to wean them

Up the side of the range, and once more he looked back,
So close were they now he could see the sun shine
In the bold grey eyes flashing of young Charlie Mac.
He saw little Empress, stretched out like a hound
On the trail of its quarry, the pick of the pack,
With ne'er tiring stride, and his heart gave a bound,
As he saw the lithe stockwhip of young Charlie Mac
Showing snaky and black on the neck of the mare,
In three hanging coils, with a turn round the wrist;
And he heartily wished himself back in his lair
'Mid the tall tussocks beaded with chill morning mist.

Then he fancied the straight mountain-ashes, the gums
And the wattles, all mocked him and whispered, 'You lack
The speed to avert cruel capture, that comes
To the warrigal fancied by young Charlie Mac,
For he'll yard you, and rope you, and then you'll be stuck
In the crush, while his saddle is girthed to your back,
Then out in the open, and there you may buck
Till you break your bold heart, but you'll never throw Mac!'
The Lord of the Hills at the thought felt the sweat
Break over the smooth summer gloss of his hide:
He spurted his utmost to leave her, but yet
The Empress crept up to him, stride upon stride.
No need to say Charlie was riding her now,
Yet still for all that he had something in hand,
With here a sharp stoop to avoid a low bough,
Or quick rise and fall, as a tree-trunk they spanned.
In his terror the brumby struck down the rough falls
T'wards Yiack, with fierce disregard for his neck – *Yiack: district on the*
'Tis useless, he finds, for the mare overhauls *upper Murrumbidgee*
Him slowly, no timber could keep her in check. *River between Tantangara*
and Adaminaby

There's a narrow-beat pathway, that winds to and fro
Down the deeps of the gully, half hid from the day,
There's a turn in the track where the hop-bushes grow
And hide the grey granite that crosses the way; *hop-bushes: native scrub*

While sharp swerves the path round the boulder's broad base,
And now the last scene in the drama is played;
As the Lord of the Hills, with the mare in full chase,
Swept t'wards it, but, ere his long stride could be stayed,
With a gathered momentum that gave not a chance
Of escape, and a shuddering, sickening shock,
He struck on the granite that barred his advance
And sobbed out his life at the foot of the rock;
While Charlie pulled off with a twitch of the rein,
And an answering spring from his surefooted mount,
One might say, unscathed, though a crimsoning stain
Marked the graze of the granite, but that would ne'er count
With Charlie, who speedily sprang to the earth
To ease the mare's burden, his deft-fingered hand
Unslackened her surcingle, loosened tight girth,
And cleansed with a tussock the spurs' ruddy brand.

There he lay by the rock – drooping head, glazing eye,
Strong limbs stilled for ever; no more would he fear
The tread of a horseman; no more would he fly
Through the hills with his harem in rapid career.
The pick of the 'Mountain Mob,' bays, greys, or roans,
He proved by his death that the pace 'tis that kills,
And a sun-shrunken hide o'er a few whitened bones
Marks the last resting-place of the Lord of the Hills.

How Polly Paid for Her Keep

Do I know Polly Brown? Do I know her? Why, damme,
You might as well ask if I know my own name?
It's a wonder you never heard tell of old Sammy,
Her father, my mate in the Crackenback claim.

He asks if I know little Poll! Why, I nursed her
As often, I reckon as old Mother Brown
When they lived at the 'Flats,' and old Sam went a burster
In Chinaman's Gully, and dropped every crown.

Crackenback claim: gold mining claim on the Thredbo River in the Snowy Mountains

My golden-haired mate, ever brimful of folly
And childish conceit, and yet ready to rest
Contented beside me, 'twas I who taught Polly
To handle four horses along with the best.

'Twas funny to hear the small fairy discoursing
Of horses and drivers! I'll swear that she knew
Every one of the nags that I drove to the 'Crossing',
Their vices, and paces, and pedigrees too.

She got a strange whim in her golden-haired noodle
That a driver's high seat was a kind of a throne,
I've taken her up there before she could toddle,
And she'd talk to the nags in a tongue of her own.

Then old Mother Brown got the horrors around her:
(I think it was pineapple-rum drove her daft)
She cleared out one night, and the next morning they found her,
A mummified mass, in a forty foot shaft.

And Sammy? Well, Sammy was wailing and weeping,
And raving, and raising the devil's own row;
He was only too glad to give into our keeping
His motherless babe – we'd have kept her till now

But Jimmy Maloney thought proper to court her,
Among all the lasses he loved but this one:
She's no longer Polly, our golden-haired daughter,
She's Mrs Maloney, of Paddlesack Run.

Our little girl Polly's no end of a swell (you   *swell: clever person*
Must know Jimmy shears fifty thousand odd sheep) –
But I'm clean off the track, I was going to tell you   *Tumbarumba: town west*
The way in which Polly paid us for her keep.   *of the Snowy Mountains*

Germanton: now called
It was this way: My wife's living in Tumbarumba,   *Holbrook – town to*
And I'm down at Germanton yards, for a sale,   *the west of the Snowy*
Inspecting coach-horses (I wanted a number),   *Mountains, renamed at*
When they flashed down a message that made me turn pale. *the time of World War I*

’Twas from Polly, to say the old wife had fallen
Down-stairs, and in falling had fractured a bone –
There was no doctor nearer than Tumut to call on,
So she and the blacksmith had set it alone.

They'd have to come down by the coach in the morning,
As one of the two buggy ponies was lame,
Would I see the old doctor, and give him fair warning
To keep himself decently straight till they came?

I was making good money those times, and a fiver
Per week was the wages my deputy got,
A good, honest worker, and out-and-out driver,
But, like all the rest, a most terrible sot.

So, just on this morning – which made it more sinful,
With my women on board, the unprincipled skunk
Hung round all the bars till he loaded a skinful
Of grog, and then started his journey, dead drunk.

Drunk! with my loved ones on board, drunk as Chloe,
He might have got right by the end of the trip
Had he rested contented and quiet, but no, he
Must pull up at Rosewood, for one other nip.

That finished him off, quick, and there he sat, dozing
Like an owl on his perch, half-awake, half-asleep.
Till a lurch of the coach came, when, suddenly losing
His balance, he fell to the earth all of a heap,

While the coach, with its four frightened horses, went sailing
Downhill to perdition and Carabost 'break',
Four galloping devils, with reins loosely trailing,
And passengers falling all roads in their wake.

Two bagmen, who sat on the box, jumped together
And found a soft bed in the mud of the drain;
The barmaid from Murphy's fell light as a feather –
I think she got off with a bit of a sprain;

While the jock, with his nerves most decidedly shaken,
Made straight for the door, never wasting his breath
In farewell apologies; basely forsaken,
My wife and Poll Brown sat alone with grim Death.

While the coach thundered downward, my wife fell a-praying;
But Poll in a fix, now, is dashed hard to beat:
She picked up her skirts, scrambled over the swaying
High roof of the coach, till she lit on the seat,

And there looked around. In her hand was a pretty,
Frail thing made of laces, with which a girl strives
To save her complexion when down in the city –
A lace parasol! yet it saved both their lives.

Oh, Polly was game, you may bet your last dollar –
She leans on the splashboard, and stretches and strains
With her parasol, down by the off-sider's collar,
Until she contrives to catch hold of the reins.

They lay quite secure in the crook of the handle,
She clutched them – the parasol fell underneath.
I tell you no girl ever *could* hold a candle
To Poll, as she hung back and clenched her white teeth.

The bolters sped downward, with nostrils distended,
She *must* get a pull on them ere they should reach
The fence on the hill, where the road had been mended;
The blocks bit the wheels with a 'sroope' and a screech;

The little blue veins in her arms swelled and blackened;
The reins were like fiddle-strings stretched in her grip;
When the 'break' hove in sight, the mad gallop had slackened,
She had done it, my word, they were under the whip.

They still had the pace on, but Polly was able
To steer 'twixt the fences with never a graze,
They flashed past the 'Change' where the groom at the stable
Just stood with his mouth open, dumb with amaze.

'Change': the end of a coach stage where the horses were changed

On the level she turned them, the best bit of driving
That was ever done on this side of the range,   *the range: the Snowy*
And trotted them back up the hill-side, arriving   *Mountains*
With not a strap broken in front of the 'Change'.

And the wife? – well she prayed to the Lord till she fainted;
I reckon He answered her prayers all the same –
He *must* have helped Polly, it's curious now, ain't it,
To see a thin slip of a girl be so game?

Did I summons the driver? I had no occasion –
The coroner came with his jury instead,
Who found that he died from a serious abrasion –
Both wheels of the coach had gone over his head.

Romance

A Memory

Adown the grass-grown paths we strayed,
    The evening cowslips ope'd
Their yellow eyes to look at her,
    The love-sick lilies moped
With envy that she rather chose
To take a creamy-petalled rose
And lean it 'gainst her ebon hair,
All in that garden fair.

A languid breeze, with stolen scent
    Of box-bloom in his grasp,
Sighed out his longing in her ear,
    And with his dying gasp
Scattered the perfume at her feet
To blend with others not less sweet;
He loved her, but she did not care,
All in that garden fair.

The rose she honoured nodded down,
    His comrades burst with spite:
Poor fool! he knew not he was doomed
    To barely last the night;
Are hearts to her but as that flower,
The plaything of a careless hour,
To lacerate and never spare
All in that garden fair.

I held her hand that I might trace
    Her fortune in its palm;
A bolder moonbeam than the rest
    Crept up and kissed her arm,
And, kissing once, was loth to leave,
So hid himself within the sleeve
That clasped the lithe arm, white and bare,
All in that garden fair.

I traced her fortune: love and wealth,-
    Tho' life, alas! was short,
But will that wealth be bought with love?
    Or love with wealth be bought?
I know not, knowing only this –
Her hand seemed waiting for a kiss,
I longed to, but I did not dare
All in that garden fair.

But she, alas! is not for me,
    And I am not for her;
Yet ever deep within my thoughts
    A faint regret must stir
A thrill of longing – that among
Those moonlit paths with lover's tongue
I might return, and woo her there
All in that garden fair.

Humorous/Satirical

Josephus Riley

The rum was rich and rare,
There were wagers in the air,
The atmosphere was rosy, and the tongues were wagging free;
But *one* was in the revel
Whose occiput was level –
Plain Josephus Riley, from the North Countree.

> *occiput: medical term for head*

The conversation's flow
Was not devoid of 'blow.'
And neither was it wanting in the plain, colloquial 'D'.
With a most ingenuous smile –
'This here is not my style,'
Said plain Josephus Riley, from the North Countree.

'And I wouldn't be averse
To emptying my purse,
And laying some small wager with the present companee,
To cut the matter short –
Foot racing is my forte,'
Said plain Josephus Riley, from the North Countree.

'I think it's on the cards
That I can run three hundred yards
(The match to be decided where you gentlemen agree)
Against your fleetest horse;
The race would prove a source
Of pleasure,' said Josephus, from the North Countree.

'To equalise the task,
This little start I ask –
The rider, ere he follows, must imbibe a cup of tea;
A simple breakfast-cup
He will have to swallow up.
That's *me* – Josephus Riley, from the North Countree.'

Then a 'knowing 'un' looked wise,
    Begged to apologise;
But might he ask what temp'rature the liquid was to be!
    Would it come from out the pot
    Milkless, steaming, boiling-hot?'
'Oh, not at all,' said Riley, from the North Countree.

    'Allow me to explain;
    I do observe with pain,
This jocular reflection on my native honestee,
    My bump of truth is huge,
    I'd scorn a subterfuge' –
Said plain Josephus Riley, from the North Countree.

    'Before the parties start
    I'll take the Judge apart
To prove, by tasting, whether I have tampered with the tea;
    And I beg to state again
    Your suspicions give me pain,'
Said plain Josephus Riley, from the North Countree.

    Then they were all satisfied
    That the match was 'boneefied,'
The bond was signed, and Riley went to 'preparate' the tea;
    But his slow, ambiguous smile
    Would have seemed to token guile
In any man but Riley, from the North Countree.

    He brought the fatal cup –
    By its saucer covered up –
The Judge examined its contents with awful gravitee,
    Then read the papers o'er,
    But could not find a flaw:
'Wade in! Josephus Riley, from the North Countree.'

Then the 'wagerer' just bowed,
    And, passing through the crowd,
He handed up the beverage unto the 'wageree;'
    And off across the flat,
    Springing gaily, pit-a-pat,
Went plain Josephus Riley, from the North Countree.

    But behind him what a yell
    Of execration fell
From lips that lent themselves to shapes of great profanitee!
    For the people of that town
    Were done a lovely brown
By plain Josephus Riley, from the North Countree.

    And here's the reason why:
    The tea was simply DRY,
You might *eat* it, but to *drink* it was impossibilitee;
    But, curious to state,
    Men did not appreciate
This hum'rous innovation from the North Countree.

    You'll understand, of course,
    That wager was a source
Of very little profit to the hapless 'wageree,'
    And, dating from that day,
    I much regret to say,
Men look askance at Riley, from the North Countree.

Jimmy Wood

A Bar-room Ballad

There came a lonely Briton to the town,
    A solitary Briton with a mission,
He'd vowed a vow to put all 'shouting' down,
    To relegate it to a low position.

Transcendently Britannic in his dress,
    His manners were polite, and slightly formal;
And – this I mention with extreme distress –
    His 'put away' for liquid was abnormal.

He viewed this 'shouting' mania with disgust,
    As being generosity perverted,
When any of the 'boys' went on the bust
    He strove his best that they might be converted.

He wouldn't take a liquor with a man,
    Not if he was to be hanged, drawn, and quartered,
And yet, he drank – construe it as you can –
    Unsweetened gin, most moderately watered.

And when the atmosphere was in a whirl,
    And language metaphorical ran riot,
He'd calmly tender sixpence to the girl,
    And drink his poison – *solus* – nice and quiet.

Whenever he was asked to breast the bar
    He'd answer, with a touch of condescension:
'I much regret to disoblige so far
    As to decline your delicate attention.

'That drink's a curse that hangeth like a leech –
    A sad but most indubitable fact is,
Mankind was meant to drink *alone*, I preach,
    And what I preach invariably practise.

'I never pay for others, nor do I
    Take drink from them, and never, never would, sir –
One man, one liquor! though I have to die
    A martyr to my faith – that's Jimmy Wood, sir.

'My friend, 'tis not a bit of use to raise
    A hurricane of bluster and of banter:
I preach my humble gospel in the phrase,
    Similia similibus curantur;

'Which means: by drinking how and when I like,
    And sticking to the one unsweetened sample,
I hope in course of time that it will strike
    All men to follow up my good example.'

In course of time it struck all men that Jim
    Was fast developing into a soaker –
The breath of palsy on his every limb,
    A bleary face touched up with crimson ochre.

Yet firmly stood he by the sinking ship,
    Went down at last with all his colours flying;
No hand but his raised tumbler to his lip,
    What time J. Woods, the Martyr, lay a-dying.

Misunderstood reformer! gallant heart!
    He gave his path to Death – the great collector.
Now…in Elysian fields he sits apart
    And sips his modest 'Tommy Dodd' of nectar.

His signature is on the scroll of fame,
    You cannot well forget him, though you would, sir,
The man is dead, not so his homely name,
    Who drinks alone – drinks toast to Jimmy Wood, sir.

Our Visitor

There's a fellow on the station
(He dropped in on a call,
Just casual – to stay a pleasant week),
He's a banker's near relation,
Strongly built, and very tall,
Not altogether destitute of cheek;
He's a descent judge of whisky,
And the hardest working youth
Who ever played a polo on a cob;   *cob: horse*

His anecdotes are risky,
And to tell the honest truth,
He's waiting here until he gets a job.

He's waiting, as I mention,
And whene'er he says his prayers,
Which he doesn't do as frequently as some,
And I fear that his intention
Isn't quite so good as theirs –
For he prays to God the work may never come.
He marches with the banner
Of the noble unemployed,
He mixes with the fashionable mob,
But while he's got a tanner   *tanner: sixpence*
He scorns to be decoyed
Where there's any chance he may get a job.

He's an excellent musician,
And the song that suits him best,
'Old Stumpy' is a masterpiece of art;
'Tis a splendid composition
As he chucks it off his chest,
Though there's something of a hitch about the start.
He's an artist, too, in colours
For he painted up the boat.
You wonder – but he did, so help me bob,
And all the champion scullers,   *scullers: rowers*
When once he gets afloat,
Couldn't catch him – if they offered him a job.

He's very unpretending,
Most affable and kind,
He'll take a whisky any time it suits;
Extremely condescending,
He really does not mind,
He'll even, when it's muddy, wear your boots.
Some think he isn't clever,

But it's my distinct belief
That there's much more than they fancy in his nob.
But he's travelling on the 'never'
And will surely die of grief
On the day when he's compelled to take a job.

To a Hatpeg

(previously unpublished – still in copyright)

There's a nice little hatpeg that hangs on the wall
That long from its owner has parted,
And though he is wandering far beyond call
Like him it is always true hearted.

Many seasons have passed since his limp Cabbage Tree
Has dangled upon the old rack
But that one single peg, always vacant must be,
For its owner will surely come back.

And though in far countries, he sadly doth roam
While hunger had forced him to beg
Till fortune grows kindly, and sends him back home,
There's an Angel who watches that peg.

One afternoon, after a long weary tramp,
And hard grafting, to which he's no stranger,
He found, that a letter, had come to the camp,
To warn him, his peg was in danger;

The words that he used, are best shown by a dash –
As he swore that no rival he'd brook,
Said he 'my fine fellow I'll settle your hash'
As the first train to Cooma he took,

When he came to that town, he bought pistols and knives,
And a sword, with a long shiny blade,
You'd have thought that his rival, had two or three lives,
By the fierce preparations he made;

cabbage tree: hat made from woven cabbage tree palm leaves – standard bush hat in nineteenth-century Australia

grafting: working

He bought a chaffcutter, an axe and a saw
With a coffin, lined neatly with satin,
Such a beautiful coffin was ne'er seen before,
With a pious inscription in Latin.

A hammerless gun, that went off at a touch,
Of green cartridges nearly a keg,
Said he 'when I've used them, there won't remain much,
Of the man with designs on my peg.

Then he planted himself, till his rival came by
From the weapons he made a selection,
Quoth he 'when he comes I shall certainly try,
And give him the warmest reception.'

So as the bold stripling, came singing along,
The Exile, sprang out from his lair,
While his rival soon warbled a different song
('Twas less of a song, than a prayer)

Then he shot him with axes, and chopped him with guns,
Till his state was too utterly utter –
When the Exile, collects all the pieces, and runs
The remnants right through the chaffcutter –

He turns the handle, with feelings of joy –
And as he puts through the last leg,
Quoth he, 'this is how I shall treat any boy,
Who dares to lay hands (hang his hat) on my peg' –

Then he shut down the coffin, well pleased to be rid,
Of the youth, who got terribly mauled for,
The sake of a hat-peg – Then tacked on the lid
A label – 'Please keep until called for' –

Read these verses sweet youth! for a moral lies there.
'Tis short, not much more than a line,
At Rosedale, are plenty of pegs and to spare –
Don't hang up your hat upon mine –